TRUE HERO

AMY KNUPP

CHAPTER ONE

*H*ayden Henry didn't usually get caught up in romantic or fanciful thoughts, but watching her best friend dance with her groom forced her to admit true love was indeed possible.

For *others*.

Not for her.

She'd tried twice. Given a relationship everything she had twice. Gotten her heart annihilated twice.

That didn't stop her from being over-the-moon happy for Sierra and Cole. They were perfect for each other, and their late-January wedding and reception had turned out to be a joyous, undeniable celebration of two souls who were meant to be together. The Honeysuckle Inn, an adorable venue an hour south of Nashville, provided the ideal combination of historical beauty and intimate coziness to enhance their big day.

After finishing the ice water she'd picked up at the bar, Hayden made her way over to two of her fellow bridesmaids, Mackenzie and Kennedy, whose eyes were also locked on the newlyweds.

"They make it look easy," Hayden said.

"I'm so happy for my little sister," Kennedy said, and Hayden did a double take when she noticed tears welling in Kennedy's eyes.

"Happy tears?" Hayden asked in shock, because Sierra's older sister had never been one to display her emotions willingly.

"Pregnant tears. Dammit, I'm ready for this baby to be here!" She laughed as a single drop cascaded down her cheek.

"You're getting close but still too early," Mackenzie said warmly, her eyes lit up. "Less than two months?"

"March eleventh. Eternity." Kennedy wiped her eyes, then settled her hands on her belly.

Hayden checked the urge to touch Kennedy's belly at the same time she checked the envy that surged through her.

Foolish girl. Babies are for other people too.

Her hormones had been playing games lately, making her think she wanted a baby, ignoring logic. Logic said it took two people to make a baby for a reason, particularly because babies and kids were a lot of work, and it was best to share that with another human.

Did people raise kids on their own all the time? Sure. Look at Eliza with Calvin. That woman was a shero for sure. But Hayden's life was overflowing as it was. Most days she could barely handle her beloved double workload, and she couldn't fathom having a baby on top of that.

She'd make do with spoiling her friends' babies—Kennedy's in a few weeks and Lena's now—as often as she could. It wouldn't be long before there were others, what with all the weddings and engagements in her circle. They were at that age where people added to their lives, hooked up with a happily ever after, then went forth and made babies.

As the bride and groom's first dance wound down, Hayden yanked herself out of her musings and returned her gaze to the lovely couple on the dance floor, not having to fake her smile. The clinking of silverware on glasses began in earnest, and Cole had his lips on Sierra's almost instantly, making the crowd laugh.

Hayden snapped to attention and scanned the room for her dance partner for the upcoming bridal party dance.

Her heart rate kicked up at the mere thought of Zane North, and then she spotted him across the way and sucked in a breath.

Literally gasped. Everything in her that was female stood at attention, because he was that delectable.

He made eye contact from the other side of the dance floor, and she swore the impact of those eyes on hers made her shaky inside. And he was still a good forty feet away, for God's sake.

Pasting a laid-back smile on her face, she started toward the dance floor to meet him halfway, keeping her eyes on him, fighting to tamp down her shakiness.

This wasn't like her at all. She wasn't shy around men, didn't hesitate to flirt with the hottest one in a room, did not physically react like this—ever.

Except to Zane.

She'd had the same reaction when she'd first laid eyes on him at Mackenzie and Drake's wedding last fall in Malta. Then again last night at the rehearsal dinner at Gabe's vacation home here on Dragonfly Lake. It had been an informal affair—a buffet-style barbecue instead of round tables of eight where she would've been assigned to sit right next to him. She'd been relieved and disappointed at the same time. Because something about Zane North set her off-kilter.

This evening, during the meal, she'd spent a span at Zane's side, every one of her senses tuned in to him, but the wedding party was a rowdy one that had kept the whole group entertained, and one-on-one conversation hadn't been necessary or possible.

So far, she'd spoken to him a handful of times, exchanged pleasantries and small talk, and found him to be quiet, with such a serious outlook that she'd worked to make him smile…and then basked in the reward when she'd succeeded.

And still, her insides quivered as they approached each other on the hardwood floor while the DJ chattered then introduced the wedding party and started their song.

As Zane, with his short sandy-brown hair, penetrating blue eyes, and rigid square jaw, held out his hand to her, he formally said, "At your service." Only the twitch of one corner of his lips gave any hint of lightheartedness.

"My hero," she said flirtatiously as she took his hand, ran her other one up the lapel of his tux, and moved her body inches from his.

"I hope you require a guy to do more than just show up in order to be your hero," Zane said, a sparkle in his eye that could make a girl swoon—even a modern, liberated girl who didn't believe in swooning.

"I'm easy," she said as his large hands settled at her waist, his warmth penetrating the fine fabric of her silver gown. "Wait. That didn't come out right."

"You're easy to be with." The teasing tone was gone from his voice, as if his words were sincere.

"You don't seem like a guy who gets nervous about dancing with a girl." The smile she shot up at him maintained a lightness, because that was her go-to mode. Fun, flirty, and out for a good time that did not necessarily *require* a man.

"Only the pretty ones."

"Are you flirting, Lieutenant North?"

"Just Zane." His reply was subdued, as if he was still adjusting to life outside of the military.

"I heard you're no longer in the Navy," she said, itching to learn more about him.

"You heard right. I almost didn't make it back to town in time for rehearsal last night."

"How long were you in?"

"I went to the Naval Academy out of high school."

"And now you're...?"

"Thirty."

He was Drake's twin, so she should've known that. But when she compared the two—she glanced around to find Zane's fraternal twin, dancing with his wife, Mackenzie—from the outside, it seemed the two men had nothing in common, especially not their age. Zane was so serious, almost restrained. Drake, who she'd gotten to know well over the past few months, was...not. Zane seemed older than he was. Drake seemed determined to never fully grow up.

"It must be weird to be out," she said.

That elicited a half grin. "Weird is one word for it."

"What do you plan to do?"

"I'm still working out some details. What about you?"

"Me?" She wasn't nearly done learning about him, but from his deflection, she sensed he didn't want to talk about himself.

Naturally, that made her twice as curious.

"Did I hear you own a store or something?" he persisted.

"I do. Henry Interiors on Hale Street. I'm an interior designer too, so I'm forever trying to balance between running the store and building my design clientele."

"Ambitious," he said. She thought she detected a hint of admiration in his tone, but when she peered up at him, his expression betrayed nothing of his thoughts or feelings.

"I like keeping busy and I love what I do." Still determined to get something more out of him, something personal, some hint about who this reticent but gorgeous man was, she flipped it on him. "Did you love what you did? In the Navy? You're a pilot, right?"

"That's right. I loved parts of it."

"But you must have *not* loved more parts than you loved. Otherwise you'd still be there?"

"This is getting deep for a wedding dance," he said, and this time when he flashed a half smile, it was more calculated than genuine.

"We can go back to the shallows."

There was a lot going on beneath this guy's surface, and it made Hayden so darn curious. But they were only companions tonight, not on an actual date, and though she might run into him periodically through the family her BFF had married into, she'd have little reason to get closer to him.

Something about that made her sad, but she shook it off.

The man was delicious to look at—and hell's bells, the biceps she'd brushed against beneath the tux sleeves were hard and substantial and made her long for a glimpse. She'd totally be open to pursuing him for a night of bicep discovery and more...*if only* there wasn't that tie between her and his family now. Sleeping with her best friend's brother-in-law could only end up one way—awkward. Besides, it'd been so long since she'd been with a guy that she probably wouldn't know what to do.

With a deep but imperceptible—she hoped—breath, she pulled herself mentally out of this man's orbit and took in the couples around them, her eyes flitting from one in-love twosome to the next. They were surrounded—Sierra and Cole, Drake and Mackenzie, Gabe and Lexie, Mason and Eliza, Kennedy and Hunter, and Jackson and Asia. Every last couple in the wedding party was married, and up till now, Hayden had told herself that didn't bother her.

But it sort of did.

Rolling her eyes at herself, she looked beyond the dance floor and spotted her dad, with his charcoal-gray hair and kind eyes. He stood alone, halfway between the bar and the cluster of dinner tables, holding a cocktail glass, watching the dancing, and something in Hayden's chest constricted at the sight of him. He looked…lonely. She knew that feeling more than she'd admit out loud.

"Something made you frown," Zane said, surprising her because she hadn't realized he was watching her.

"My dad just moved back to Nashville," she said, nodding toward the man in question. "He'd never acknowledge it, but I think he's having a hard time."

"With living here?"

She shook her head. "He's happy to be back—he says he likes being close to me and my brothers—but he retired recently. That's hard enough, but I'm pretty sure he's used work to keep from missing my mom. It's been six years since she died."

"And now he finds himself with an unsure future," Zane said.

Something in his tone caught Hayden's attention and made her think he could be speaking about himself as well.

"Does he have friends here?" Zane asked.

"He does but I don't think he's stayed in touch with them. He moved to Texas after my mom died—got a transfer from his company, saying he needed a change. He's buried himself in his job to the exclusion of everything else."

"Could you encourage him to see his old friends?"

As her dad spotted her, she waved her fingers at him and smiled, then said, slowly, thoughtfully, "I could do more than encourage him. His birthday's coming up in a couple of months. He'll be seventy. I could throw him a party and invite everyone he's ever known."

With a quiet chuckle, Zane said, "Or a small party with a few of his closest friends."

"No reason to think small," she said, her mind spinning, plotting, committing to the idea. "Seventy's a big deal, and my dad deserves it." It would give him something to look forward to, reintroduce him to his old circles, and be a way for everyone who loved him to honor him on his milestone birthday.

"You said you have brothers. They could help, right?"

She scrunched up her face in consideration. "Seth might. Cash, no. Holden, who knows? But they're boys, and party planning isn't really their thing. I'll be better off doing it myself, and maybe Sierra will help me."

"Is your dad a social guy? Will he appreciate it?"

"He and my mom were always social. They have a billion friends in the area. I think he's just…still not used to being alone. He's the kind of man who needs a partner." Hayden sifted mentally through her parents' friends, the people she'd known her whole life, thinking surely there must be some single or widowed women he could spend time with.

A loud, feminine cackle reached them from behind Hayden. She turned toward the sound to find Zane's aunt Liz, his mom, Faye, and the ladies' other BFF, Geraldine, in a huddle at the edge of the dance floor.

"How old is your mom?" she asked Zane.

"Sixty-five, I think?"

"Totally age appropriate. She's not involved with anyone, is she?"

"A man?" His furrowed brow told her he'd not considered such a thing, and he shook his head. "I don't think she's been with anyone since my dad died, and that was sixteen years ago."

"Maybe she's due," Hayden pressed, "for some happiness and companionship?"

"What exactly are you getting at?"

"She and my dad…both single, alone, in need of companionship…"

"You think setting them up is the answer?"

"You don't?"

"I wouldn't know. I've been away for a long time."

"Maybe she could use a little nudge. I know my dad could."

"A nudge named Hayden?" His hint of a grin was back, and she felt the reward deep inside.

"I'm always up for a sidekick," she said. "We can introduce them after we're done dancing."

Her lightness faded when he shook his head, went back to being Mr. Serious, and said, "I'm not one for interfering in other people's lives. I'll leave that to you." He said it as if he didn't approve, and she frowned at his stoic tone.

This guy had the tough outer shell of a walnut. He might be tempting to look at, to fantasize about getting to know better, but with his recent major life change and his uber-serious outlook, there was nothing easy about him.

She'd joked about herself being *easy*, but really, she kind of was—not in the promiscuous sense but in the way that she didn't take life too seriously. She was an incurable optimist, liked having fun, and thrived on bringing joy to others, whether it was by helping them create a perfect-for-them "nest" or introducing them to someone they could share happy times with.

She glanced at her dad, still alone, then angled enough to see Zane's mom again. Everything Hayden knew about Faye North said she was a kind, capable woman, a strong woman—she had to be to raise five boys, most of whom were loving, well-adjusted humans.

The more she thought about it, the more she believed her dad and Faye North could bring some happy moments to each other.

"I guess the mission is mine alone then," she finally said, forcing a nonchalant smile up at him, ignoring the hitch in her heartbeat when he gazed intently down at her for a solid two seconds.

Obviously, she and Zane North had nothing in common

except, she could swear, maybe an attraction. Didn't matter. She could be friendly to him, dance with him, and not let his grumpiness get to her. Not let his holy hotness get to her.

And she could introduce her beloved dad to an awesome lady who just happened to be Zane's mom. She didn't need Zane's approval.

As the song wound down to the last few notes, she closed her eyes for a moment and inhaled the essence of this sexy man regretfully, knowing he and she were not destined to get any closer.

It'd been fun while it lasted, she thought, then said, lightly, "Thank you for the dance, kind sir," shot him a friendly smile, and made her way toward her dear father.

CHAPTER TWO

*N*early an hour had passed since Zane and Hayden's dance, and Zane was still hot and bothered.

Or maybe *again* was a better word than *still*, because his means of cooling off after having Hayden Henry in his arms for approximately four minutes had been to escape outside to the brisk January night air and freeze his nuts off.

He'd spent a good quarter of an hour on the inn's wrap-around porch, gazing over the partially frozen expanse of Dragonfly Lake. It was desolate and deserted and reminded him of the times on the carrier when he'd steal a few moments of blessed solitude on the stern, staring out at the vast, monotonous sea. Minus the frozen nuts.

When he'd come back in, he'd kept his distance from the dance floor, mainly because he was acutely aware that Hayden was still on it, sometimes with a group of women and other times with one of a parade of men, each of whom Zane had the inexplicable urge to punch the charming grin off his face. Fighting had always been more Cole's MO than his, but then Zane had been all sorts of fucked up ever since he'd taken that final flight off the boat—the one where he'd had to let someone else control the plane because his time in the Navy was over.

He swallowed down the uneasiness that thought brought with it and found an out-of-the-way spot against the back wall, far from the bar, far from the dance floor—yet he could still see Hayden's brunette updo bouncing around the floor and catch flashes of her wholehearted smile as she laughed with her friends. He couldn't deny he was enjoying that view.

Though she was apparently driven and motivated professionally—a turn-on in itself—she also had a carefree spirit that was foreign to him but still drew him in. As she raised both arms and swung her intriguing hips, she seemed to be fully in the moment, loving her life.

He could use a good dose of loving his life. He'd almost forgotten what that felt like.

As one song ended and the next started, the DJ announced it was time for a line dance, which drew a throng to the floor and expanded Zane's circle of peace—until he spotted Drake, Mason, and Gabe heading his way.

"The longer you stand back here and leer at Hayden, the closer you verge into creeper territory," Drake said with a wide grin as he settled against the wall to Zane's left.

"Aren't you supposed to be line dancing with your wife?" Zane shot back.

"She's doing okay without me." Drake gestured to the front row of dancers, where Mackenzie was in the middle of the other bridesmaids, the bride, and several other women. "We'd rather catch up with our wayward brother."

"There's literally nothing to catch up on," Zane said. "I've been home barely over twenty-four hours. Nothing's changed since then."

"I guess we're all still reeling from your bombshell," Gabe said, not unkindly, just matter-of-factly, which was what kept Zane from becoming defensive. "Why didn't you tell us ahead of time you were coming home for good?"

"I wasn't sure it would actually happen until my ass was on that plane coming home."

"Were you afraid *you* would change your mind or they would?" Mason asked perceptively.

"Both. The military does love to jack with a person's plans."

There'd been days, though—good days when his landing

grades were an OK-3 or he'd gotten an attaboy from the air boss —when Zane had nearly weakened, reverted to his original life plan, and decided not to resign. It had always been his plan to stay in until retirement, and the idea of derailing from that, still, to this day, left him twitchy. But resigning was the right decision. He knew that in his bones.

Gabe leaned against the wall on Zane's right, his eyes skimming over the dance floor and resting on Lexie while he spoke. "How long have you been thinking about resigning?"

"I started right after Mom's heart attack." He'd mostly been able to talk himself out of it back then—until Andre Weber's death.

"That was over a year ago." Gabe stated the obvious as Cole ambled up to them.

"Had to finish out my commitment." Unfortunately, that had given him plenty of time to waffle, and waffle he had.

"What made you quit?" Drake asked.

It wasn't a topic Zane wanted to get into, here, now, or anytime with anyone, but he needed to get them all off his back about it for good.

"The Navy's not the right place for me anymore," he oversimplified.

"What are you planning to do instead?" Gabe asked.

"I'm hoping to work for the family business," he answered, glancing around for anything that might distract his brothers, because this was not the time or place he wanted to discuss this subject.

"North Brothers Sports?" Cole asked as if it was the most off-the-wall thing he'd ever heard.

"Is there another family business I don't know about?" Zane snapped.

"What do you have in mind with NBS?" Gabe asked Zane, shooting a *chill the hell out* look at Cole.

"You could fly our corporate jet," Mason said. "We contract with a company but I can hook you up with them."

"I'm not interested in being your chauffeur," Zane said

without hesitation. "I'd like to discuss possibilities, but not here, not tonight."

"Fair enough," Mason said and finished the last of his beer.

The truth was, Zane didn't know where he'd fit in the company. What he did know were three things:

One, the Navy had soured him on flying.

Two, he had no interest in being a glorified taxi driver for his CEO oldest brother or the rest of upper management.

Three, he believed he owed it to the company, to his family, to do his part in helping NBS operate and flourish.

NBS was a hell of a legacy, built from nothing by his dad and uncle. Mason and the rest of their brothers and cousins had helped guide it from a local company to a national contender in the sporting goods industry.

Zane was grateful as hell for the company and his family's dedication, because, as one of Harry North's sons, he'd benefited financially—handsomely. To the tune of a seven-digit bank account balance. Between that and the nest egg he'd managed to save for himself with his salary from the past decade, he had the luxury of not having to jump into any job right away. He'd be fine financially if he took several years to figure it out.

But he sure as hell wouldn't be fine mentally.

"You've got time to figure things out," Gabe said in his well-intended, encouraging way. Some things never changed. "You need to relax. Decompress. You need some recovery time."

"Perfect opportunity to distract yourself with a certain brunette. You two seemed close on the dance floor." Drake held his beer up and pointed it casually toward the line dancers.

"A distraction is the last thing I need," Zane said.

"How 'bout a beer then?" Cole suggested, adding with a laugh, "My treat." He garnered the attention of one of the wait-staff who was collecting empty glasses from the tables.

The server, a good-looking woman who couldn't be more than about twenty-two, made her way toward them with a wide smile as she took in the five North brothers, and Zane supposed they made quite a sight. They weren't small guys, any of them, and none of them had ever had a problem attracting women. It only took him an instant to recognize there was less preening and posturing than in the past among his brothers, and it hit him—again—all these assholes had found their "true love."

Their mom's phrase, not his.

"What can I do for y'all?" the server asked.

"My brother here needs a drink. What do you want, Zane? Beer? Whiskey? Shot?"

"Sprite please," Zane said without hesitation, and he could feel the confusion among his brothers.

"Sprite with what?" Drake said.

"Ice," was Zane's response. "You ready for another?" He pointed at Drake's bottle.

"Can we get a round of the best Macallan you've got?" Mason asked.

"Sure thing. I'll see what he has." The server nodded toward the bartender.

"And the Sprite for me," Zane repeated.

As the server hurried off to the bar, Zane's brothers eyed him with varying amounts of confusion.

"You don't drink anymore?" Drake asked.

"I thought Navy pilots played as hard as they worked," Cole added.

"Most of them do." Zane shrugged. "I just quit doing stuff that could alter my judgment. Too much at stake on a daily basis."

"Makes sense," Gabe said, "when you're flying billion-dollar planes every day."

"One celebratory drink won't hurt tonight," Mason said. "None of us has to drive—or fly—anywhere."

"Did you find a room?" Cole asked.

"I found a couch." Zane nodded at Gabe, who'd offered the couch in the lower-level family room of his four-bedroom vacation home here on the lake. Zane had wavered too long, arrived to town too late to get in on one of the rooms in the inn, and all the bedrooms in Gabe's place were spoken for as well. Zane hadn't been too concerned. Had figured he could just make the hour-long drive back to their mom's in the city tonight and have the place to himself, as she and the rest of the wedding party were staying at the lake.

The blond server returned with a bottle of scotch, five glasses, and what looked to be a Sprite on ice. She poured the amber liquid into the first four glasses, then met Zane's gaze with a questioning brow arch.

He nodded his acquiescence, silently acknowledging that he'd initially refused the liquor out of habit and that there *was* cause for celebration. Cole's nuptials, for one. He truly liked Sierra, or what he knew of her so far. Being home, for two. Though he might not be able to see his future exactly at the moment, he was confident he no longer had any business flying million-dollar jets for the Navy.

When they all had their glasses with a finger of scotch, Zane double-fisting with his Sprite, Mason raised his. "To Cole, the star of the show."

"That'd be my hot wife," Cole said with a laugh. "To all my douchebag brothers."

"To moments worth celebrating," Gabe added.

Zane was next in the round robin, and all four sets of eyes were locked on him.

"To family," he said with a nod, meaning it.

"To hookups that turn into more," Drake said with a nudge to Zane's forearm, and Zane's four whipped brothers laughed and howled in agreement.

They clinked their glasses and swigged their liquor, and Zane had to admit Mason had good taste in scotch.

The line dance had ended at some point, and the crowd on the dance floor had shrunk. Before he could check himself, Zane realized he was scanning the room for Hayden.

"I don't believe it," he said when he spotted their mom across the way, next to Hayden—and her dad.

Mason and Gabe had gone off to meet their wives, but Drake and Cole were apparently still within earshot, because they both looked at him, then followed his gaze toward the trio.

"What? Hayden talking to Mom?" Drake asked.

"She's trying to set up Mom with her dad."

"Set up our mom?" Drake asked, his brows shooting up as if the idea had promise.

Cole's response was a slow grin and a head shake. "Hayden's a steamroller."

"I get that sense," Zane muttered.

"She got her sights set on you?" Drake asked, his amusement clear.

"No." Zane's answer was immediate if not accurate. She'd made it pretty clear she was interested, with the periodic glances his way, the flirty looks, the private but brief smiles he could swear were just for him.

Was he that out of practice? Reading her all wrong?

It'd be better that way. But he didn't think he was.

He watched as a couple came up to Hayden, the woman pulling her into a hug and acting as if they hadn't seen each other in a long time. He also didn't miss that his mom pulled Hayden's dad out of the way, closer to her, presumably so they could continue to talk—and she kept her hand on Mr. Henry's forearm for several seconds.

"Hayden's got a good heart," Cole said. "According to Sierra, she's been hurt pretty badly in the past, so she isn't looking. Matter of fact, it's a joke between them that Sierra would set her up with one of my brothers or cousins."

"See?" Drake said. "Might as well be you."

"Hayden said no every time. Emphatically." Cole shrugged as if Zane was shit out of luck. "Sorry, man."

Zane let out a scoff. "Hear me when I say I'm in no position to handle a woman in my life. Casual, serious, or otherwise."

"Hey, I get it," Cole said. "Major life changes tend to fuck with the head."

"Precisely. I don't even know where I'm going to live, other than with Mom for a while. Feels like I'm a clueless eighteen-year-old again."

"Except when we were eighteen, we thought we knew every damn thing," Drake said.

What he left unspoken was that Zane's actions as an eighteen-year-old had harmed their twin closeness. Though all of it was buried, not spoken of, the tension between them still existed, still kept a pronounced distance between them, and Zane knew that was on him.

"Let us know if we can do anything," Cole said, the middle North brother catching Zane off guard yet again with his genuine concern and caring. It blew the mind what finding the right woman had done for their black sheep brother.

"Thanks," Zane said. "Better go get your bride."

"Don't have to tell me twice." Cole placed his empty whiskey glass on a passing server's tray, then headed for the woman in white.

"I'll let you hold up the wall," Drake said. "I've got a woman to see to."

Zane leaned back to do exactly that, his eyes doing the seek-out-Hayden thing, which had apparently become a habit in the past hour and a half. The surge in his heart rate when he found her was immediately counteracted when it registered she was on the dance floor again, with another guy. This time, his cousin Connor—biggest ladies' man alive now that Drake was out of commission.

Zane might not want to get involved with Hayden, but he sure as hell couldn't deny that the sight of her in his cousin's arms did not sit well. Not at all.

CHAPTER THREE

*I*t was nearly one a.m. when Hayden walked out into the frigid January night—minus a coat—after the reception.

Though she'd gone out of her way to buy a coat that worked with her bridesmaid's gown, she'd apparently left it somewhere earlier in the chaos, maybe in Sierra's room, maybe at Gabe's gorgeous vacation rental. She wasn't worried about it. It would turn up later, and in a few minutes, she'd have the heater in her SUV going full blast and warming her.

As she opened the driver's door, she realized she was smiling, still riding the high of her BFF's special day. There'd been so much love in that reception hall, nothing but good feelings all around, and it was impossible for her to hold on to any kind of sadness or loneliness just because she was dateless. Besides, her dad and Faye North seemed to have hit it off and even danced together; that gave her all kinds of hope.

The Honeysuckle Inn was more than a century old and had two parking lots, one for overnight guests and one farther out for people attending events. The event lot was mostly deserted as Hayden made her way to her vehicle—there were only two other cars, neither of which she recognized. Most likely those drivers were spending the night somewhere, because the last of the guests had left around midnight, when they'd had to shut down.

Twenty more feet, she counted in her head, anticipating both the heater and removing her four-inch heels. She unlocked her Santa Fe, climbed in, making sure the long gown was clear of the door, and shut herself inside. She exhaled as she took in the silence, then hurried to shove the key in and get the heater going.

Except nothing happened when she turned the key.

She tried it again. Four times. Because maybe those first three were a fluke or someone was playing a joke on her?

But no.

Hell's bells. Now what?

She grabbed her bag and dug out her phone, then googled why her car might not start. She tested the lights, which worked, then tried the ignition again. Still nothing. According to her good friend Google, it could be the starter or ignition. Bottom line, did it matter? She was pretty sure the jumper cables her dad had bought her eons ago were in her assistant Elena's car, and even if she did have them, there was no one around to give her a jump.

Plus…one a.m. The world, at least this small town, was asleep, and she was exhausted. She'd been on the go since before seven that morning, spending a couple of hours in Henry Interiors, reassuring herself everything was in order for a potentially busy retail Saturday without her, before she'd headed out to the bridal luncheon and the bridesmaids' spa appointments.

She and Sierra had always been each other's go-to in emergencies like this, but no way was Hayden bothering the bride tonight. She'd better be deeply involved in some wedding-night aerobics by now.

All three of Hayden's brothers lived here in Dragonfly Lake, but she hated to call them for help. Seth had left the wedding a couple of hours ago and was likely asleep. If she called any of them, she'd never hear the end of it, and while she could take a lot of crap from her brothers—all of them older—Uber was easier.

She swiped to the screen with the Uber app, opened it, had to look up the inn's address, then entered it and…

No Ubers available in her area?

What the…?

Dragonfly Lake was tiny, but it was only an hour from Nashville. That was practically a suburb these days, wasn't it?

She went to the App Store and typed in *ride service* and was about to download another app she'd heard of when a man appeared at her driver's-side window and nearly scared the pee out of her. She let out a non-graceful gasp-scream kind of thing and pressed her hand to her racing heart as recognition dawned.

"Zane," she said, also in a gasp, even though he likely couldn't hear her on the other side of the door. She leaned her head against the headrest for a moment as she took a personal inventory and made sure she hadn't in fact peed herself, then slid the window down a few inches.

"Problems?" he asked, leaning close to the open window, his breath clouding in the cold air and further steaming up the glass.

"What are you doing here?" She glanced around the lot again to see if he was with his brothers, but it was still deserted, still just the two other cars.

Zane pointed over his shoulder at one of them, a black sporty-looking thing. "My rental. I couldn't tell it was you in here, but it didn't seem normal for any woman to get in by herself and sit for so long without the engine and heat running. Not in this cold."

She filled him in on the situation, then said, "Apparently there's no Uber this far out."

"You're not staying at the inn?"

"I have an early appointment with a potentially big potential client."

"That's a lot of potential," he said with a half grin. "I don't have jumper cables but I can give you a ride."

"Back to Nashville? It's an hour from here."

He let out a gravelly laugh, as if he hadn't done it for a while. "I know how far it is."

Hayden studied his handsome, hard-angled face, looking for a hint of whether his offer was genuine or one of those where he felt obligated to offer but was dreading a yes. In total Zane style, his face told her nothing.

"And then you're going to drive back here?" she said. "That would be dumb."

"Not driving back here. I neglected to make arrangements in advance due, in part, to not knowing for sure whether I would be Stateside in time for the wedding. As of yesterday, all the rooms were full, so Gabe offered me a spare couch in his rental house. But I can crash at my mom's in the city. I'd be happy to drive you home, unless you'd rather sit here and debate for the rest of the night, in which case, could you at least let me in out of the wind?"

The mere suggestion of spending the night together sent a flash of heat through her, idiot that she was, since he'd said that as a joke.

She snapped out of it and made a decision. Though she didn't love having him go out of his way, at this point, it seemed like the best option.

And the opportunity to stretch out her time with Zane, such as it was, for one more hour was definitely appealing. Maybe she could crack that tough outer shell and get to know him better.

"I'll take you up on the offer. If you're sure."

Zane stood there in the moonlight, looking like a dream in that tux, his eyes burning into her as he took a second and a half to answer. "I'm sure."

Without giving him time to reconsider, she dropped her phone back into her bag, closed the window, removed the key, and opened the door.

"Thank you," she said as her feet slid to the pavement. After Zane closed the door for her, she eyed him, then spontaneously stretched up and laid a quick kiss on his rough cheek. "My hero, part two."

———

ZANE HAD BEEN STUNNED to discover the woman in the SUV was Hayden. Stunned and a little bit elated, if he was honest with himself. Having her kiss him though?

Stunned didn't quite cover it.

Shit.

Those lips…

The sparkle in those eyes, full of teasing and mischief...

His blood pounded through his veins. From a friendly kiss on the cheek.

Because he wanted this woman.

He didn't *want* to want this woman, didn't want to want any woman.

He'd kept that human urge in check for so long out of necessity that extending his dry spell was no big deal—or it wouldn't be if he wasn't staring down a good hour in a small, enclosed space with a beautiful, alluring woman who hit all his damn buttons.

All that went through his mind in a flash as his senses spun from the feel of her lips.

As he gazed down into her sure-of-herself, flirtatious eyes, he could tell she was amused to think she'd thrown him off his game. She had, but she didn't need to know that, so he kept his gaze locked on her blue eyes, their connection sizzling in the air between them for a moment. Her pupils grew bigger, telling him she was as affected as he was. He brushed a stray strand of hair out of her face, let his knuckles skim over her cheek briefly, and hovered close, checking the urge to lean in and kiss her properly. Then he took his tuxedo jacket off and slid it over her shoulders.

"Thanks," she said. "I misplaced my coat."

With a smile and a shake of his head, he couldn't help but be further intrigued. Hayden seemed like she was at the top of her game and had her shit together—she had to be to run a retail store and a design business—and yet there was a scattered, less-than-organized side of her that hinted of barely controlled chaos that made her seem real.

"I'm sure it'll turn up eventually," she said as they started toward his car.

They made their way to the rented Mercedes in silence, so close their arms were almost but not quite touching, their steps not too hurried, as if they were both savoring the closeness.

Zane opened the passenger door for her and helped her settle in, which turned out to be a process thanks to the dress and the heels and the low bucket seat. He held her arm as she tucked the fine fabric around her legs. As she leaned forward, his jacket fell open, treating him to a tantalizing view of her cleavage.

He went rock-hard in a millisecond and stepped back, as if that would cool down the heat that shot through him. Frankly, he wasn't sure an hour-long cold shower or an ice bath could accomplish that.

After shutting her in, he went around to his side, paused, and sucked in a breath of frosty air, but it didn't do a thing to ease the thrumming of his blood.

Once he lowered himself into the driver's seat and shut the door, he nearly swore out loud, because damn, this was a small car, and he couldn't help but breathe in Hayden's sensual feminine scent.

It was going to be a long hour.

"Where am I taking you?" he asked once he had the heat up all the way—solely for her benefit, because he was burning the fuck up—and was rolling out of the parking lot.

"I guess I need you to drop me off at my Hale Street place since I won't have a car to get to the store in the morning."

"Hale Street," he repeated, trying to recall where that might be. "I don't think I know it."

"Ah, you probably wouldn't if you've been gone for a while. It's near downtown, so head like you're going there. It's a cute little block-long street—the Wentworth Hotel is at one end—that's been completely redeveloped over the past few years. Now it has shops and restaurants and apartments."

Zane knew of the Wentworth. It was a landmark historical hotel that, last he knew, had seen better days. Ironically, he'd met the owner, Burke Wentworth, tonight at the wedding. "Did they refurbish the hotel as well?"

"Sierra's company did all the restoration work, as a matter of fact."

That explained why Burke and his significant other, Ivy, were guests.

Hayden shifted in her seat so she was half facing him, her hand coming to rest on the console between them. She wore delicate silver rings on two of her fingers—but not the ring finger, he noted with satisfaction. The femininity of the jewelry on her fingers captivated him. He took in the sight of her small hand as he reached a stop sign, and couldn't help wondering what it'd be like to have those fingers touching him, teasing him, tending to his body…

He blinked away that line of thought, forcing his mind back to the conversation. "And you live on Hale Street? Or your shop is there?"

"Both. Sort of," Hayden said with an adorable self-conscious laugh. He really needed her not to be adorable. "My shop is there, Henry Interiors, and I have an apartment upstairs from it, but I also have a house about twenty minutes away."

"That sounds complicated." He didn't understand women in general, but he was beginning to believe there wasn't a chance in hell he would ever be able to understand this one with all her contradictions and complexities. *If* he were going to try, which he wasn't.

"It's probably something I need to change, but I haven't decided what to do yet," she said. "I bought the house in large part to use the oversized garage as a workshop for furniture refinishing. I rent the apartment because I sometimes work long hours, and it's easier to just go up the stairs."

"So if you sell the house, you're out of a workshop."

"Right. And if I let go of the apartment, not only will I not have a nearby bed to lay my head in after a fifteen-hour day but I'll have upstairs neighbors who could be loud or annoying or interfere with my business." She shrugged, then took her hand away to pull his jacket tighter against the not-yet-warm air blowing out of the vents. "My brother says I need to choose one and simplify, but it's not that easy."

"I have the opposite problem. I'm staying with my mom until I figure something out."

"Maybe it'll feel good to be 'home' for a while?" She pulled her knees up, still covered by the silver gown, and he noticed she'd removed her shoes, her toes peeking out for a moment. Toes with sparkly silver polish. She hugged her legs to her and wrapped the sides of his jacket around them, and…damn.

Zane wanted it to be his *arms* wrapped around her, nestling her close, keeping her warm.

He quashed that idea. "Maybe for a week or so," he said. "I love my mom, but I don't want to live with her. You said you have brothers?" he asked. The longer he kept her talking, the less he would think about how close she was, how good she smelled.

"Three of them. They live in Dragonfly Lake and run Henry's Restaurant, which they inherited from our nana on our dad's side."

"She didn't include you?"

"She did. When she got sick five years ago, she offered it to me and my brothers. I'd earned my degree in interior design a few years before, had been working as an assistant in the industry, and loved the job if not my supervisor at the time. I adore Henry's, have so many good memories there, but I've never aspired to do anything in the food industry. My brothers decided to take on the challenge, and I was torn."

"I can understand that. You studied to be a designer for years, but your family business means a lot too."

"Even more so when my nana died. Long story short—which isn't always my strong point, so you're welcome—the boys took it on as owners. I just bartend on weekends during the summer."

"Which means you work basically three jobs."

"Only in the summer, and bartending is only one day a week."

"Do you ever think about stopping? It sounds like you have your hands full without it."

Hayden bit her lip for a second, hesitating. "I guess I still feel bad for turning down the career opportunity. Sierra thinks that's why I work so much."

"Because you feel bad?"

"Partly. And if my design business is a success, it shows I made the right decision. Right?"

"Sure," he said. "That sounds like the right decision." He sure as hell understood feeling obligated to work for the family business though. "You get along well with your brothers?"

"Mostly. They're rowdy, overprotective thugs, but I love

them. Cash is the oldest—he was in the Navy too, so you'd probably have something to talk about. He's a chef. Seth's the middle of the boys, the business brains, and I'm closest to him. Holden is a year older than I am, and we clash sometimes, probably because we're a lot alike. He's Mr. Social and manages Henry's front of house."

"You must know Dragonfly Lake pretty well. I think I went boating there about twice as a teenager, but that's it."

"We lived there until I started second grade. After that, I spent big chunks of the summers there at my nana's. Summers at the lake were the best."

They spent the rest of the drive with Hayden telling him stories about growing up at the lake, her brothers, her entrepreneurial nana, whatever Zane could get her to talk about. He loved listening to her, her voice, the way she told a story, her take on things—always with a twist of humor—and if he kept her talking, it made it easier to avoid thinking about how damn much he was attracted to her.

His life was currently unsettled as hell. The plan—because he was a planner to the nth degree—was to get it settled, career, home, maybe a dog, in the next few months. For his own sanity. There was no room in his head for distraction by a sexy brunette. They were already too connected for a one-night stand—hell, his mom and her dad were going on a date—and more than a one-night thing with anyone was out of the question for him.

She directed him to Hale Street, and as he drove down it, she pointed out some of the businesses.

"Clayborne's, that's owned by Kennedy's husband, Hunter, and is, in fact, where they met. Kennedy's part owner of Sugar Babies"—she pointed to a quaint-looking bakery on the opposite side of the street—"along with Violet Morello and Ivy Gibson, who were at the reception. Those girls do sugar right, so if you ever need a sweet treat…"

He tamped down hard on any thought about sweets and treats and Hayden and…

Jesus. Get yourself under control.

"Looks like we'll have to pull around to the alley," Hayden

continued, oblivious to his internal battle. "Midnight Moonshine was playing at Clayborne's tonight. I'm sure they were filled to capacity and then some. There's my store."

He was already going about ten miles per hour because there were cars parked on both sides of the street and people out and about, a lot of them for nearly two a.m. Slowing further, he checked out Henry Interiors, eager to see it, to gather more intel about this woman, whether that was smart or not.

The storefront consisted of a door in the center, flanked by huge floor-to-ceiling panes of glass on either side. The window displays—a large, unique cabinet of some kind on one side and a plush sofa on the other—were dimly illuminated, and the words *Henry Interiors* were painted in simple white letters on the glass. At a glance, his impressions were of class, style, and comfort, and his admiration for the owner grew.

The top levels of the old buildings on both sides of the street looked to be apartments with balconies.

"Frank's Diner has the best blueberry ice cream in the known universe," she said, pointing to the darkened storefront two doors down from hers.

At the end of the street, the Wentworth Hotel, indeed refurbished to be a magnificent linchpin to the neighborhood, stood in grand but understated glory. There was no question it was once again thriving.

"Turn right before the hotel," Hayden said. "At the florist. Amelia did all the flowers and arrangements for Sierra tonight. Then you're going to take a quick right into the alley."

He did as she directed and eventually pulled into a narrow spot behind her building, next to a large storage shed. A flight of stairs went to a single door on the second floor.

As he put the car in park, Hayden touched his hand where it rested on the gear shift, jump-starting his pulse again, and he froze for a moment, steeped in indecision. Without looking at her, he was ninety-five percent certain it was an invitation, an opening. One he shouldn't consider.

Still not glancing her way, because he knew if he did, that would sway everything, he casually removed his hand so he could stop the engine and remove the keys. He would walk her to the door like a gentleman.

"Zane," she said, her voice stopping him with his hand on the keys, still in the ignition. He made the error of looking at her then, making eye contact. She quickly averted her gaze, blew out a gust of air, a self-deprecating exhale. "I'm sorry. I thought I was seeing signs that you like me. I'm out of practice at this. Obviously." She laughed at herself, shook her head.

"I do like you," he said before he could think it through.

"Yeah," she said as if she didn't really believe it. "Embarrassing. Anyway—" She moved her right hand to the door handle, as if to get out.

Zane caught her left hand and tugged it lightly toward him, causing her to face him again, and he leaned into her and kissed her before she could say more.

After a second of hesitation, she shifted her right hand to his neck and kissed him back.

He went from zero to lost in her in half a second flat, drowning in the softness of her lips, the heat of her breath, the boldness of her hand holding him to her. He allowed it for a handful of seconds, long enough to register her sweet taste and breathe in her scent, something sensual with a hint of spice to it. Like the woman herself.

With gargantuan effort, he pulled back from the kiss, cradling her cheek with one hand, unwilling, maybe unable to completely break the contact. Not just yet.

"Do you believe me?" he managed in a rough, half-there voice.

She blinked and lifted those dreamy long lashes to meet his gaze. "Huh?"

"I like you, Hayden." He let out a rumble of a laugh, because *like* seemed like such an understatement for the way his blood raged through him, every last drop heading to his dick.

"Come upstairs with me," she invited.

Seconds ticked by as he gathered his control, summoned the sense God gave him. "That seems like a bad idea. I'm not in a place where—"

"You don't want entanglements."

"No." But damn did he want tonight. Just a night…

"I get it, Zane. I do." She lowered her gaze as she wove the tips of their fingers together. "Here's the thing. I don't do relationships. I haven't been on a date for more than two years. It's been an embarrassingly long time since I've even had a fling, but I don't remember ever feeling a pull like I feel with you tonight. Do you feel it too?"

There was no way he could lie, even if it would be smarter. "I feel it too," he said, his voice barely more than a growl.

"I can't help but think it would be an absolute disgrace if we didn't allow ourselves a night of heaven together," she said, adopting more of a drawl, her lips curving into a hint of a smile. An irresistible damn hint of a smile. "Let's spend one night together, Zane. Then we go our separate ways."

When she put it that way, he didn't have to give it a second's deliberation. He'd be a fool to say no.

"Pretty sure that's the best offer I've had in my life."

Without wasting another moment, he pulled the keys out, exited the car, and hurried around to her side. Her lips were on his the second she stood, and it took some effort, but he got the door shut, then led her to the stairs.

CHAPTER FOUR

*H*ayden had never had a man turn her legs to jelly before, had never truly understood the expression…until now.

As they made their way up the stairs—nineteen god-forsaken stairs, to be exact—toward her apartment, her legs were weak and shaky.

From a single kiss.

Zane had woven their fingers together, and she relished the strength and warmth and size of his hand, so much larger than hers. She'd not noticed before how much of a turn-on a man's hands could be.

Something told her—maybe the throbbing ache deep in her lower abdomen—that tonight was quite possibly going to redefine sex for her.

As she stole a glance up at his face, his chiseled, handsome face, she confirmed that she and her ovaries were totally on board for that redefining.

At the landing in front of her door, she dug through her bag for her keys, thinking she should buy one of those porch lights that came on automatically when it got dark, because she never remembered to turn hers on. Never really knew when she'd end up sleeping in her apartment or when she'd make the drive all the way home.

As she dug, the bag slipped out of her hands, probably because they were shaky, too, thanks to the sexy, hulking man right next to her. He picked it up for her and handed it back.

With a sheepish grin, she said, "Thanks."

Finally, she got her fingers on the bulky key ring and pulled it out—and accidentally dropped it as well.

As she laughed quietly, he teased, "How much did you drink tonight?"

"Half a glass of wine plus a few sips of champagne for the toast…hours ago. I think my clumsiness is your fault."

Normally she'd imbibe more at a wedding, especially her BFF's, but the meeting tomorrow was that important to her. She needed to not have a fuzzy brain.

He bent down again and picked the keys up, which was handy, because legs…jelly… When he stood to his full height, towering quite a few inches above her in spite of her heels, he peered down at her, his body close, his heat reaching her in waves.

"How is it my fault?" he asked in a low, intimate voice as he pushed a stray curl out of her face again, sending a shiver through her.

She lifted her empty hand and hovered it over his chest, then ran it up his lapel. "You make me nervous," she said softly, honestly, summoning her courage.

The low growl that emanated from his throat resonated deep inside of her and revved her blood further, and she wondered whether she might be in totally over her head.

"Nothing to be nervous about," he said, brushing his knuckles over her cheek, so close she could feel his breath. "I've got the door."

He held up the key ring, which admittedly had a lot of keys on it, and she pointed out the right one, then he turned away to unlock the door.

Whereas she was still shaky, inside and out, he slid the key in as if there was nothing to it. Hayden made up her mind right then and there that she would get to *him*, do her best to rattle *him* before the night was over. Preferably in the next five minutes.

As he eased the door open, she was jolted back to reality momentarily as she wondered what state she'd left the place in. She wasn't known for her tidiness outside of her business—who had time? It'd been a few nights since she'd slept here.

Who was she kidding? She didn't have a maid service, and there was no way she'd left her apartment in the state she'd want it to be in for having company over.

"Um," she said, entering ahead of him when he stepped back for her to do so, then flipping the light on, "I should warn you… my place is probably not neat and tidy."

"Okay," he said with a quiet laugh.

"Which is to say, it might be a disaster."

The back entryway, where they now stood, had the washer-dryer closet, the second bath, and the spare bedroom attached. Straight ahead, a short hall led to the galley-style kitchen, and she could see it hadn't miraculously cleaned itself since she was last here. There were a few dishes in the sink, the toaster sat askew on the quartz counter, and a stack of unopened mail lay awaiting her attention on the opposite counter. Under her breath, she said, "Could be worse."

She led him farther inside, switching on the recessed lights over the kitchen counter, setting her bag down next to the mail, and looking ahead to the living room to assess its state. Before she could get a view of it, Zane caught her hand in his and drew her into him.

"I could be easily distracted," he said as he slid his hands over her sides, to her waist.

"Yeah?" Forgetting the living room's condition, she stood on her toes, wound her hands up to the back of his neck, and kissed him.

His reply was to plunge his tongue into her mouth and press her up against the cabinets with his solid body. Their mouths still plundering each other, he slid his tux jacket from her shoulders and let it drop to the counter, then he ran his hands up and down her sides, over her hips and back again, as if he'd been dying to explore her curves all evening.

When his thumb trailed over her breast, even with the gown

and her strapless bra between them, she shuddered and arched into him, letting out a moan that might've embarrassed her but didn't, because he lit her on fire like she'd never been lit before. All of her nerves seemed to stretch toward him, enflamed with need, dying for him to touch her, all of her.

Before she could register it, Zane's hands wound around to her butt and lifted her onto the countertop right next to the bag and the mail that she no longer cared about.

Her dress had a high slit in front, to one side, and he used that to his advantage within a single heartbeat, his palm making contact with her bare thigh. She relished the feel of his skin on hers and ached for more.

Zane was apparently on the same page because, with his other hand, he had the long gown up around her thighs in no time, baring her legs, freeing her to wrap one around him and draw him in even closer.

She ran her fingers over his bow tie to see whether it was a clip-on or something she could untie and peel off him.

"A real one," she said to herself.

"No clip-ons for the North boys. My dad taught me to tie one of these when I was six or seven."

"My dad did *not* teach me to untie one, but I've got this."

"I heard that about you," he said, amused, and she snapped her gaze up to him.

"Heard I untie bow ties?" She didn't remember ever doing this before. Maybe after senior prom years ago? If so, it was unmemorable.

"Heard you can be determined. *Steamroller*, I believe, was the word Cole used."

"He got that straight from Sierra. Some days, she just calls it stubbornness." As she said it, she released the tie and pulled it from his neck in victory, smiling.

"I'd call it hot."

His lips were back on hers in the next second, and one of his hands was on her thigh, caressing, working its way higher. The other was at her shoulder, where each side of her dress was held up by two thin straps and a thicker strap that fell off the shoulder and rested on her upper arm. He pushed the straps off one shoulder, giving him better access to her breast.

Still kissing her, he managed to get all the straps on both sides out of his way, then dipped his palm beneath the fabric of the dress and her lingerie, moving it down, freeing her breasts. The feel of his fingers on her nipple was electric, awakening a direct connection to her core and making her squirm against him for more.

Hayden had managed to undo the first few buttons of his shirt, but he seemed intent on distracting her from that. When his tongue laved over one nipple, his fingers still teasing the other, she gave herself over to the sensations and let her head drop back, supporting herself with her hands on the counter behind her.

"Do you want—" She broke off with a gasp, because, oh, my God, he had a talented tongue. "Bed?" she eventually managed.

Zane swirled his tongue and caught the tip of her nipple between it and his teeth, growled, which vibrated across her already burning-up skin, and said, "Later."

His more immediate plan turned out to be driving her out of her ever-loving mind right where they were. He showered attention from his tongue, lips, and fingers on her breasts, then gradually trailed a path of kisses lower, over the gown that was still bunched around her middle, until all his amazing, maddening attention was centered at the apex of her thighs.

She felt the dampness and heat of his tongue swirling over the thin material of her thong. As her head fell against the wall behind her, she shamelessly arched her hips into him, aching for his mouth on her flesh.

He took his sweet time teasing her, exploring, pausing to hook her leg over his shoulder, and then, at last, he moved her thong to the side and laved her skin directly. She nearly launched off the surface at the first touch, gasping, trying to breathe, then deciding oxygen wasn't so important.

This man… He was a master of using his tongue as a glorious, enrapturing weapon.

"I'm going to…" *come, explode, die…* She didn't know which

and lost all ability to think as he drove her higher and higher until she came apart, oblivious to everything except the sensations exploding through her body.

He coaxed more out of her with his mouth, his fingers back on her nipples, lightening his touch, seeming to know just how much contact she could take. She melted into him, savoring the aftereffects of the most earth-shattering orgasm she'd ever experienced.

When she started to recover her wits and coherent thoughts, her heart rate closer to normal and her breathing steadier, she registered the attention he was still giving to her body. Slow, adoring attention, with his mouth, his hands, an occasional nip from his teeth.

He took his sweet, diligent time exploring all of her exposed flesh, her breasts, her neck, her collarbone, her calves and feet. When he unfastened the tiny buckles on the ankle straps to release her shoes, she breathed out her relief. Zane worked his way back to her inner thighs, laving, nibbling, making her feel treasured. Adored. And burning up with need *again*. Already. The way he was owning her body...

"Oh, God," she gasped when his tongue reached her center again, and then she was rendered unable to speak actual words and merely let out incoherent sounds as he took her over the edge. Again. In record time.

As she let her heart get back to non-redline levels, gradually noticing the hardness of the countertop below her, the wall behind her head, she let out a depleted laugh.

"You're going to kill me with all this attention, and you haven't even had any pleasure yet," she finally managed as she sat up straighter, pulled him to a full stand, curling her legs around his middle and tracing her finger over his lower lip.

Zane grinned, like fully grinned, for the first time since she'd met him, and hell's bells, did he have a breathtakingly handsome face. A growl came from his throat, a low, sexy, male sound that reached her on some primal, cellular level. Like, even if she couldn't see him or touch him or be touched by him, that sound alone would jump-start her biological need to procreate.

"I've had pleasure," he said, his voice rough, gravelly. "Your body...seeing it, touching it...so much pleasure..." He bent in to kiss her lips again.

She lowered one hand to his pants—still fully buckled, buttoned, intact, for the love of God—and easily ascertained he was hard as granite and in need of some attention, which she was all too eager to shower on him. He gasped as she stroked him through the fabric.

"Now would be a good time for that bed you mentioned," he said in nearly a whisper, his breath brushing over her ear in an erotic way.

With a playful grin, she leaned back enough to see his face, took in the lust-heavy lids, the strain of need. "Are you...*rattled?*"

"That's one word for it."

She pressed a playful kiss to the tip of his nose. "Good." She managed to slide her bare feet to the tile floor, her body riding down his hard one the whole way. "Going to take me a minute to be able to walk," she said, holding on to him as he grasped her upper arms to steady her.

Before she could adjust to the blood returning to her limbs, Zane swept her up in his arms cradle style, and she let out a surprised yelp.

"Which way?" he asked.

She pointed to the open door on the left side of the living room. With four long strides, he carried her into the bedroom and shut the door behind them. The streetlights came in through the sheer, gauzy curtains and the partially opened blinds that covered the large window on the Hale Street side. They illuminated the room enough for him to see his way to the queen-sized bed.

Hayden noted the clothes strewn everywhere, the books scattered on the padded bench at the foot of the bed, the shoes littering the super-deep white shag rug, but none of it seemed to faze Zane as he carried her single-mindedly to the bed. The bed she had, in fact, made, her one concession to neatness. She could overlook the clutter and the mess, but when she climbed into bed at night, she wanted to pull back neat sheets and blankets, not fall into a lumpy mess.

He set her on the mattress, lifted her dress over her head, and placed it meticulously on the easy chair nearby. When he turned back to her, she'd unfastened her bra and tossed it carelessly over the side of the bed. With her fingers under the thin sides of her thong, she peeled it down her legs and off.

Even in the dimness, she could see the heat in his eyes as he watched her, taking in every inch of her body with his burning gaze.

"Your turn," she prompted, and he got busy unbuttoning his own shirt as she watched. "Want help?" she asked, propping herself up on her elbows, her eyes on his belt.

He shook his head as he whipped his shirt off, then proceeded to undo his pants as he kicked his shoes off. When he shoved his pants and briefs down his legs together, his erection sprung free, and Hayden felt the knot of need tighten deep inside of her. She'd have to trust in the universe that that thing would fit just fine. She was game to give it a college try.

After he'd shed his socks, he lowered his body over hers, and her hand went to stroke him, unable to resist exploring, touching him, relishing the feel of velvet-soft flesh over steel.

Zane groaned and raised his body, catching her hand after only a few seconds of contact. "It's been a long time. Don't want to go too soon."

As he laced his fingers with hers, she noted that his hand was shaking, so instead of pushing him, teasing him as was her first instinct, she relaxed into the thick comforter, sank into the soft memory foam, and let him control everything. With pleasure.

He kissed her, slowly, thoroughly, keeping his body raised just off of hers, and she sensed that the contact would push him too far too fast. She could be accommodating for a bit, but the teasing, having his body so close but not quite touching, his heat engulfing her, was driving her mad, and her body pulsed with need for him. Again.

"We need protection," she said before they got any closer,

starting to rise. She knew she had condoms in one of her bathroom drawers.

"I've got it." After a sweet kiss to her jawline, he moved to the edge of the bed, sat up, and dug through his pants until he found his wallet.

Seconds later, she heard the rip of a foil packet, and when he turned back to her, he was sheathed. She couldn't help herself—she reached for his shaft again, and instead of pulling back or stopping her, he groaned and braced himself over her on his forearms. His arms were shaking slightly too, his biceps bulging but not seeming at all strained, which told her the shaking was desire, all for her. It got to her, really got to her that this hot, sexy man could be that turned on by *her*...

He lowered his body to hers, at long last, as she felt like she'd been waiting her whole life for this man to drive into her and turn her inside out. She felt him at her opening, then he eased inside of her, stretching her, the friction buzzing through her.

"Doing okay?" he asked, restraining himself.

She breathed out an "Mmm," then pulled his face to hers and plunged her tongue into his mouth the way she needed him to do with his body.

Zane surged into her all the way, and she caught her breath, overwhelmed in a good way, so many good ways. He stilled, as if he himself needed a moment, and Hayden tried to be patient and half as considerate as he'd been, fighting the need to arch into him, swirl her hips against him. She pressed kisses to his jawline, burrowing her fingers through his short hair. He was biting his lip, his eyes closed.

"You feel...incredible." Letting out a breath of a laugh, he added, "That word doesn't do you justice. Jesus."

"Back at you," she whispered, meeting his gaze for an intense second.

Then he began moving in and out of her, eliciting a gasp from her. She wrapped her legs around him, drawing him in, meeting his every thrust, climbing toward release already. Never in her life had she had a three-O night, but she was well on her way.

Zane North was a magic man, she thought, and she kept a

silent, joyful laugh to herself, a combination of amusement and astonishment and sheer ecstasy.

Within moments, their intensity notched upward. Hayden lost all ability to think, became overloaded with physical sensation, lost in this man, as if her sole purpose for being on this earth was to give and receive pleasure with him.

He reached between their bodies and touched her right above where they were joined; she went off like a bottle rocket, clinging to him for all she was worth as she rode the waves of yet another orgasm. She felt him stiffen and still, felt his gritty "Fuuuck" brush over her ear as he came as well.

Aftershocks of bliss ricocheted through her for long seconds, making her moan in appreciation. He rested his weight partially on her, and she savored the feel of it, breathed in the male scent of him, running her hands gently up and down his back, relishing his strength in the ridges of muscle, the tone of his butt. Her military guy was cut and fit, no two ways about it.

Her military guy *for the night*. She allowed herself a private smile because that was ideal.

But actually, what would be the harm in a *few* nights? They were both dedicated to not getting their hearts involved, but she wouldn't mind entwining their bodies on a semi-regular basis. Consenting adults, physical release, hella good orgasms…

Zane shifted, moving his hands to the mattress on either side of her shoulders, holding himself up in a half push-up as he kissed her slowly and thoroughly. She couldn't help herself; she slid her hands to his biceps, running her fingers over the hard bulges that supported him.

As their bodies slipped apart from their intimate connection, he pulled back from her lips and frowned. "Be right back," he said. "Bathroom?"

She pointed to her en suite, and as he headed that way, she curled onto her side to watch him walk away, appreciating the play of shadows and light over his narrow hips and perfect ass. The door closed, and the gap beneath it lit up when he turned on the light.

When she rolled to her back again, the smile was still on her face and her body still buzzed from that man's skills. The smile slipped away at the thought that he might not be on board with seeing her again. That would be sad but maybe smart.

"Tonight, though…" she whispered, and the grin was back.

She'd convince him to stay tonight. Another round or two broken up by sleep would be heavenly. Though she'd be tired for her morning meeting, she'd be energized in a different way. A little more time with Zane would be worth it. Now to convince him.

The bathroom door opened and Zane came out. Naturally, she drank in the sight of him, not minding that he'd left the light on and the door open as he made his way to the bed. When her gaze reached his face, though, she noted he wasn't looking at her. In fact, his face, averted toward the floor, was drawn in a frown.

He didn't look as over the moon with lust as she was. He didn't look anything like she'd expect a man to look after getting his rocks off with a no-strings, willing woman. And she was still naked and everything, but he didn't even know. Because he wouldn't look at her.

"Zane?" She rose to her elbows as he reached the bed and lowered himself to sit on the edge. "Hey. You okay?" She swung her legs to the floor, sitting next to him, several inches separating their thighs.

Still not looking at her, he breathed out heavily, and her hope of continuing their night started to dissipate. He hunched forward, bracing his elbows on his thighs, running both hands over his face.

As Hayden's brain started racing on what the actual hell was going on, he lifted his head, pressed his lips together, then said, "The condom broke."

CHAPTER FIVE

*H*ayden stopped breathing as Zane's words sank in and sucked out all of the joy and contentment of thirty seconds ago.

Silence weighed heavily in the room as she tried to wrap her mind around what he'd said. She reached over and flipped on the lamp on the nightstand, illuminating the room in a low, ambient light that did nothing to lend comfort at this moment.

"You're sure?" she finally asked, running her hands up her arms as the chill of the night washed over her. Her head, so far, was rejecting the news.

With a loud exhale, Zane nodded in response, his hands over his mouth. Then he reached down to the floor and picked something up—the empty wrapper, she realized—and scrutinized it. He shook his head and said, "Not expired."

Not expired. Just broken. Useless.

For the first time in her life, she'd just had unprotected sex.

Surely the universe couldn't be that cruel, could it? It was just one time…

She knew that rationale was ridiculous even as she clung to it.

"A pregnancy right now would *not* work for me," she said, more to herself than anything. "There's already not enough hours in the day."

When she'd first opened Henry Interiors, the retail store, it had taken some time for foot traffic to pick up, as Hale Street was still in the redevelopment stages back then. It'd been easy to find time, while she manned the store, to work on her interior design business, to meet with potential clients, to work up designs and bids, to process the business end of it. Now that the store was in its third year, retail business had grown exponentially and was, quite frankly, on the verge of kicking her ass. In a good way. Her design clientele was growing as well.

"Elena would kill me," she said out loud.

"Who's Elena?"

Zane's voice drew her out of her deep dive into her own world. "My assistant. Also known as a godsend. She jokes that she's actively looking to clone me for my own sanity."

Hayden mostly suspected she was too late as far as sanity was concerned. But Hayden thrived on the challenge, fed on the energy of both her burgeoning businesses.

"Maybe we're fine," Zane said. "How's the timing of your cycle?"

The timing of her cycle… She let out a self-deprecating laugh. "Oh, good question."

Shit. She sucked at keeping track. Didn't even try. Hadn't ever needed to. Even with Patrick and Brian, she hadn't had any true scares. Matter of fact, with Brian, they hadn't had sex that often, which should have clued her in that he was getting it elsewhere, but that was neither here nor there at this moment.

"I don't know," she said quietly, racking her brain, trying to come up with any concept of when her last period had been. "It's been…a while. More than a week. More than two weeks, probably."

Which meant the timing for a pregnancy was…all too possible.

Still naked, she suddenly felt super exposed, so she stood and scanned the floor for her silky salmon-colored robe. She found it in a pile in front of the built-in floor-to-ceiling wardrobes that lined the walls on the way to the bathroom, picked it up, slipped it on, and tied it in front.

When she glanced back at Zane, she realized he'd put his

boxer briefs back on. It was a disgrace to cover that body but probably for the best. They had shit to figure out.

Shit like a potential pregnancy.

"Not enough curse words in the known universe," she muttered as her brain dived further into the possibility of conceiving a baby.

Was it just hours ago that she'd looked at Kennedy's seven-month-pregnant belly and wished, if only a tiny bit, that she was in the position to have that?

Sweet God above, she did *not* want that!

"Oh, God." Hayden sagged heavily against one of the wardrobe doors and covered her face with both hands, as if she could hide from reality.

As her heart raced with honest-to-god fear and nausea rose in her throat, she felt hands on her upper arms. Large, gentle hands grasping her, reminding her that, at this moment, she wasn't alone. She lowered her hands and looked at him, registered the intent in those arresting blue eyes.

"Hey," he said. "It's probably going to be okay. We've got a fifty-fifty chance here, right?"

"I don't love those odds." She lowered her gaze to his bare chest and couldn't help running a finger down it even if her mind was locked on their situation and unable to truly soak in the pleasure a chest like that could evoke.

"Fifty percent chance of rain, you're probably not even going to take an umbrella." He caressed her upper arms.

Hayden laughed. "I can't seem to remember an umbrella even if it's raining when I walk out the door." Realizing she must sound irresponsible, she added, "Just so you know, I've never had unprotected sex in my life. So you're safe that way."

"I haven't either."

She let out another laugh, but it wasn't one full of humor, more like an edge of hysteria. "Look at us. We have something in common."

"Couple things," he said dryly, obviously referring to their current dilemma. "We're borrowing trouble. I thought you should know about the condom, but it doesn't mean we've been sentenced to eighteen years—"

"Plus nine months," she said, because, hell's bells, she hadn't even begun to consider an actual child. She was too caught up in the thought of a pregnancy and how *that* would rock her entire world. "You're right. Borrowing trouble, and that's a waste of time." She straightened, met his gaze again, and forced a sort-of smile. "We're probably fine."

"But if we're not, we'll figure it out. Together. You're not in this alone, Hayden." The intensity in his eyes shook her to her soul and made her almost believe him, even if she didn't have the slightest clue what being together meant in this case. She couldn't begin to think that far ahead. Hoped they didn't have to. "I'm damn sorry about the condom."

"It's hardly your fault. And it's going to be fine." She straightened and said it with more confidence than she felt. *Fake it till you make it.*

If only that would work for *not* getting knocked up…

"It is." Zane stepped his delectable body away and went for his pants, pulled them on, then he picked up his shirt.

Hayden settled onto the edge of the bed to watch him button his shirt, because one, it was like watching live art, and two, it beat the heck out of thinking too hard. There'd be time for that later.

Though she'd been fantasizing about a full night with him just minutes ago, him leaving would be better now. Things had gone weird and stressy, at least for her, even if she was determined to believe everything would be fine. And even if there was a part of her that thought, *Shove that stress down and get him naked one more time!*

When he tapped her chin lightly, she realized her lips had curved up into the beginnings of a smile at that thought.

"We should exchange numbers. Just in case," he said, then he seemed to backtrack. "I mean, we'll probably see each other often enough, what with my brother and your best friend being married now…"

"True. Or at least once they're back from their honeymoon. But we should definitely exchange numbers." *In case.*

She rose and led him back to the kitchen, to the bag where her phone was, and the sight of the counter… If she was a blusher, that would do it. She'd never think of that counter quite the same again.

Leaning a hip against it, she dug her phone out, unlocked it, and handed it to him. He entered his number, then sent a message to himself. She didn't hear a text notification, had no idea if his phone was even on him, come to think of it.

After he handed it back to her, he took her other hand in his, surprising her. He ran his thumb over her fingers, his eyes on their hands as he said, "If this goes to worst-case scenario, you let me know."

She nodded.

"Promise?"

Hayden glanced up into his eyes, then got caught up in them again, because his stare was once again piercing into her, as if to convey that he meant it, cared about this.

"Promise," she said. "I wouldn't hide it from you, Zane." Then, mostly for her own benefit, she added, "Everything's going to be fine anyway. You'll run in to me at a random North family barbecue in a year and realize you forgot all about me."

That would be preferable to having to notify him in a couple of weeks that they were going to be parents, but even so, if she was honest with herself, the thought of Zane forgetting her made her a little sad.

"Impossible," he said in a low, rumbly voice she wouldn't forget anytime soon.

Knowing this could be the last chance to have him to herself, Hayden tugged him to her, stood on her tiptoes, and pressed a kiss to his lips. A goodbye kiss.

Except instead of goodbye, his reaction was to pull her hips into him with those big, capable hands and turn the kiss from simple to complicated. Lingering. Mind-scrambling.

With a short exhale of a laugh, he broke the contact of their mouths and shifted the embrace to something a little more along the lines of friendly and caring. She could feel, though, his body had reacted, his erection pressing into her.

That gave her some measure of satisfaction. She would cling to that later, after he was long gone and she was, once again, all alone.

———

ZANE CLIMBED into his rental car, tossed his tuxedo jacket on the passenger seat, started the engine to get the heat going, and let out a breath that he felt like he'd been holding on to for days.

Fuck.

What moment was it, exactly, that he'd weakened and made the wrong decision tonight?

Giving Hayden a ride home?

No. He couldn't leave her stranded in the middle of the night.

Kissing her in the car?

Well, that wasn't his brightest move, but it was recoverable. He could have kissed her in the front seat of his car for a week straight and not been in his current fucked-up situation.

Undoubtedly it was the moment after the kiss when he'd let himself be convinced that, as long as they both had no delusions about a relationship, it would be okay to indulge in a few hours of mutual pleasure.

He clenched a fist and resisted the urge to pound the steering wheel, clenched his jaw so hard he could break a tooth, then held in the stream of swear words that exploded in his mind. Because control was his middle name, and yelling and beating things wouldn't do a damn thing to change this situation.

As if to prove that, he backed calmly out of the parking space and pointed the car toward his mom's house.

Hell. He was an expert in risk mitigation. He was alive today because he'd learned *when* to take a risk and *which* risks to take in things far more complex than sex.

Tonight, he'd ignored everything he knew and followed his dick instead of his brain. Didn't matter that he didn't do it often. Didn't matter that he'd tried to be responsible by using protection. He knew condoms weren't one hundred percent. Nothing was except not going up those stairs to Hayden's apartment.

For years, Zane had been the guy who had his shit together. He'd known his path in life from an early age. From four or five years old, he'd wanted to fly planes. Now his life was more unsettled than it had ever been, his future unclear, and if Hayden did get pregnant, he didn't have a fucking clue what he'd do—other than be a responsible human being and take care of his kid. Whatever that entailed.

As he drove along nearly deserted streets, in his mind he saw a sleek, high-dollar, supreme-performing fighter jet blazing through the clear blue sky, and then, *boom*, it lost a wing in midair and spiraled out of control toward the deep, fathomless sea.

Zane only hoped the pilot could eject in time.

CHAPTER SIX

*S*unday morning, Hayden stood by the live-edge walnut-slab dining set in the back corner of the sales floor of Henry Interiors, barely managing to keep a lid on her excitement. She kept her eye on her newest design client, Jane Johansen, who wound her way through the various room displays toward the main exit at the front of the store.

Next to Hayden, Elena Morales, her assistant and frequent lifesaver, still sat at the table where they'd met, playing it cool, jotting some final notes from their meeting on her tablet.

Jane and Tom Johansen were old-money, had a grand seventy-four-hundred-square-foot 1920s home in upscale Belle Meade, and were updating all the common areas—salon, foyer, game room, entertainment bar, and more. Violet Morello, owner of Sugar Babies Sweet Shop three doors down, had introduced them, warning Hayden that Jane had a heart of gold and a penchant for gossip, and most importantly, deep connections to rich, high-society women who would be an extremely desirable market for Henry Design.

The bell over the door chimed as the diminutive sixty-something woman walked out to the sidewalk with a final smile and finger wave over her shoulder, then turned right and made her dignified way past the store's windows and out of their sight.

Hayden let out a happy laugh and hugged Elena as soon as her tall twenty-eight-year-old assistant popped out of her chair.

"We did it," Hayden said as they swayed together in a celebratory dance. "Oh, my god, we did it!"

"Let's be real. *You* did it. She liked your designs so much that she went with them even though we weren't the lowest bid," Elena said.

Sydney, one of Hayden's full-time store employees, peeked out from the mostly open sliding barn door that led to the back room. Hayden had heard her arrive about fifteen minutes ago for her store-opening eleven a.m. shift. While Sydney, Marley, and Trinity were strictly retail employees, Elena was Hayden's right hand for her separate interior design business, although she was well versed in the retail business as well.

"Did she sign?" Sydney asked, her perfectly shaped dark brows rising in question.

"Yes, ma'am." Hayden held up the electronic tablet where they'd accessed the relevant documents. She threw her head back, eyes closed, savoring the moment.

Whenever she landed a new design client, it reaffirmed that she was doing what she was meant to be doing. Not that she truly doubted it, but there was always a small part of her that had to have validation—likely the part that still felt guilty for not joining her brothers in their nana's bar and grill.

Sydney let out a whoop, said, "Hold, please," then disappeared into the back room again.

"I just have one question," Elena said to Hayden, suddenly serious, her tone scolding.

"I know, I know," Hayden said. "The timing."

"How in the *hell* are you going to pull this off? You can't be two places at once."

"If we couldn't start in three weeks, she would've gone with the other company. I'm sure of it."

Elena conceded, nodding. "Better get on that cloning project. We'll be right in the middle of the Wilson project in three weeks."

"I know. I'll figure something out."

"I know you will," Elena said. "Just make sure it doesn't include you giving up sleep completely."

Hayden had ideas for how to handle it. Of course she had ideas. She had business stuff running through her mind twenty-four hours a day, and one of the possibilities she was considering was giving Elena more responsibility. The idea was solid; it was just…hard for Hayden to act on.

Elena was a design student, an overachieving straight-A one, nearly done with the program, and her potential was why Hayden had hired her more than a year ago. Elena was fully capable of overseeing the in-progress Wilson project. She was more organized than Hayden was, truth be told. But it would be the first time Hayden entrusted such a big part of her business—either of her businesses—to someone else, and there was still a stumbling block somewhere in Hayden's head.

"Time to celebrate, ladies." Sydney stood in the doorway to the back room and held up an open bottle of champagne and three flutes.

"Yes!" Hayden said, and she and Elena walked to the back room for a toast.

The store officially opened in a minute or two, so they'd keep their celebration and their alcohol out of sight.

It wasn't until Hayden raised the glass flute to her lips that she remembered—there was a chance she could be pregnant. Champagne might not be the best thing for her right now.

After a pause, she took a sip, knowing one little swallow wouldn't hurt. Some would say alcohol in moderation would be fine, and maybe that was true, but she'd figure that out later. *If* she was pregnant.

She set the flute on the high-top counter in the break area, her smile fading.

"You okay?" Elena asked, watching her carefully.

Hayden nodded and forced the smile back on. "I haven't eaten anything yet. My stomach is a little off."

"Got you covered," Sydney said as she walked around to the other side of the counter to the kitchenette and picked up a teal bakery box. "I brought a half-dozen muffins."

"Cherry almond?" Hayden asked.

"I'm not dumb." Sydney—and the rest of Hayden's staff—knew very well what Hayden's favorite Sugar Babies flavors were.

"Godsend." Hayden helped herself to the box, holding it out for Elena, who grabbed the chocolate chocolate chip.

At the first bite of sweet cherry, crunchy almond, and slightly warm cake, Hayden let all the what-if thoughts go and decided maybe carbs could fix everything.

The bell on the front door chimed, and Sydney snapped into action, setting down her blueberry muffin by her nearly empty champagne glass and heading toward the sales floor.

"Hel-lo," Sydney purred quietly before she reached the door between the back and main rooms.

Elena and Hayden exchanged a raised-brow look, then Elena stepped away from the counter so she could check out the person who'd entered.

As soon as she did, she let out a tongue-roll growl. "He's not on the right team for me, but even I can admit he's a tall glass of water."

Men weren't frequently their customers, with the exception of designers, who were becoming more common, interested enough in Hayden's one-of-a-kind merchandise that they overlooked her position as a competitor in the design realm. Wondering if it was a designer she'd met in the past, Hayden shoved the last of her muffin in her mouth and moved just enough that she could see out the open door to the sales floor—and promptly got the food stuck in her throat, coughing and sputtering.

What the Sam Hill was Zane doing here?

Her mouth still full, she leaped out of the line of sight before he could spot her, her eyes wide in disbelief as she frantically chewed and tried not to choke. She leaned against the floor-to-ceiling shelving unit of stored accent pieces, her heart thundering in her chest.

As Elena came back into the room, Hayden managed to swallow her food, her mouth suddenly parched.

"The gentleman asked for *you*," Elena said, her brows raised nearly to her hairline. "I don't get the impression he's here to buy a sofa."

Hayden was big on selling sofas, but she hoped Zane wasn't here to buy anything. She could admit, if only to herself, she wanted him to be here to see *her*.

"Thanks," Hayden said. "Do I have crumbs on my face?"

Checking her face, Elena shook her head. "You look gorgeous." Then she narrowed her eyes. "If a little sleep-deprived. I didn't see the circles under your eyes until now. Nice job with the makeup." With a knowing look, she glanced back toward the sales floor, as if seeing Zane, who was thankfully still out of Hayden's sight, in a new light.

That speculation prompted Hayden to brush her hands together to get rid of any signs of her muffin and then step toward the doorway before Elena could say more.

He stood in profile to her, about twenty feet away, gazing at a rack of pillows in every color and size. She couldn't help but pause for a moment and admire—him, not the pillows.

He was tall but not too tall, maybe around six foot or a little over, and his body was...fit. That's the word she thought of. *Damn fit.* There wasn't an ounce of fat on him, she knew that firsthand, and he wasn't thick with muscles but rather slim and well sculpted. A pilot's body, was all she could conclude. They probably couldn't have too much bulk to fit in a cockpit. At any rate, everything about him appealed to her. Too much.

"Zane," she said, and he turned toward her.

Damn, his face was a pretty sight when he met her gaze. And by *pretty*, she meant hot, masculine, manly. She could swear he had a direct line to her female hormones.

He gave her his half smile as he turned toward her. He wore a lined brown winter jacket, unzipped, over an olive-green Henley and dark denim jeans. It was obvious he'd shaved since she'd seen him, as his jaw looked clean of the rough stubble she'd run her fingers over just hours ago.

"Hayden, how's it going?"

She couldn't miss his once-over, his eyes drifting from her

dove-gray jacket to her scallop-necked shirt, down her slim black pants to her classic three-inch pumps.

"Good," she said cautiously. "What are you doing here?"

Please don't say furniture shopping.

"I'd like to talk to you in private."

That sounded less fun than she'd hoped. Maybe furniture shopping wouldn't be so bad.

Elena had busied herself straightening the pillows on a nearby love seat, her back to them, acting as if she wasn't listening, but she was six feet away and hanging on every single word, Hayden knew. Store tasks, like straightening pillows, weren't remotely in Elena's job description.

Sydney, too, hovered on the other side of the pillow rack, Hayden realized. With a grin, she said, "It will greatly disappoint my employees, but we can talk in my office."

"Take your time," Sydney sang out, her grin audible.

Hayden was definitely going to have some explaining to do, at least in their eyes.

She led Zane through the merchandise-cluttered back room, sliding that door closed once he was through, and then into her tiny office, beyond the break area. She closed that door too.

"I did say private," Zane said with amusement. "Nosy employees?"

"In a word, yes. They're wonderful people and good friends, but let's just say we don't get a lot of good-looking Navy pilots through our doors."

"We could go upstairs if you'd prefer."

"No." *Hell no.* Upstairs they'd be *too* alone. "This is good. I'll be able to hear if they get swamped and need me." Which they wouldn't. Sundays were not one of their busier days.

She'd always known her office was tiny—that was by design, in fact, because she spent very little time in it—but she hadn't been prepared for the effect of sharing the space with Zane North *and* having the door closed. Good lord, he was standing a foot and a half away from her—because there wasn't space for more—and she could smell him, could practically feel him breathe.

"Have a seat," she said, trying to shake herself out of her hyperawareness of him.

Instead of hard, uninviting guest chairs, Hayden had two plush barrel chairs in front of her desk so when she and her employees met, they were comfortable. Zane took the far one, making the compact chair seem miniature.

After a moment's debate on whether to sit next to him in the other barrel chair or to put her desk between them, she walked around her French-country-style antique desk. It was white with gold accents and definitely not very practical, but it was small and pretty and she liked the vibe of it—and the space it gave her from this man who seemed able to affect her on a cellular level without even trying. She lowered herself to her white executive chair.

"So…" She left the word hanging, inviting him to get to whatever he'd come to talk about.

"So…" He rested both arms on the too-small arms of the chair, tapping the fingers of one hand, obviously not at ease. "I was up most of the night thinking about our situation."

"Potential situation," she corrected. "Assuming you mean a pregnancy."

Zane nodded. "Fair enough. I researched the morning-after pill. Have you thought about that?"

"I… No." She folded her hands together and rested them on her desk, leaning forward, sorting through her thoughts.

The truth was, she'd convinced herself after he'd left that the chances of a pregnancy were minuscule and that worrying about it at that moment would be pointless. After an insanely busy week of hard-core wedding prep on top of her two jobs, she'd fallen into an exhausted sleep, one where she found herself lying in the same position when her alarm went off.

She hadn't been in this situation before, and the morning-after pill was barely on her radar. It hadn't occurred to her at all.

As she thought about it now, her gut feeling was…not as relieved as he appeared to be.

She frowned and met his gaze. "So you're saying we don't even know if there is a baby but you want to get rid of it?"

"That's not what I'm saying at all." He pressed his lips together, as if preventing himself from blurting out whatever flashed into his mind first, seeming to consider his next words. "First off, my opinion is secondary here. That's not to say I'm not involved. If you're pregnant, I'm involved one hundred percent. But the bigger burden is yours, regardless, and I respect your right to decide what happens to your body."

She felt her shoulders relax by a degree, then nodded once and waited for him to go on, because frankly, she was reeling now that she had enough time to breathe—and think.

"The window is narrow for the pill—seventy-two hours—so I wanted to be sure *you* had that option if *you* wanted it," he said.

Leaning farther onto her desk, she ran her hands over her face, trying to wrap her head around that option. "Three days…"

Three days to decide if she wanted to wipe out any chance of conception with this guy she barely knew. *This* decision wasn't even about the guy or how well she knew him so much as it was about *do you want to have a baby or don't you?*

She did. Someday. She wasn't ready yet, but someday she wanted to be a mom, a wife, on top of a successful career woman.

"Technically two and a half," he said, his tone gentle and sympathetic.

What if she took that little pill and then never got pregnant in her life?

What if this was her only chance to have a child?

Was she willing to give that up just because the timing wasn't ideal?

Zane was watching her, as if letting her come to her own conclusions, which she appreciated.

"How can a person make such a gargantuan decision in two and a half damn days?" Hayden asked rhetorically. She ran one hand through her straight-as-a-board hair, unconcerned about messing it up what with much bigger issues to worry about.

Seconds of silence passed with her thoughts racing, internal arguments going back and forth. Then she felt his hand on hers, and she looked at him as he clasped their fingers together.

"This is just an observation," he said, "not an attempt to sway you either way. Just guessing here, but I suspect a lot of women would say *Get me the pill* without thinking. Because it's that black-and-white for them. It doesn't seem black-and-white for you."

"No. It's not."

"So tell me something, Hayden Henry, how do you normally handle decisions? Decisions that aren't so potentially life-changing. Run-of-the-mill daily decisions. Are you impulsive and go with your gut? Or do you deliberate for weeks?"

"Somewhere in the middle," she answered quickly. "Sierra's impulsive, and she makes me look slow, but I like to think through my options."

His thumb was brushing back and forth over her fingers, and she watched it, taking a mental side trip to consider how much skill must be in that thumb, those fingers, in order to pilot a fighter jet. When her inappropriate brain started veering toward what other skills his hands had, she pulled away and sat up straighter. "What about you, Zane?"

"As a pilot, I've had to learn to make split-second life-or-death decisions, but this isn't mine to make."

"What if it was?"

He studied her pensively, as if he was analyzing her down to her gray matter. "I think if I were in your position, I'd give it another twenty-four hours. You have time. This is too big to rush."

Hayden was nodding before he finished his sentence, because that seemed a hell of a lot smarter than blurting out *Get me the pill* and "taking care" of it today.

"So tell me this," she said, her voice low just in case anyone was in the back room, "what would you do if I didn't take the pill and ended up pregnant?"

He averted his gaze and swallowed, as if he was trying to get that possibility down. "Specifics, I don't know. Generally, we'd figure things out."

"Really?" Was this guy for real? He was saying the right things in this very wrong situation, but did he mean them?

His gaze shot up to meet hers, his brows rising. "Really. Last I knew, you didn't get yourself pregnant."

"No," she said slowly, trying to believe that he wouldn't desert her.

Of course, if he did desert her, and *if* she was indeed with child, she would figure it out. In fact, that was probably a safer route to think about now and later. *If* she was pregnant.

He clenched his jaw for a second and then looked intently into her eyes again. "I realize you don't know me at all—that's the folly of our situation—but the first thing you should know is that I don't shirk my responsibilities. Ever."

The way he said it, the way he stared at her with those arresting blue eyes, she wanted to believe him. She had no doubt *he* believed what he said. But, she knew, sometimes things changed. People changed their mind. So she merely nodded half-heartedly, also knowing there was no point in debating.

"Do you want kids, Zane?"

He blew out a breath and rubbed his hands down his face, let out a sort of scoffing laugh. "Question of the day, huh? If you're talking someday, yes. I guess I always envisioned having kids eventually. I like kids. Family's important."

"Just not today," she said with a laugh that didn't quite work.

"Hadn't planned on it this soon, no."

"Well…" She sat back in her chair, adding space between them, breathing in air that was a little less full of Zane. Because he was overwhelming, and if she were a fanciful girl, she might really want to be sucked in by all that was Zane North. But she wasn't. She was a practical girl. A two-business-owning girl who did best when she relied on herself. "It seems like a long shot, doesn't it?"

"Fifty-fifty," he said just like he had last night.

Damn his math and his logic. "You're not going to let me positive-think our way out of this, are you?" she joked.

"If I thought it would work, I'd be all for it." His expression became distant for a moment, troubled. Hinted that he was going through a tough time even without their current predicament.

Hayden studied him, wanting to know more, wishing she

could help him sort through whatever was bothering him. Wishing he would open up to her about something besides kids and pregnancies.

She grasped then that her self-protective approach of cross-that-bridge-if-we-get-to-it was not working for him, and she relented a little.

"I don't need twenty-four hours," she said, scared as hell but listening to her gut as well as her heart. "I'm not getting the morning-after pill. If I'm pregnant…we'll figure things out."

Or *she* would. Whatever she needed to do, *she would*. She had a strong support system in the very best girlfriends and her dad and brothers. She wouldn't lock Zane out if he wanted to be involved, but she couldn't help being skeptical and maybe scared to believe in him.

And, she reminded herself, she didn't know that she needed to. Not yet.

That bridge she would cross *if* she got to it.

CHAPTER SEVEN

Zane had been back in Tennessee for barely more than forty-eight hours. Forty-eight hours and he was still waiting for some semblance of relief to set in. Instead, it was as if he'd stepped from one hot zone into another, this one entirely of his making.

That was not a position he was used to being in. He was used to making sure shit went right.

Two days back and he was sleeping in his childhood room, among his and his brother's sports trophies and video game posters and Cardinals paraphernalia.

Two days back and he might've gotten a girl pregnant. *Him.* The guy who'd always had his shit together and then some. The guy who left as little as possible to chance.

He stood at his bedroom window, looking out over the dark backyard, the lawn a winter brown, the trees leafless and stark in the illumination from the kitchen window. He'd told his mom he was napping, and she hadn't pointed out that he wasn't a napper, had let him have the time to himself he so desperately needed.

Time alone on the boat had been hard to come by, but he'd been able to, at times, drift to the back corner of the ready room and keep to himself in a room full of aviators. Here, it was harder. He loved his mom, loved his family—even the newest additions, his brothers' wives—but it was impossible to be just a spectator, not with them peppering him with questions about everything from living on a carrier to flying a multimillion-dollar F/A-18 to what made him decide to come home to what he planned to do with the rest of his life. He appreciated that they were interested in his life, that they were making an effort to reconnect, but he wasn't in the right frame of mind to be so sociable.

It'd been six hours since Hayden had decided not to take the morning-after pill, and he was still processing all the ramifications.

If the decision had been his, would he have had made the same one? Probably not, he could admit. He didn't like leaving things up to chance. But he could also admit that there was probably a hell of a lot more to it than he could ever imagine, being a male. While he couldn't fault Hayden for making that decision, could actually admit to respecting it and admiring her for not taking the obvious "easier" way out, he could try to make a plan for how to handle every possible outcome.

In theory.

And now he had to sit through more family time. The very thing he'd longed for the past few months was too much too fast, between the wedding festivities and tonight's upcoming Sunday dinner. The North family had always been as loud as a Navy squadron. Add in the women and it was at least a squadron and a half. And he just craved peace.

He could hear his brothers and sisters-in-law arriving though, and he'd already flaked on helping his mom with prep beyond tossing her bean recipe in the crockpot to simmer, so he put on his friendly family face, shoved down the incessant might-be-a-father worries, and headed downstairs.

The whole gang was indeed present and accounted for—except Cole and Sierra, of course, who'd flown off to the island of Jiva for a two-week honeymoon. His mother was gracious when he apologized for not helping more, telling him he needed recuperation time and that she fully intended to take care of him for as long as he would let her. He'd bitten down on the urge to tell her that wasn't going to happen and simply hugged her. She was the best mom ever but would never understand his need for solitude.

A couple of hours later, after a hellaciously good home-cooked meal of fried chicken, biscuits, baked beans, and fries—a definite upside of staying with his mom—the family sat around the table, chatting, drinking, finishing up the fresh-baked apple and cherry pies that had filled the house with a killer aroma all afternoon. Now that just about everyone was married, both table leaves were necessary—his mom at the head, Mason, Calvin, and Eliza on one side, Drake, Mackenzie, Gabe, and Lexie on the other, and Zane at the foot. The barrage of questions about living at sea had subsided some time ago, and he was content to listen in on the others' conversations.

When Gabe sat up straighter, shared a look with Lexie, and cleared his throat, Zane sensed something was up even before his brother said, "We have some news to share."

The table quieted down as much as a three-ring circus could quiet down, and all eyes focused on Gabe expectantly.

"We're pregnant," Gabe said with a wide-ass grin, as if it'd been all he could do to wait till after the meal to make the announcement.

The fucking irony, Zane thought as the rest of the table broke out in howls and squeals and congratulations. Their mom was on her feet with her hands over her mouth in half a heartbeat, then she went around the table and threw her arms around Lexie, then Gabe, tears shining in her eyes. He reminded himself that for a newly married couple who was so obviously gaga for each other, the news was full of happiness and optimism and good feelings.

"It's early," Lexie said as she sat back down. "Really early, so we're only telling family for now."

"We couldn't keep it to ourselves," Gabe admitted. "So keep it on the down low for another few weeks, please."

Zane set aside his angst for his own situation, stood enough to lean over and kiss Lexie on the cheek, and said, "Congrats, you guys." As long as they were happy, he was happy for them.

The North family was apparently exploding. He couldn't help the thought that he hoped he wasn't part of that expansion.

It took a couple of minutes for the excited buzz and the questions to die down, with Zane mostly observing from his end of the table, and that's how he spotted Mason giving Eliza a raised-brow look over four-year-old Calvin's head. With a grin that seemed to be bursting with anticipation, Eliza nodded at her husband, and Zane knew what was going to happen before Mason could say a word.

"There must be something in the water," Mason said, "because this guy"—he picked up Calvin and pulled him on his lap—"is going to be a big brother. We're having a baby too."

Something in the water indeed, Zane thought.

Calvin's eyes went wide and he looked to his mom, speechless.

"How does that sound, kiddo?" Eliza asked him, grabbing his small hand and rubbing her forehead to his. "How would you like a baby brother or sister?"

"I want a brother!" Calvin blurted, making everyone laugh.

"We'll have to see what we get," Mason said.

Faye made a trip around to their side of the table for more hugs and tears and congratulations.

"Is this a conspiracy?" Mackenzie said, laughing. "Just so you know, I'm not succumbing to peer pressure."

"Two more grandbabies," Faye said, her voice teeming with joy. "I couldn't be happier."

"We need a toast," Drake said, raising his beer bottle, and everyone did the same with whatever they were drinking, Lexie and Eliza with hot tea, Zane noticed. "To making the North family bigger." He glanced at Mackenzie and then added, "Courtesy of my brothers...for now."

"Amen," Mackenzie said.

Zane added to himself, his *other* brothers.

"I'm planning to redecorate Mason and Gabe's bedroom for Calvin when he stays with me," their mom said, her face lighting up. "I could turn Cole's room into a nursery at the same time so all these grandbabies can come to Mimi's any time."

Talk turned to design ideas and what theme Calvin would like, and Zane got up to help himself to another soda. As he was pouring a can into a glass with ice, everyone but Gabe and Mason headed upstairs to make plans for the redesigns. Zane couldn't have asked for a better opportunity to hit them up for a job.

"You guys want something else?" he asked from the adjoining kitchen.

"I'm good," Mason said, and Gabe asked for a bottled water.

Zane took the two drinks back to the table. "Talk to me about NBS. What kind of role can I fit into there?"

To his surprise, his brothers just eyed him for a few seconds, causing an uncomfortable silence, and Zane wondered what the fuck he'd said wrong.

"Do you not want me there?" he asked.

"Of course we want you there," Mason said, and he sounded genuine in spite of the hesitation.

"Then what?"

Mason and Gabe shared a look—a brief one, but a look—and then Gabe said, "Are you sure that's what you want to do?" Zane got the impression the two had discussed this previously.

With a shallow laugh, Zane said, "What else am I going to do?"

Mason sat back in his chair and said, "You could do anything. Seems like you're at a crossroads where the choice is yours. What do you *want* to do?"

Instead of blurting out that he didn't fucking know, Zane studied his brothers, trying to read between the lines.

"What we're trying to say," Gabe said in his equitable way, "is that we want you at North Brothers Sports if you really want to be there, but there's no obligation."

"I call bullshit," Zane said. "Dad set it up so that all of us would be taken care of. I've already shirked that duty for more than a decade. I should pull my weight."

"I don't think Dad ever intended for any of us to be roped in," Mason said.

Gabe nodded and leaned his elbows on the table. "You've

been through a hell of a change. I suspect you've got enough money that you could be set for life if you never worked again. So why rush the decision?"

"I need to do something now. I'm not cut out to be unemployed."

"Gabe," Lexie called from what sounded like the top of the stairs. "We need your opinion up here."

"My decorating skills are in high demand," he said with a laugh and went upstairs.

"Here's the thing," Mason said. "You'll always be welcome at North Brothers, but I want you to *want* to do it, to feel some kind of passion about it if you're going to go that route. The last thing I want is you feeling forced to be there, whether by your misinterpretation of Dad's intentions or your own stubbornness. If I thought right now you were burning to work for us, I'd find a position to accommodate you tomorrow. I don't sense that though. I sense you trying to make a hell of an adjustment to civilian life and settling for something you feel obligated to do, which you absolutely aren't. Let's give it a couple of months and see if you're still interested."

Zane bit down on his frustration. "What am I supposed to do in the meantime?"

"Learn how to relax," Mason said. "Figure out how to lighten up. You're strung tight, man. You always tended that way, but the Navy has increased that tenfold. Probably understandable considering the nature of your job, but you're home now. You can loosen up, enjoy life a little."

Zane studied his oldest brother, weighed whether confessing his situation would help his case or not. Decided it couldn't hurt. Besides, he needed to get someone else's thoughts on it. He was making himself nuts trying to figure out what the right thing to do would be. "If I tell you something, can you keep it to yourself?"

"Of course," Mason said, leaning forward.

Zane turned his soda glass around and around, making sure this was the right decision. He knew he was being premature, but he also knew the last thing he wanted was to be caught with baby news and have his life be in as much upheaval as it was currently.

"There's a chance I got someone pregnant," he said quietly. Sure as hell didn't need anyone overhearing.

"What do you mean a chance?"

"I mean condom failure big-time, and from what I gather from her, the timing was pretty damn good for conception."

Mason's brows shot up. "You've only been home for two nights."

"Only needed an hour or so."

Mason shook his head, grinning. "Maybe should've taken longer to think things through."

"Fuck you. My point is I need some direction. North Brothers can give me that."

"Or you could find it on your own and make sure it's a direction that really works for you. If there is a baby, it won't be here in a couple of months."

"I thought I knew for my whole life what direction would work for me," Zane said. "Turns out I was wrong."

"Flying worked for you for a long time."

"Until it didn't."

"You don't want to fly anymore? If you don't want to fly the NBS jet, you could get a commercial license."

Zane blew out a breath. "The military put me off of flying. Something I never thought could happen."

Mason studied him with raised brows. "That's why I think you should give it some time. If you still want to work for North Brothers in two months, we'll talk."

Frustration pumped up Zane's blood pressure, but he didn't let Mason see how much. He merely narrowed his eyes and asked, "That your final answer?"

Mason returned his scrutiny, then said, "That's my final answer. Late March. Talk to me then. And good luck on the woman situation. Keep me posted."

Without a word, Zane calmly got up from the table, set his empty soda glass on the counter, then walked outside to the patio to cool down.

CHAPTER EIGHT

ugar Babies Sweet Shop, just down the block from Henry Interiors, was often Hayden's Sunday morning refuge, where she could concentrate on some of the duller parts of her businesses, otherwise known as paperwork. She usually timed her visit to coincide with the opening of the Angry Cat Bookstore, which adjoined the bakery on one side and offered the world's best coffee.

Today's project was ordering materials for the Johansen project, and while shopping for supplies was normally fun, this list was so long that she was ready to be finished. That and she didn't understand some of Mrs. Johansen's choices, but for what she would make on the job, she could overlook some eccentricities.

She was sorting through a stack of loose-leaf pages, swearing at herself for her perpetual lack of organization, when the door to the otherwise empty bakery opened. As she looked up, her heart started racing and her mouth went dry.

"Zane, what are you doing here?"

"Hey," he said, smiling when he saw her, and that smile...it did things to her.

Instead of going to the counter and ordering something, he pulled out the chair across from her and sat. She couldn't deny that a thrill shot through her at his friendliness.

"It's my mom's birthday. She loves cupcakes, and a little bird said this place is the best."

Hayden recalled saying something like that the night they'd ended up at her place. "The little bird was right," she said, grinning and gesturing toward the counter. The employees—Jilly and Kellen—were both in the back, though Kellen had poked his head around the corner when the bells on the door rang.

"What do you recommend?"

"For cupcakes? From today's flavors?" She got up and went toward the filled-to-the-brim case. "The birthday cake is one of my favorites. Strawberry if you like fruit flavors. You can't go wrong with double chocolate. Ohh, and creme brûlée is delicious. No, wait, s'mores. Definitely s'mores."

Zane laughed. "Is that all?"

"Well, the apple crumble with marshmallow filling is to die for too."

Since they were at the counter, Kellen came out with a smile and a "What can I get for you?" He was a tall, skinny, quiet high school kid who worked weekends, when the owners, Kennedy, Violet, and Ivy, didn't come in.

"I need to get a couple dozen cupcakes," Zane said. "A variety." He got multiple of each of Hayden's recommendations first, she noticed with some satisfaction, then added some vanillas and some bacon maple syrups. "Did you already have one?" he asked Hayden.

She shook her head. "Not yet. I started with coffee."

"Add whatever she wants, plus another creme brûlée for here."

"I'll take a s'mores."

"And coffee?" he asked Hayden.

"It's next door. Today they have mocha almond, Jamaican dark, and regular. Though it sounds boring, the regular is the best around. What do you want? I'll have Cooper get you one."

Once he chose a regular brew, she went through the arched doorway to the bookstore, where she found Cooper wrapped up in his wife, Georgia, both of them behind the main checkout counter. When they saw her, Georgia rushed over to help her.

"You two are so cute," Hayden said.

"I find a little flirting can go a long way to softening the grumpiest man," Georgia said in a hushed voice. "Even when you're married to him. What can I get you, Hayden?"

She ordered Zane's coffee, paid, said goodbye, and went back to the bakery to find Zane sitting at their table, looking as if he was going to stay awhile, and yeah, there was that little zip of a thrill through her blood again.

"Here you go," Hayden said as she set his steaming cup down then took a seat across from him.

"Looks like you were working. You okay with some company?"

"If it's a tall, good-looking Navy pilot," she replied before she could think it through. Georgia's words of wisdom about flirting popped into her head, even though Zane didn't seem grumpy.

"Guess it's my lucky day." He pushed the plate with her cupcake on it across the table to her. "What are you working on?"

"I'm ordering materials for my latest design job. It's a huge project, seven rooms in total. An old home in Belle Meade."

"Nice. That sounds like a good chunk of change for you."

"My biggest to date," she said, unable to curtail her excitement. "Getting into the Belle Meade crowd is priceless."

"I'm not sure I'd know good design if I saw it, but you must be good."

"I hope so. This client is, let's just say, persnickety."

"How long have you being doing this?"

"Design?"

He nodded as he unwrapped his cupcake and took a bite.

"I got a job as an assistant straight out of college, ten years ago. I left there after my supervisor repeatedly took credit for my designs. I always dreamed of having a store to sell my repurposed, refinished furniture, and when redevelopment started here, I specifically wanted a store on Hale. So I started the wheels turning on the store and opened it. This is my third year in business. I also hung my shingle out as a designer, and they're both growing rapidly, keeping me busy."

"That surprises me not at all," he said between bites. "You

were right about this place. Both places. The cupcake and coffee are excellent."

"I'd never lead someone astray about cupcakes," she said with a laugh. "So…birthday party for your mom today?"

"Weekly family dinner tonight," he said as he took the lid off his coffee. "North family thing. Sunday night dinners. Everybody comes."

"I've heard about those," she said. "They're famous."

"Sierra?"

"Sierra. I think it's cool that you guys still get together regularly, even with everyone busy and getting married and whatever else."

"You know, when I was on the boat, I longed to be a part of it again. It's been good…mostly. But living at home in my thirties…" He shook his head. "I need to find my own place. Going from zero family to all family, all the time, is rough when you're an introvert."

"I'm not an introvert but I still like living by myself," she said. "Of course, I'm rarely home. What do you have in mind? Apartment? House? Ready to buy something?"

She knew from Sierra that all the North boys had sizable bank accounts thanks to North Brothers Sports.

"I want out sooner than I could buy something," he answered. "I love my mom but I don't want to live with her."

"I get it." An idea popped into her head, and she weighed it as she took another bite of her decadent cupcake. The desire to help him solve his problem surged, so she went for it. "You could rent my apartment for a few months. Have it to yourself, the whole thing. Move in tomorrow. Stay as long or as short as you like. That would give you time to get settled and decide whether you want to buy something."

"And where would you stay on your late nights?"

"I can drive home. That's what I did for the first year. It's not that big of a deal."

"I don't want to make things more complicated than they already are between us."

"Not complicated," she said. "I'll have Hudson Bennett draw up a simple sublease, month to month, no long-term obligation."

He looked at her pensively for a good minute as he continued to eat his cupcake. He asked about rent, she quoted him what she was paying, and he didn't blink.

"You can keep my furniture there so it's furnished," she said, not pausing to consider why she was pushing him.

"You make it tough to say no," he said with a half smile.

"Then say yes."

"I don't want to make you move your stuff out. Your clothes and things you might need during the day."

"Well…" Again, she pulled off a chunk of cupcake as she checked in with herself and avoided a too-quick decision. "If it would make you feel better, you could take the second bedroom. It's almost as big as the first, queen-sized bed, its own bathroom, and I can keep some of my clothes in the master. Just for emergencies. I'd check in with you before stopping by though. Always. It'll be your place."

His cupcake devoured, he wadded up the wrapper and looked off into the distance, as if still undecided.

"Zane," she said, reaching across the table and putting her hand on his without thinking about it, "it's a solution to your problem. Take it. Hale Street is a great place to live. Three restaurants plus a bakery within walking distance. Clayborne's has amazing fried mushrooms and ham and cheese melts."

He stared down at their hands, making her feel self-conscious, and then he wove their fingers together briefly and squeezed before releasing her. "Okay," he said. "I'll take you up on the offer. But the master is still yours, closet and all. And if you need to crash there some night when you work late, just let me know. We'll be pretend roommates."

As she looked into his eyes, she saw heat in his that matched the flare deep inside of her. "That sounds…complicated," she said.

"I'll leave that decision up to you. Just know your bed is available whenever you need it."

The bed where they had… Yeah. She'd need an iron will if she was going to spend the night down the hall from him. By herself.

"So it's a deal?" she asked.

"It's a deal."

She didn't know if that was good news or bad news…but a shiver—the good kind—went through her as they shook on it.

CHAPTER NINE

*H*ayden had woken up with a knot in her stomach the following Saturday morning, as if her body knew, even before her brain did, that it was fourteen days today. Fourteen days since the sex.

Today was test day.

Google had told her the fastest she could have a reliable answer was between seven and twelve days, and she'd forced herself to wait the extra two to be sure. Or maybe to put off knowing the truth.

She'd bought a test on the way in to work at Henry Interiors—a three-pack of tests. Sydney had been there to open before her, and the customers had been nonstop. A good thing—unless you needed to steal a few minutes to disappear and take a pregnancy test.

Now it was going on one p.m., and for the first time, store traffic slowed to a single browser who was content to not have one of them help her. Trinity was due to start a shift at one, so without hesitation, Hayden told Sydney she had to take care of something upstairs before Zane arrived. He was scheduled to move in around three.

"Take your time. I got this," Sydney said, brushing her dark dreadlocks out of her face and smiling, as if Hayden wasn't about to do something that could change her entire life. Not that

Sydney knew a thing about what was going on. No one else did except Zane, unless he'd told someone.

"Thanks. Text if you need me." Hayden grabbed her purse and hurried out the back door.

After a pit stop at her car to get the drugstore bag, she climbed those nineteen stairs, thinking how vastly different this was from when she'd climbed them that night with Zane. Then, she could barely make it up from wanting him so badly and couldn't wait to get where they were going. Now, it felt like they were leading her to some kind of torture chamber.

For two weeks, Hayden had waffled between pushing this possibility out of her mind and wanting to pour her troubles and worries out to a trusted friend. Problem—her BFF, Sierra, was not only out of the country on her honeymoon but was now Zane's sister-in-law. The other women Hayden was closest to all happened to be related by marriage to Zane's family as well—Mackenzie and Lexie. She didn't feel right about asking any of them to keep such a big thing from their husbands, and unless there was reason, none of the rest of the North family needed to know.

She'd worked her way into total awkwardness for sure.

There were a lot of other dear women in her life—Sloan, Eliza, Asia, Lena, and Kennedy only a few of them—but this was intensely personal. Hayden had decided to take the test alone.

Once upstairs and inside, she pulled out the box of tests as she headed toward the master bath, dropping the store bag on the bathroom floor once she got there.

Then she stood facing the toilet, thinking maybe she wouldn't be able to pee even though she'd needed to for the past half hour, and read the directions.

"Easy-peasy, lemon squeezy," she said as if she were getting ready to brush her teeth or put on lip gloss.

Less than a minute later, she'd peed on the test, set it on the vanity to determine her fate, and finished on the toilet. Once she was put back together, she washed her hands, and her eyes happened to land on the test panel area.

"What the—" She grabbed it, glancing at the timer on her

phone that was counting down from two minutes. There was more than a minute left and the lines were both there, making a plus sign.

"Oh, God." Her empty hand flew to her mouth as her heart started thundering. "Oh God, oh God, oh God." Her lungs felt empty, so she sucked in air repeatedly as she reeled.

She'd convinced herself—mostly—there was no way. What were the damn odds that she had sex once in, what, a year? And got knocked up?

She heard Zane's deep voice in her mind, saying, *Fifty-fifty*.

Her breath came fast and she couldn't get enough air. As she started to really panic, it hit her she must be hyperventilating. She picked up the paper bag from the floor and stuck it over her mouth, breathing in and out.

Once she started to level out and feel less light-headed, she lowered herself to the closed lid of the toilet and giggled semi-hysterically. When they'd handed her the paper bag at the store, she'd thought it odd they didn't use plastic until they explained they were out of plastic. Now she thought maybe someone was looking out for her.

She was still laughing sort of crazy-like when she heard a noise at the other end of the apartment. She bolted up and rushed into the bedroom, listening for another sound. At the same moment she walked into the living room and had a clear view through the galley kitchen to the door, said door opened, and there was Zane, a large duffel over his shoulder and a moving box in his hands.

Shit. Zane.

He looked up and froze when he saw her.

"I'm a little early. Got done loading up and figured I'd come on over instead of sitting around for another couple of hours."

"It's fine," she said, her voice not quite right. "I just came up for a few minutes to take care of something."

Idiot. He's the one person you need to tell most.

She cleared her throat. "I came upstairs to take the test. To see if I'm pregnant."

He was still standing in the doorway, hands full, just staring at her.

Hayden took a few steps toward him, ending up in the kitchen. "I am."

After a moment he unfroze, came all the way in, and lightly kicked the door shut behind him. Meeting her in the kitchen, he slid the box from his arms onto the counter, then let the duffel fall to the floor, hard enough she was sure it would be audible in the store below.

Zane leaned heavily against the counter and covered his mouth with both hands, still silent, no longer looking at her. Absorbing, she knew. Just as she still was, only she'd had time to close her mouth.

From in the bathroom, her timer sounded, had been sounding, she realized, only she hadn't registered it till now. Without explaining, she went for it, the thought flittering through her mind that what if the official answer had changed now that the full time had elapsed?

Ridiculous thought, she knew, and when she picked up the test, she verified it.

Still pregnant.

Those lines couldn't be any brighter.

Zane appeared without a sound just behind her, startling her when she saw him in the mirror. He glanced over her shoulder at the test, then met her gaze in the mirror.

"Those things are pretty accurate, aren't they?"

"Pretty sure." She remembered the three-pack and said, "I have two more chances to get a better answer," as she picked them up off the counter.

After a noisy exhale, he said, "I suspect a false positive is extremely rare."

"Yeah," she said on her own gusty exhale. "You're right." She knew he was right, but she stuck the two extras in the bag—hopefully she was done hyperventilating for the time being—and would take them with her. In case she wanted to double-check.

"How are you doing?" he asked, his voice going quieter, more intimate.

She faced him directly instead of through the mirror. "Oh,

you know." She could barely get the question to sink in, let alone come up with an answer. "I swore a little. Hyperventilated a little. That was right before you walked in, so I haven't had much time to process."

"Yeah. Going to take some processing." After a couple of seconds when it seemed like he went understandably introspective, he returned his attention to her. "Come here."

Before she could respond, he pulled her the last few inches into him and put his arms around her, surprising her. It took a heartbeat or two, but then she sagged into his chest and wound her arms around him and just…breathed.

Breathed in his scent, clean and masculine and reassuring. Breathed in what it felt like in his arms, as if she wasn't alone in this.

More than a minute must've ticked by with neither of them moving, both of them just standing there, holding on to each other, as if their little sphere was an escape from reality.

Then Hayden could no longer keep the thoughts from rushing into her head as if a dam had broken. First and foremost —it was way too early to conclude that she wasn't alone in this.

She straightened and, without looking at him, picked up the paper bag and walked out of the bathroom, mainly because the bathroom was no place to have whatever conversation they needed to have.

They needed to have a conversation, right?

Aimlessly, she ended up in the kitchen and mindlessly set her bag down before leaning against the counter, not seeing anything.

It took a while for Zane to come out of the bedroom. When he did, he entered the kitchen and hoisted himself up on the cabinet opposite her. Hayden was still reeling so hard she didn't know what to say.

"Based on your morning-after-pill decision, I assume you plan to go through with the pregnancy?" he asked.

She didn't have to think hard to answer that one. "Yeah." It was everything else that stumped her. "If you don't want to be—"

"Don't say it," he cut in. "I said I'd be in it and I'm in it."

"You can change your mind."

If he didn't want to be involved, then the sooner she knew that, the better.

"Hayden."

She met his gaze at his sharp tone.

"It's my baby too."

Baby. Not just a pregnancy but a baby.

"Yeah," she acknowledged. "I guess we're having a baby together."

They continued to stare at each other across the six feet or so of kitchen, and then, at the same time, they both said, "Shit."

And then they both broke out into laughter. Stress laughter? Probably, but damn, did it feel good. And then they seemed to feed off each other and laugh a little harder.

Hayden hadn't seen Zane laugh that hard ever. That fact, more than anything, sobered her quickly.

"Shit," she repeated. "What are we going to do?"

Her question was somewhat rhetorical, but he answered anyway.

"Don't know yet." He slid down from the counter. "We'll figure it out, but not right now. We both need some time for the situation to sink in."

"Truth." She moved closer to him, thinking they barely knew each other at all, and now they were supposedly going to go through one of the most intimate events two people could go through.

Weird. As. Anything.

With the corner of her mouth quirking upward, she said, "My name is Hayden Eloise Henry. I'm thirty-two years old. My birthday is June second." When he raised his brows, clearly confused, she continued, lightly, "We're going to have a child together. These seem like things you should know about your baby mama."

He shot a lopsided closed-mouthed grin back at her. "That's as good a starting point as any. I guess we have nine months for the rest."

"I guess we do," she said, her humor slipping away once again. "And somehow I need to get my rear back downstairs and act like everything's fine."

"How late do you work today?"

"Till we close at seven."

He grabbed her hand, then sandwiched it between both of his. "Good luck with the everything's-fine act. Let's talk later. Maybe tonight if you're not too tired."

She nodded, thinking she was already too tired—for anything.

She took her bag, went out the door, left the tests in her car, then went inside the store, determined to sell a sofa or two and act like her entire world hadn't just raced right off the rails.

———

AFTER HAYDEN LEFT, Zane closed the door of his new apartment and stood there, staring at the wood panel, not really seeing it.

He was going to be a father.

"Whoo," he said on an exhale, and he stepped away from the door.

His box was still on the counter, bag on the kitchen floor. It said a lot that that was everything, all the belongings he was moving in with him. He didn't need much else, but he suspected a dad would have more than a bag and a box.

"Not a dad yet," he allowed. "Technically." Then he did what he usually did when tough emotions threatened—he busied himself with what needed to be done.

After heaving the admittedly big-ass duffel onto his shoulder and picking up the box, he headed to the doorway he'd seen near the entry, pretty sure that was his bedroom. He hadn't seen more than the kitchen, master, and master bath, but that was fine. He was grateful for the easy, if temporary, solution to his problem. From what he'd seen, Hayden's decor was tasteful and not too feminine outside of her bedroom.

He pushed the door open to his room and took in the barest details—queen bed with a navy-blue comforter and entirely too many throw pillows, built-in wardrobe along one wall that would hold all his clothes and five other people's, TV and stand at the foot of the bed, a nightstand. It'd do just fine.

He set both the box and bag on the bed and unzipped the duffel, started unpacking his clothes and putting them away. As he moved on autopilot, his mind veered to Hayden. The pregnancy. The goat fuck of pressure that entailed.

The timetable for him to straighten out his life had just tightened, and Mason was determined to make him wait. Damn him. It didn't matter if his brother's decision was well intentioned; Zane needed his career in place. If there was a flicker of doubt in his mind about working a desk job, he ignored it.

On the upside, Hayden seemed like she had her act together. She certainly appeared to know what she wanted out of life.

Sitting heavily on the bed, job unfinished, he realized he didn't actually know if Hayden knew what she wanted. He didn't know much of anything about her.

And she would be the mother of his child.

The discomfort of that reality had him shooting back off the bed, pulling out his supply of boxer briefs, rolling them neatly, and sticking them in one of the drawers.

Without opening the box, he strode out of the bedroom, through the kitchen, into the living room, trying to pry his mind off uncomfortable topics. On the exterior wall, there was a tall double window and a French door that went to a balcony. A gray L-shaped sectional was the main furniture in the room, its back against the window and facing a mounted TV. On the side toward the master and kitchen was a dining area with a small table and four chairs. And scattered throughout were accents and decor pieces he was beginning to understand, after seeing her store and now this, were one of Hayden's trademarks.

He went around the table to the French door, opened it, and went out. On the small balcony were more signs of Hayden's taste—two outdoor chairs, a table between them, and a mini shelf on the end that probably held plants in the summer.

Grasping the wrought iron railing, he stood and surveyed the street below. Across the way were a bar, a boot store, a music store, a women's boutique, and a spa. Down the way was the Wentworth Hotel, where even now, midafternoon, people were coming and going. In fact, there were pedestrians everywhere, even though it was only about forty degrees. Without giving it much thought, he pushed away from the railing and went back in, shot through the length of the apartment, and went out the back door. He'd never thought he'd see it happen, but suddenly he found himself with way too much fucking aloneness.

At the alley between the bakery and the mosaic place, Zane passed to the Hale Street side of the buildings, not noticing much of his surroundings.

He needed to make sure Hayden had good health insurance and a doctor she trusted. They needed to secure a doctor's appointment as soon as possible.

Robert Pendleton had always been the North family's lawyer, and Zane made an entry on his mental checklist to call him and figure out a trust for the baby.

By that time, he was at the end of the street and took a left on Peach Boulevard, and there was the door to the bookstore that had the damn good coffee.

As he went inside, he knew what kind of book he was after. Information was vital, and he and Hayden had a lot to learn, so he asked the clerk where the pregnancy books were, spent several minutes browsing and selecting three, then checked out.

The only other action he could take was one he was good at—taking care of details for Hayden. That had been his go-to when his dad died, his way of helping as well as his way of shutting down emotions he'd had no earthly clue how to cope with. At fourteen years old, he'd taken care of the house and family for his mom while she was too devastated to function.

Not to say that Hayden was devastated. He didn't really know what she felt, and he needed to remedy that.

If he could get her to agree, he'd get to know her better tonight over a dinner that he would provide for her as soon as she got done with work.

He took out his phone and sent her an invitation, feeling marginally like he was doing something worthwhile.

CHAPTER TEN

$\mathcal{H}$ ayden could easily get used to having Zane cook dinner for her after a long day at work.

She *wouldn't*. But she could.

It was weird to knock on that apartment door and wait for him to answer, but she did, making the point that the place was his now, and she wouldn't abuse that. When she heard a distant "Come in," she shrugged and opened the door.

The sight that met her eyes was something she wouldn't forget anytime soon. He was straight ahead in the kitchen, wearing athletic shorts that revealed his strong, muscled legs and a black tee that allowed his biceps to peek out at her. He had a kitchen towel over his shoulder and a skillet in his hand, and the smile he flashed at her as she reached the edge of the kitchen was genuine and full and she was sure had won him his way with more than a beautiful girl or two. This one she was keeping all for herself.

"Hi," she said. She came all the way into the room and ran her hand up his back—without thinking about what she was doing—as she looked into the pans and on the counter. What she didn't do but sincerely wanted to was press a kiss to his slightly scruffed cheek. "Wow. This looks incredible. Something you should know about me: I could easily get used to being spoiled. So you might want to switch to your B game. Or C."

He laughed and said, "Something you should know about me: half-assing it isn't in my DNA."

"Point taken. Judging by the smell, you can cook."

"It'd be smarter to judge by the taste, wouldn't it?"

"Ready and willing, sir." As soon as the words came out of her mouth, the potential suggestiveness of them hit her and she cringed. "For dinner," she added.

On two plates that sat on the counter next to the stove were hand-breaded chicken breasts with red sauce and melted cheese served over pasta. There was a spot to the side on each one for the asparagus he was cooking.

"Have a seat," he said, flipping off the burner.

"Ooh, you're going to serve me?"

With the hot pan in hand, he turned slightly, met her gaze, and sent her a flirtatious, panty-melting half grin. Or was it just his regular half grin and the flirtatiousness and panty-melting were all in her interpretation?

And while she was pondering important questions and he was plating the veggies, Hayden wondered what the proper protocol was for dining with a man you'd spent exactly one night and a couple of half hours with but were venturing into parenthood together. The attraction was practically pulsing between them, and yet it seemed…unwise to pursue.

Once they were seated across the table from each other and they'd started eating—a fantastic dinner, as it happened—Zane set down his fork and said, "Got something for you. Be right back." He disappeared into his bedroom and came back before she could swallow the food in her mouth.

On the corner of the table, next to her plate, he set a stack of three books. "I couldn't decide which you'd prefer, so…"

Hayden picked up each of them, read the titles, and couldn't help smiling. "You bought me pregnancy books." His thoughtfulness was endearing. "Thank you," she said as she flipped through the top one and noticed multiple illustrations of expanding bellies and fetuses.

"I figured you could choose the one that sounds best and I'll read it too."

Between that and his culinary skills, she was beginning to feel lucky as a leprechaun with her "choice" for her baby's father. She knew better than to trust a leprechaun though.

She tilted her head slightly. "Are you sure? There's probably all kinds of vagina stuff in here."

That elicited a quiet laugh from him as he retook his seat. "I can handle vaginas."

When he winked at her, she shook her head and laughed.

He had, as a matter of fact, handled hers quite wonderfully. She felt a tightening deep within her body at the thought and pressed her legs together in response.

"Okay, then, vagina whisperer. I'll pick one tonight and let you know."

They ate a few bites in silence, and then Zane said, "I was hoping we could start getting to know each other better. Seems like it would be smart."

"Smart," she said, nodding. "Yes." She was absolutely curious about this man, but in light of their situation, she was off her social game, a little nervous around the edges—because what if it ended up he couldn't stand her?—and, frankly, cautious. There was a crap load at stake for both of them, as well as their child, so playing it smart was a priority.

It'd be a disaster if she were to fall for him and he were to break her heart, for example. Far better to keep her heart out of the mix.

"So tell me five things I should know about Zane North."

He studied her as he chewed, as if thinking of how to answer. "That's too broad. What do you want to know?"

Everything, she thought. *The good, the bad, the ugly.*

"Start easy. Middle name."

"Austin."

"What's your call sign?"

"Nope," he said curtly.

"Your call sign is Nope?"

"Nope. I'm not telling you my call sign."

She finished a bite of pasta with flavorful red sauce. "Why

won't you tell me?" she asked, a little disbelieving. "What's the big deal?"

"Well…" He chewed some more, then swallowed and took a drink of his ice water. "You have to understand that most call signs are *not* like the movies."

"How not?"

"Movie call signs are bad-ass, like Maverick and Iceman. Real call signs are more often than not embarrassing, often coming from a fault or a weakness."

"No," Hayden said, thinking that would be cruel.

"Google it."

She decided to believe him.

"So yours is embarrassing," she said. "Okay. What is it?"

He conveniently shoved another bite of food in his mouth and shook his head.

"You really won't tell me?"

Another head shake.

Hayden let it go. For now. Naturally, she was dying to know, and she wouldn't forget any time soon. "What's your dream job?" she asked instead.

He didn't blink, kept staring at her, then said, "It used to be flying for the US Navy."

"So you need a new dream job, huh?"

"Or just a job. I'm going to work for the family business. As soon as Mason cuts the Yoda/life counseling bullshit."

"What's going on?" She knew Mason fairly well, thanks in part to the three-day Mediterranean tour that was Drake and Mackenzie's extended destination wedding reception last fall. Being "stuck" on a private yacht with all the Norths, minus Zane, had been an unforgettable experience all the way around, and she'd come away closer to the whole family. Mason had his stereotypical oldest sibling traits, but according to Sierra, Eliza had leveled him out quite a bit and made him more human.

Zane scowled, shook his head minutely, and she thought the topic might be off-limits, but then he said, "I went to him for a job with North Brothers Sports. He won't hire me for two months because he says he can tell I don't really want to do it. Gave me some shit about finding what I *burn* to do."

"Is he right?"

"I don't burn to sell sporting goods, but that's irrelevant. I'd do whatever job we agreed to and I'd do it well. I've already done the thing I burned to do, and I don't burn to do it anymore."

"Flames can go out."

"Exactly," he said.

"Do you have any interest in flying some other way? Outside of the military?"

He hesitated. "No. Not as a job. Been there, done that."

"Fair enough," she said, but his hesitation made her wonder what his true hang-up was.

The mood of the room had plummeted, so she tried to turn that around with some easier questions. "Dogs or cats?"

He perked up, jabbed a bite of chicken, and answered, "Dogs. You?"

"Either. But right now, neither. I can barely take care of myself some days." She left it unspoken that she didn't yet know how she would manage a baby, but she knew she would. Somehow. "Rock or country music?"

"Rock."

"That explains the shirt," she said of the old, faded Stone Temple Pilots tee he wore. "I like both but if I had to choose, country. Do you run for fun or because you're being chased?"

He let out a quiet laugh. "The question reveals a lot about the questioner. Which are you?"

"Being chased," Hayden said unabashedly. "Otherwise running is a bad idea. I bet you're in the 'for fun' club."

"I'm in the had-to-stay-in-top-shape-for-my-job club. I haven't run since I've been home. I need to though. I can feel it. It's like a sickness."

"A sickness that makes you healthier. Hmm." She shook her head dismissively and continued. "Chocolate or vanilla?"

"Are we talking ice cream?"

"Sure."

"Vanilla with chocolate chips."

"You're a complex man, Zane North. If it's ice cream, I'm choosing Moose Tracks. It's vanilla with baby peanut butter cups, chocolate fudge, and a caramel swirl."

"Not surprisingly even more complex," he said, shaking his head with a grin.

Undeterred, she went on, "Make lists or wing it?"

"Lists all the way."

"Same. We have something in common," she said happily.

"I bet we could find more."

"It sounds like you're an optimist," she said. "So am I."

"I'm more of a realist."

"Do you like sports? NFL? MLS? NHL?"

"Titans and Bears for football, Cardinals for baseball, Predators for hockey."

"I like the Predators and the Titans but where did the Bears come from?" she asked.

"My cousin Logan has always been a huge Packers fan. Bears are their rivals."

"Ah, so you aren't all *yes, sir.* You have some contrariness in you."

"Probably why I couldn't stay in the military for my whole career." He kept his tone light, but she wondered if there was more to that statement as well. She wanted to understand why he'd left, sensed it was important, but now didn't feel like the right time to ask.

Though they'd been talking nonstop, they'd managed to eat too, and their plates were empty. "You can teach our kid to cook anytime," she said, and then she realized that might sound as if she saw them as a family, all of them living together, happily ever after. Which she didn't. She didn't know what she saw.

He saved her by saying, "Do you cook?"

"I wouldn't call it that, really. I'm good at frozen pizzas and microwave dinners."

He frowned but then tried to hide it as he pushed back from the table.

"I won't force them on you," she said, also standing and gathering her plate and water glass.

They carried everything into the kitchen. "I was thinking more of the health factor now that you're pregnant."

"Oh," she said. "Microwave dinners have veggies in them. All four food groups usually."

"If sodium counts as a food group. Maybe I'll cook you some real food."

"If it's like tonight, I'm in."

Once he'd emptied his hands of plates and glasses and napkins, he turned and leaned his backside against the cabinets. "I'm trying not to overstep my bounds here, but nutrition is important for a pregnant woman."

"Yeahhh," she said slowly, frowning herself. "I'm sure you're right. I haven't had time for anything to sink in, to be honest. I'll figure it out though."

"While we're on the subject, we need to get you a doctor's appointment as soon as possible. Do you have an ob-gyn?"

"You're kind of controlly, aren't you?" She smiled to soften it, but he needed to know she was capable of growing a baby and taking care of herself just fine.

Zane blew out a breath. "Maybe a little 'controlly.' Maybe a lot. I'm not going to lie. This is hard."

"What's hard?" she asked as she washed her plate off and stuck it in the dishwasher without thought. She *had* lived here part-time for almost a year.

"Relying on others isn't my strong point. Mitigating risk is what I do, and now, having you pregnant… Everything's out of my control."

"Not everything," she said gently, moving closer, very much taking his concerns seriously. "You can cook me a healthy dinner anytime." She said it with a grin, but that faltered slightly when he reached out and took both her hands.

"And the doctor's appointment?"

"I'm already on it. I texted my friend Lena today. She's a nurse for an ob-gyn practice *and* has a newborn baby. I'm calling her practice first thing Monday morning."

"Do you have good health insurance?"

"I better. It's what I offer my employees. I haven't had to use it much."

"Okay. At least you have some." He frowned again. "Am I supposed to go with you to your appointments?"

There was just enough lost little boy in his expression that she softened a little more toward him. "I'll go to the first one by myself. They have to test and make sure I'm actually pregnant and then do a physical exam." Even though he'd seen her naked before…holy awkward.

He gave a curt nod.

"Did…you want to go?"

"I don't know. I want to be there for big things. Like ultrasounds."

"We can do that." She had no idea when an ultrasound might be. Good thing she had three books to study. "So here's a question. Have you told anyone?"

"I told Mason that I might've gotten someone pregnant but not who and not that it's for sure."

Her gut clenched a little at the thought of his family finding out. She *knew* his family. Was that better or worse than not knowing his family? *Let's face it. Either way stinks because now you're that girl.*

"I haven't told anybody," she said, and it had been killing her. "I didn't want to hit Sierra with it on her honeymoon, plus once I tell her, I hate to force her to keep it from Cole, and…tangled web what with you being his brother."

"I see what you mean. I agree it wouldn't be right to ask Sierra to hide something from her husband." He was quiet for a while, thoughtful. "You need your best friend through this."

"Truth."

"I think we should tell our families. Or…I'd like to tell mine, I guess, in part because of that tangled web. It's your call on your family."

Her family. Her brothers. Oh, *that* would be fun.

As tempting as it was to avoid the discomfort of telling her family, she knew if she kept them in the dark longer than Zane's family, they'd be upset.

With a deep inhale, she said, "We should tell them around the same time, I guess. Especially if your mom and my dad keep seeing each other."

"We can ask them to keep it to themselves," Zane said.

Hayden nodded, grateful for a little time to get used to it herself before too many others knew. "Let's wait a bit for everyone else then. Until…"

"Until we're ready. Maybe three months in. End of the first trimester. That's what a lot of people do, right?"

"Right."

Like it had a few times throughout her busy day, the fact that she was pregnant hit her like a wrecking ball and took her breath for a second. She pulled one of her hands out of Zane's and pressed it to her chest, as if she could slow her galloping heart.

"You okay?" he asked, his brow furrowing.

After a slow inhale, she nodded. "It's just…a lot."

"I know." There was so much understanding and patience in those two little words, in his tone.

Before she could say more, he tugged her forward, and then he was kissing her, and that battle she'd been fighting since she'd arrived, that one where she wasn't going to succumb to their overwhelming attraction…

Yeah. Out the window.

What started out as a gentle, soothing kiss didn't take long to spark hotter. When she felt his tongue at the seam of her lips, she opened to him, put her arms around him, and allowed her body to fall all the way into his. The feel of his erection pressing into her stoked a corresponding ache between her legs.

Maybe she would've plummeted just as easily if he wasn't such a good kisser, but…he was so good, so attentive and tender and then, just seconds later, *not* tender, in a good way, making her believe he couldn't get enough of her. She never wanted this kiss to end, wanted to be connected to him for decades—and then her stupid brain reminded her she was. Connected. By a baby.

It took some doing, but she straightened, backed away enough to break the contact of their mouths, tried to unscramble her brain. "I'm not sure this is a good idea."

Zane let out a shaky exhale that said he'd been way into it, just like she had been pre-brain interference, and he lowered his hands to her hips. He held her gaze for a second, two seconds, then said, "Yeah." He lifted his chin, carrying his gaze to the ceiling. "I guess we should figure out us."

"I guess we should."

He returned his gaze to her face, then took both her hands in his again, which put some extra space in between their bodies. "We need to get to know each other better, figure out how well we get along. Without sex muddying things up."

"Yes." Because sex muddying things up with this man could make her fall.

She couldn't fall.

She averted her eyes, because his were so intense, and she sort of loved that about him—and sort of hated it at the same time, particularly when she was trying so hard not to get swept away.

Next thing she knew, his lips were on hers again, lighter now, and once the surprise wore off, she laughed into the kiss. "Kisses are okay though?"

He pulled away enough to make eye contact, grinning fully, no half smile this time. "Kisses are okay though. Don't you think?"

"I mean, we have to get to know each other, which means spending time together. If kisses happen, they happen. They won't muddy."

"Agree."

He pressed another one to her mouth, and then she stood up straight, used every ounce of willpower she could summon, and ended it.

"But I'm so tired I can barely stand. We need to clean up this mess, and then I need to go home before I can't keep my eyes open."

"You're welcome to stay here. In your bed," he added quickly.

She pressed her lips together as she took in his handsome face. "Muddy. And I've got a crap ton to process."

"I'm sure you do." He straightened and peered down at her again. "You've had a hell of a day. I've got the kitchen tonight. We'll make the rule whoever cooks, the other person cleans, but that starts next time. On a day when you don't learn you're going to have a baby."

"You," she said, trying not to wilt from the wave of fatigue that hit her, "have a deal. Thank you, Zane. Next time, I'll take you out. For healthy food," she tacked on.

"We'll figure it out. We'll figure all of this out."

"We will." She went to the table and grabbed her new books, kissed him short and sweet as she walked back through the kitchen, then went straight for the door. "Night, Zane."

Once the door closed behind her, she exhaled and closed her eyes.

After summoning enough energy, she went down the stairs, all nineteen of them, thinking she was in a big, fat mess. In more ways than one.

CHAPTER ELEVEN

A week ago, Zane wouldn't have believed he could get sick of being alone.

By Wednesday evening, after four full days of living in Hayden's apartment, processing her pregnancy news, avoiding her, and avoiding most humans in general—he'd even skipped Sunday dinner, unsure how to act normal when nothing was normal at all—he was about to climb the walls.

He got up from the plush sectional in the living room, where he'd been reading the archives on a blog about fatherhood, and paced through the kitchen, into the bathroom on the back of the building, not because he needed to use it but because its window looked out on the parking area.

Hayden's SUV was there, telling him she was downstairs, rocking her business world. It gave him some unexplainable comfort to know she was nearby.

Did he want to see Hayden? Hell yes. There wasn't an hour in the day when he didn't think about her, wonder how she was doing, whether she was taking good care of herself.

At the same time, he needed space. Space to let his new reality settle into his brain.

He was going to be a father. Someone was going to call *him* Dad. How did a person ever comprehend such an enormous status change?

Maybe speaking the words out loud to someone else would make it real or easier to imagine. He had yet to tell the specifics to a soul, preferring to wrangle with it on his own first.

And he and Hayden had much to discuss. Eventually. That space he needed was as much to comprehend impending fatherhood as it was to build up some resistance to a woman he found irresistible. Had she not slowed things down Saturday night, he would've taken her to bed again, without a thought, without an ounce of self-control.

That's what she did to him.

That's what he needed to get a handle on, because it was vital for him to approach this momentous event in his life with his head on straight and his dick in his pants.

As he wandered into the kitchen, his phone buzzed with a text. It was from Drake.

Gabe and I are at Clayborne's for dinner. Get your ass over here and join us.

He and his twin hadn't spent any time alone, and it was beginning to feel obvious. He missed his brother, missed the closeness they'd once shared. Zane needed to repair the damage somehow. Soon. Maybe dinner tonight could be a start.

You treating? he typed back.

Only because you're unemployed, Drake responded, knowing full well that would get under Zane's skin.

"Bastard," Zane said aloud, then typed back, *Be there in a few.*

He changed into jeans and a Henley, grabbed a coat, and headed out the door and down to street level. Ignoring Hayden's SUV and the fact that she was steps away inside the building, he walked down the alley, then took a right at the narrow walkway between buildings to reach the Hale Street side. With a wave at Violet Morello through the bakery windows, he headed across the street to the bar and grill.

When he walked through the door, he took in the long bar against the wall, the high-top tables scattered, the compact stage in the front as he scanned for his brothers. The place was crowded, and he finally spotted them at a table along the wall.

As he approached, he realized Cole was there too, and before he could sit, Mason came striding up to the table from a different direction.

"You didn't tell me *all* of you fuckers were here," Zane said. He was actually okay with that; this probably was the time to break the news to them.

"We weren't when I texted you," Drake said, stuffing a pita chip with hummus in his mouth.

"Who ever thought we'd see the day when Drake is on time and Mason's the late one?" Gabe said. He and Mason were both still in suits, while Drake and Cole looked somewhere between casual and business casual.

"I'm a changed man." Mason grinned, then gestured to the couple at the next table to see if he could take one of their spare stools. They nodded, and he pulled it up to the head of the table and sat.

"Never underestimate Drake when there's a drink involved," Cole said.

A server came up to their table and took drink orders from the three latecomers. Zane's mindset was such that he didn't hesitate to order a beer.

"Y'all ready to order more food yet?" the twentysomething woman asked, her blue eyes friendly and warm.

Zane's brothers started rattling off their orders, so Zane glanced at the menu and ordered a grilled chicken sandwich and sweet potato fries.

"Thanks, Zoe," Drake said, and she hurried off to put in their order.

"Welcome back from the honeymoon," Zane said to Cole. "When'd you get in?"

"This morning," Cole answered. "Went home and crashed in bed all day, then Sierra dropped me off here and went to visit Hayden."

While his brothers threw out lewd comments about what else besides crashing Cole and Sierra had done in bed all day, Zane's thoughts went, yet again, to Hayden. He suspected she would tell her best friend she was pregnant tonight, and he was glad she finally had someone to lean on. He wanted to be that for her too, as soon as he got a handle on his attraction to her.

Cole filled them in on his adventures—outside of the bedroom—with his bride in the South Pacific, with Drake asking about places he and Mackenzie had apparently been last year.

"Giovanni Rossi, you had him snowed," Cole said to Drake. "He had nothing but complimentary stuff to say about you."

"He's a good guy. Helped me pull off an island-hopping surprise for Mackenzie when we were there."

"How'd you all get out of the house on your own tonight?" Zane asked, still a little blown away that all these lunkheads were suddenly married.

"Wednesdays are Mom Day for Calvin," Mason said. "Mom and son time, Eliza's weekly thing since the tour started last week and she'll be gone every Thursday night to Sunday. Tonight it's pizza and that new kids' movie in the theater."

"How'd week one of single dadding go?" Gabe asked.

"No problems. Little man went to Mimi's Friday after preschool, then had a slumber party with her Friday night. I don't know who loved it more, him or her."

"And how'd Eliza do on the Steele Hearts bus, being pregnant?"

"The trip wore her out, but she came home revved up and inspired and talking a mile a minute. If you know her, you know that's not her usual mode, unlike some women." He grinned at Drake, and Zane was already figuring out that Mackenzie talked a lot.

"I guess I better study up on Steele Hearts," Zane said, "if my sister-in-law's playing with the band. They any good?"

The unanimous opinion around the table was yes, and Mason told him Tucker Steele, the lead singer, and his wife, Gin, were frequent customers here at Clayborne's, along with the rest of the band.

"Apparently that recording studio down the street is always booked," Drake added with a nod.

"I saw a brunette woman with a bodyguard go in there from

my balcony yesterday," Zane said. "She looked like someone important in the music industry."

"Probably Joey Bloom," Mason said. "Eliza says she's working on an album."

Zane didn't know Joey Bloom from Eve and figured he needed to dip into country music if he was going to live next door to a recording studio in Nashville.

"Joey's a cool cat," Drake said.

"Figures you'd know her," Zane shot at him.

"She came in with her bodyguard, who I'm pretty sure is her boyfriend, and bought a bunch of workout equipment." Drake looked smug, as if he deserved kudos for *not* having dated her before he met his wife.

"How's Lexie doing? Is she feeling okay?" Mason asked Gabe, reminding Zane that, including his own situation, more than fifty percent of the North brothers were in the process of increasing the world population.

"She's dealing with a little morning sickness—at all hours of the day. She and Eliza are texting back and forth a lot."

"It's a North baby boom," Drake said. He held up his beer bottle. "Cheers to you two for carrying on the family name."

They clinked their beverages, water glasses for those who hadn't been served yet, and Zane told himself a better opportunity wouldn't come up.

"Three," he said when the rest of them were taking a swig.

All four heads turned his way.

"Three what?" Cole asked.

Zane set his glass down and ran a hand over his short hair, taking reassurance from the high level of noise around them that no one would overhear. "Three of us carrying on the family name."

Drake laughed at first and then seemed to register Zane's meaning and he sobered instantly. "Come again? You…" He tilted his head. "I didn't know you were seeing anyone."

"*Seeing* would be a bit of an overstatement," Zane said, feeling heat creep up the back of his neck. When all four of his brothers stared at him, obviously waiting for more, he laid out the facts. "I was with someone the night of your wedding." He nodded at Cole. "We had a condom fail. The timing was apparently spot on."

Mason sat back against the barstool backrest. "Damn. I was hoping it was a false alarm."

"Explains why you didn't make it to the couch in the lake house," Gabe said.

"Who is she?" Cole asked.

"Hayden Henry," Drake said with certainty before Zane could answer.

He nodded once, then leaned forward over the table. "It's confidential. You four and, I'm betting after tonight, Sierra, are the only ones who know. If you tell your wives, please ask them to keep it to themselves."

"What about Mom?" Gabe asked.

"I'm planning to tell her. Soon."

"Shit, bro," Drake said. "How's Hayden?"

He didn't admit that he didn't exactly know. "Adjusting. It's still new."

"Sierra will be there for her," Cole said. "*Is* there. Probably getting an earful right now, huh?"

"She planned on telling her. Didn't want to lay it on her during your trip." Zane admitted to himself he'd been shit for support for Hayden the past four days. He had to do better.

"How do you feel about it?" Gabe asked.

Zane let out a half laugh and rubbed his forehead. "I'm still figuring that out. Still shell-shocked. Overwhelmed. Worried as fuck."

"Welcome to the scared-as-fuck fathers-to-be club." Gabe picked up his beer bottle. "Sweet mother of God. I would've thought Drake would be the one—"

"Hey," Drake said. "I've always been responsible."

"And lucky," Zane threw in. Because though he himself had never been a saint, even back in high school, Drake had fucked circles around him. Based on odds alone, his twin should've been the one in this unfortunate situation. Not that he wished it on him, most days, but irony was a son of a bitch.

Zoe showed up with a tray full of drinks and mozzarella sticks Mason had ordered, then distributed everything as silence fell over their table. Even Drake refrained from chatting her up.

"Entrees will be out in a few, gentlemen," the server said and headed off to another table.

Once she was gone, Zane took a gulp of his beer, and his brothers bombarded him with questions, many of the same questions that'd been churning through his mind nonstop. Would they get married? Would he share custody? How would he share custody? Were he and Hayden together?

"We're amiable," he said. "Planning to figure out things together."

"Talk to Robert Pendleton," Mason said.

"Already have." The family lawyer, who'd helped Zane with his will before he'd deployed the first time, had given him even more to consider, if that was possible.

"You got a due date yet?" Gabe asked. "Ours is August thirty-first."

"And ours is September fifth," Mason said.

Zane shook his head. "She hasn't been to the doctor yet but whatever nine months from your wedding day is," he said to Cole, who grinned and shook his head.

"I'll expect you to name him after me," Cole said.

"Cole seems a little masculine for a daughter." Zane took another drink of his stout beer.

"You don't have a due date but you know it's a girl?" Drake asked.

"Known fact that fighter pilots have daughters," Zane said.

Cole pulled out his phone, and Zane was ninety-eight percent certain his middle brother was googling that.

"Colleen," Gabe suggested.

"Colby," Mason added.

"Collette," was Gabe's next suggestion.

"Columbia." Mason gave Gabe a look of challenge.

"Columbine," Gabe said, raising his chin back.

"It's like they've been scouring baby name websites or something," Drake said.

"Guilty," Gabe admitted, laughing.

"Glad you two are having a grand time with this," Zane said, shaking his head at these morons. He was about thirty or forty steps behind coming up with a name.

"I, for one, am here to be supportive," Drake said as he beckoned to their server. When Zoe got to their table, he said, "I need a round of shots, please. Mezcal."

"Five?" she asked, meeting each of their gazes and receiving a nod from all but Zane. He hesitated, because a fuzzy head had never been his friend.

"Do it," Drake said to him.

"If ever there's an appropriate time for Mezcal, I think you're staring it in the face," Cole added.

"You still haven't decompressed post-military and now this," Gabe said.

"You won't be as free to do shots in a few months," Mason said, and that was the argument that pushed Zane.

He nodded to the server.

A few hours later, every last one of his brothers had ordered multiple rounds of shots, beginning with supportive *oh, shit* ones and progressing to *congrats, you're gonna be a father* ones. Funny how Mezcal—and brotherhood—could make that transition so easy.

When Zane stood up to leave, he realized it was a damn good thing he only lived half a block away.

CHAPTER TWELVE

ednesday evenings in February at Henry Interiors were reliably slow. So slow, in fact, that Hayden had insisted Marley go home an hour ago. She'd had exactly one customer since then—Fallon from World in Pieces Mosaics next door had come in for a lamp she'd had her eye on for a couple of weeks.

With five minutes till closing, Hayden was straightening the retail floor and adding a subtle, classy Valentine's flair by placing red and pink heart-shaped throw pillows on random sofas, love seats, and chairs. It wasn't a big holiday for a home furnishings store, but Sydney had had the pillow idea last year and insisted they dig out the heart stock again this year. Though Hayden wasn't the most romantic of souls, she did try not to bah humbug the day of love—at least not in her business realm.

When the bell on the door tinkled, she straightened with her professional smile on, prepared to greet the last-minute customer with as big of a welcome as she'd give the first one of the day. The woman who came through the door wasn't a customer though.

"You!" Hayden squealed, then tossed the last heart pillow askew on a cloud-white love seat and rushed over to Sierra. She threw her arms around her taller friend and didn't let go.

Sierra hugged her back, saying, "It's so good to see youuuu."

At the familiar citrus-vanilla scent of her friend and the welcoming, loving embrace, all the emotion of the past two-plus weeks rolled over Hayden like a rogue tidal wave. She clung to Sierra, her throat swelling up, eyes filling like a freshwater spring.

"Hay?" Sierra said when she started to straighten and Hayden only held on tighter. Sierra relaxed once again, accepting the extended hug, until Hayden let out a sniffle. "Hayden, what's wrong?"

What a flipping mess she was. Hayden held on for another three seconds, sniffed again, then pulled away and wiped her eyes, stunned at her own breakdown out of nowhere.

"I have a lot to tell you," Hayden said.

Sierra looked alarmed. "Is everybody okay?"

Hayden nodded, because depending on your definition of okay, everybody was. No one had died. No one was sick.

She glanced around the store, seeing that all except the last pillow she'd tossed was in place. "It's a long story. Can you let me close and… Do you have to rush home, or can you ride to my dad's with me? I won't be there too long and we can talk on the way there."

"I don't have to rush home. Cole knows I'm here. What can I do to help? Because you're killing me with the suspense."

"I'm ready to go. Let me turn out the lights and get my bag."

On her way to the back room, she checked the time to make sure it had hit six o'clock. It was three minutes after. At the back door, she peeked outside in spite of herself, curious whether Zane's sports car—he'd purchased a brand-new silver Jaguar— was parked in his spot beyond the storage shed. It was, and it gave her heart a jolt of warmth to know he was upstairs. And then she shook her head at her ridiculous self as she went into her office, pulled on her coat, and grabbed her overstuffed work bag and purse.

She hadn't seen Zane since she'd left his apartment Saturday night—since they'd agreed not to muddy things up with sex. She'd heard him a couple of times. During quiet moments before she opened the store, there'd been subtle clunks from above that most people wouldn't think twice about. But she had. Twice, thrice, and more, wondering what he was doing, what he was wearing, whether he was thinking about her.

"You coming?" Sierra called from the barn door to the main room.

"Just finding my keys." She unzipped an exterior pocket and pulled them out, then dragged both bags up to her shoulder.

Hayden locked the back door, hit the lights for the back room and sales floor, glancing toward the front to ensure the window display lights stayed on. Then she followed Sierra to the front, locked up, and got into Sierra's truck, parked at the curb in front of the door.

"Can you bring me back here afterward so I can get my car?"

"Sure, but why don't you just sleep upstairs? You look exhausted, Hay."

"Thanks, friend." Hayden lowered the visor and peered at herself in the mirror. "Ew."

Sierra started the truck and pulled away from the curb. "To your dad's condo, right?"

"Right." Hayden sagged into the seat, so stinking tired, maybe more tired than she'd ever been in her life, even though it was several hours earlier than she quit most nights. Two weeks into this pregnancy and it was kicking her ass.

"Did I give off some sign that said I was going to be patient?" Sierra asked. "Because I'm not. What is *up*? Why the tears?"

And that was all it took. The waterworks turned on again, her eyes filling, throat clogging with emotion.

"Hell's bells." Hayden dug through her purse for a tissue. "You haven't even told me about the honeymoon. I want to know all about Jiva."

"And I'd planned to do exactly that until you grabbed on to me like a stage-five clinger. Tell me everything. Your reward will be honeymoon deets."

"Bossy." Hayden sat up a little straighter and took in a fortifying breath, wondering where to start. "So you know how you've always threatened to set me up with a North brother?"

"Oh, my God. You and Zane?"

"Me and Zane. It was such a fluke." She explained about her car and Zane happening by at one in the morning and rescuing her.

"Fluke or destiny," Sierra said.

"Or a bad decision," Hayden said, and yet, even with her current situation, she couldn't truly feel bad about the night she'd spent with Zane. Half night. Whatever.

"Was it bad?" Sierra asked.

"Hell no." The reply came out with zero hesitation. "It was good." Hayden let out a sigh that might've verged on dreamy. "So. Damn. Good."

"Yeah?" Sierra's grin was audible.

Her lips spread into their own smile. "Oh, yeah." She fanned herself as if she was having a hot flash.

Sierra let out a howl and held up her hand for a high five. "The drought is dead!"

Hayden smacked her hand with glee, then sobered. "The night, however," she said in a dramatic voice, "was cut tragically short with the breaking of the rubber."

"What? Oh, shit. And you're not on the pill." Sierra turned onto a less busy street that led to Hayden's dad's condo.

"Nope. Not on the pill."

"Did you get your period yet?"

"Nope. Got me a positive pregnancy test instead."

"Shut up!" Sierra hit the brakes, jolting the truck to a halt. Thankfully they hadn't been going very fast.

Hayden couldn't help it—she craned her neck around to see if anyone was behind them. "What are you doing?"

"Freaking the fuck out because my best friend, last I knew, my very *single* best friend, just told me she's pregnant," Sierra said.

"You need to pull over to the side at least. Or you could keep driving."

"I can't drive when you're pregnant."

Hayden laughed at the stupidity of that statement. As the laugh faded, she said, "We're going to be here for a while then."

Sierra pulled over to the curb, leaving the engine on for the heater. Hayden glanced around the residential neighborhood. It was fully dark, with a few streetlights scattered, and most of the homes were lit up, but no one was out and about.

"Does Zane know yet?" Sierra asked, pushing her seat back and turning slightly to face Hayden.

"He knows."

"And?"

"Well." Hayden raised her brows. "He keeps things to himself, so there was no big freak-out in my presence."

"That sounds about right, from what I know of him. Which isn't much. I still can't believe he resigned from the military without telling his family in advance. Cole says he's always been the private, steel-control one."

"Believable." Hayden launched into the story of Saturday, when Zane had walked in right after the test, and then that evening's dinner, where they hadn't managed to decide much of anything, other than no sex.

"So he's in it with you," Sierra said. "I'm not surprised at all. Their mama raised them right."

Hayden nodded pensively. "I guess I don't quite understand what 'in it' means yet, you know? I haven't heard from him since Saturday night."

"But you haven't contacted him either, right?"

"It's"—Hayden blew out a shaky breath—"risky."

"Because you like him."

"Too much."

"What would you do if you weren't pregnant? See him again?"

Without deliberation, Hayden shook her head.

"Really?" Sierra pressed.

"Really. For so many reasons."

"Because of Brian." Sierra stated it instead of asking.

Hayden watched a car pull into a driveway down the block and realized her jaw was clenched tightly. "Partly. And let's not forget Patrick."

"I know they both devastated you, but they're assholes who

were too stupid to see what they had. You have to get past that sometime."

"Yeah. Apparently not today. And not with a baby on the line."

"But you and Zane have a deadline of sorts for deciding whether a relationship beyond parenting will work. You really need to get to know him. Better to do that now, before the baby's born, because your lives will be rocked when there's a bambino in the picture."

"Maybe."

"Maybe? You know I'm right."

Hayden nibbled on her manicured thumbnail without actually biting it, wishing she had any kind of sane argument for that, but she didn't. "Fine. Probably."

"Did you talk about how you'll handle raising the child once it's born?"

Hayden again shook her head.

"What do you want?" Sierra persisted.

A semi-hysterical laugh bubbled out of Hayden. "Want? I want to go back three weeks for a do-over."

"Of course. But you have to move forward, start figuring things out."

"I know," Hayden said curtly. "I can't even think about specifics yet."

"Did he say anything about getting married?"

"Bite your tongue, woman. He didn't, and if he had, I would've told him no. I don't need a husband to have a baby. Besides, a lot can happen in eight and a half months."

Like, their chemistry could evaporate, especially since she was going to balloon up and lose her figure. Or Zane could decide he didn't like Hayden that much after all. Happened all the time, folks, and she'd rather not be legally attached if and when.

"Well, you can't avoid each other for eight and a half months," Sierra pointed out.

"We probably could..."

"You will *not*."

Hayden let out a half grin. "No. Probably not, considering he's leasing my apartment."

A look of amusement skittered over Sierra's face. "Because things weren't complicated enough, so you decided moving him in literally on top of you was a good idea."

"He was looking for a place. I was helping him out."

"You have a good heart," Sierra admitted. She craned her neck back as if stretching. "Oh, Hay. You're in quite the tricky situation. But Zane is a good guy. He's not going to shirk his responsibilities, whatever you two decide those are. If you have to get knocked up, might as well be with a hot, rich North boy."

Hayden tended to believe exactly what Sierra said—that Zane wasn't going to shirk his responsibilities. What she was so much less sure about were his *non*-responsibilities. Like her. Their relationship, if that word was even appropriate in this situation. She didn't want to be his responsibility, and if there was ever going to be anything romantic between them, she'd have to be careful to distinguish between his reasons for being with her—out of responsibility or because of genuine feelings?

And she still wasn't anywhere close to that bridge.

"We should get going to my dad's," Hayden said. "I didn't specify which evening I'd drop by, and he likes to go to bed early."

Pivoting to face forward again, Sierra smiled and said, affectionately, "Gotta get Mr. H. his beauty rest," then put the car into gear and pulled away from the curb. "I'm going to say one more thing on the subject. For tonight."

Hayden tensed slightly at her friend's tone, sensing she wasn't going to like whatever it was.

"It's time, Hayden. You need to get organized and learn to delegate. You're killing yourself as it is, between the store and the design business, plus party planning for your dad, and God knows what else you've got going on. Now that you're with child, you have to slow down. I mean it," she said before Hayden could get a word out. "It's not just *your* health anymore."

"Yes, Mom."

Sierra narrowed her eyes at her.

"Okay," Hayden said. "I know this. I've been meaning to. Trying to. It's...not easy. I've built up everything myself."

"I know you have. And you've done a fantastic job with all of it. All. Of. It. Including hiring really good, trustworthy people. You need to use them better. More. And hire some more."

Hayden exhaled, knowing her friend had a valid point. She'd known it for some time and was trying...in her mind. Working up to it. Because it was hard. Trusting others with her business babies was hard.

"Hayden?"

"Yeah. I hear you, you evil hag," she said lightly.

The fact was, Sierra was wicked good at business. She'd been running her own remodeling company for years now, and on top of staying booked year-round in an industry that was often seasonal, she was becoming more and more known as a TV personality and a revered expert on restoring historical homes. The woman was creating her own empire.

"Have you thought more about promoting Sydney to manager?"

"Of course." She thought about it all the time. But in order to do that, she'd need time to sit down and figure out how much extra she could pay her and what additional duties Sydney could take on and...and...

The nitty-gritty details melted her down, because, as Sierra had mentioned, her days were already overflowing with to-dos.

"Do you want me to help?" Sierra offered.

"You have enough to do, including your new husband. I'll figure it out."

"Soon."

"Soon," Hayden agreed, because she knew she needed to rest more. Her body was telling her that. "I'm ready for my reward now. Tell me all about your South Pacific luxury honeymoon."

It was Sierra's turn for a dreamy sigh. "Heaven. Just like Mackenzie said. Like, we lived in a postcard world for two weeks."

"Naked?"

With a laugh, Sierra said, "A lot of naked. But we toured a

bunch of islands in the area too. The owner, Giovanni, has more brothers than Cole and they all have island resorts. Can you imagine? All of them are breathtaking."

"The brothers or the islands?"

"Both!" She parked the car at the curb in front of Hayden's dad's place and they got out, Sierra still talking about the beaches and the music and the food in the South Pacific. There were lights on inside, so when they got to the front door, Hayden tried the lock, and finding it unlocked, she pushed the door open as she called out.

"Hey, Dad."

He came around the corner into the small entryway, look-ing...guilty? Not thrilled to see her? He smiled, but there was something beneath it. "Hey, honey. What are you doing here? Oh, hi, Sierra."

"Hi, Mr. H."

"We came to finish up the guest list for the party and get Mom's old address book."

It was old-school, a spiral-bound book bursting from having index cards shoved in with extra contacts, and the entries on the pages had often been crossed out and replaced, sometimes multiple times for one family. But her dad had held on to it because it was the holy grail of their contacts, their friends, their lives, really.

"Oh, was that tonight?" her dad said. He stood in the doorway to the living room, hands on his hips, like he was hiding something.

"We said an evening this week. Is tonight not good?" Hayden asked.

"Well—"

"Did I hear my daughter-in-law's voice?"

Faye North breezed into the entryway, a wide, welcoming smile on her face. Hayden noted her hand clasping familiarly to her dad's forearm, couldn't miss the softening effect the woman had on him as he relaxed slightly and made room for her to stand next to him.

"Faye," Sierra said happily, managing to hide any shock. Or

maybe it was just Hayden who was stuck on the seeming inti-macy they'd walked into. Mrs. North's—*Zane's mother's*—shoes were off, and her silver hair, which had been perfectly in place at the wedding, was slightly mussed.

Mrs. North stepped forward, arms open, and Sierra met her in a hug. "I hadn't expected to see you until Sunday dinner," Mrs. North said. "What a pleasant surprise. Can you girls come in? I'd love to hear about the trip."

It was she who motioned welcomingly to the living room, as if she was comfortable here, while Hayden's dad still looked awkward and a little embarrassed.

"We don't want to interrupt," Sierra said.

"Did you two have dinner?" Hayden asked as she registered a faint hint of food aroma lingering. "I'll just get the address book and we'll leave you to your date."

"I'll grab it." Her dad disappeared into the office all too willingly.

"Come on in," Mrs. North said warmly. When she turned to lead them into the living room, Hayden met Sierra's gaze, her brows raised, both of them holding in a laugh.

When they entered the living room, which was open to the dining room, they could see the remains of an intimate *candlelit* dinner—two mostly empty wineglasses, napkins, plus a single dessert plate with two forks on it between the two places, as if they'd been sharing.

Her dad had busted out candles? Hayden hadn't known he had it in him.

And then, she froze as she spotted an overnight bag on the sofa. A pink and gray overnight bag. Clearly Mrs. North's.

Hell's bells. Her dad had an overnight guest.

"Here it is," Simon said as he came back into the room, holding out the tattered booklet that was so familiar and, like every other reminder of her mother, beloved.

Hayden moved to him to accept it, while Mrs. North asked Sierra about her and Cole's long transglobal trip home.

"Thanks, Dad. I really only had questions about three couples." She pulled out her phone, where she'd entered the guest list. "What do you think about the Mullenses, the Worthingtons, and the Giddingses? Are they a yes to invite?"

He frowned. "They all sound okay. Are you sure you want to do this, buttercup? You look exhausted."

"Totally sure, Dad. Just had a long couple of days. We're going to leave you two alone, and I'm going to bed early tonight."

"You need to take better care of yourself."

"Yeah, Sierra already lectured me," Hayden said, grinning to soften her impatience. "I will. I promise." To Sierra, she said, "About ready?"

"Anytime. I'll show you all the pictures Sunday," Sierra told Mrs. North.

Hayden hugged her dad, who stood there still a little awkward and stiff. "Love you, Dad." Then she whispered, "I'm happy for you. Enjoy your date."

At those words, he relaxed more, pulled her in tighter, and said, "Thanks, buttercup. Love you too."

After a round of goodbyes and hugs—Mrs. North even hugged Hayden, and Hayden couldn't quite wrap her head around the fact that her baby's grandmother was hugging her— she and Sierra walked calmly, silently to the truck at the curb.

Once inside, doors shut, lights off, they both burst into laughter.

"Mr. H is romancing my mother-in-law!" Sierra let out.

"I can't even… What have I done? I introduced them for a possible date, not a slumber party!" Hayden said, grinning.

"I'm not so sure there will be slumbering."

"Stop."

They talked about the two senior lovebirds the rest of the way home, laughing, celebrating her dad's potential happiness, giggling over the fact that he most likely had a better love life than his daughter.

"Oh, pretty sure you could compete," Sierra said, "if you'd just let yourself."

Just like that, with that little return to her own problems, all the merriment seeped out of Hayden. She exhaled loudly. "Yeah. If only it were that easy…"

"Hey, it could be. Just start with getting to know him. Things will fall into place one way or another."

"Look at the new Mrs. North, handing out advice like candy."

"Just trying to pay it forward. There was a time when you advised me to play it cool with Cole, and look where that got me."

"Blissful and well-serviced, if I had to guess," Hayden said dryly.

"Guilty." There was not a hint of remorse in Sierra's voice.

As they pulled up in back of Henry Interiors, Hayden glanced up at her apartment—*Zane's* apartment. The exterior light was on, shining like a welcoming beacon. Part of her longed to give in to it.

She leaned across the truck cab and hugged her friend. "Thanks for listening. Love you. Talk to you soon."

"Anytime. Let's do dinner soon."

"For sure." Hayden slid out of the truck and let herself into her Santa Fe.

With a wave, Sierra drove off, and Hayden sagged into the seat. She was dragging big-time. The thought of her bed—the one at home, twenty minutes away—was tempting. But…

She wanted to see Zane.

It scared the shit out of her to want to see Zane, to give in to that desire, but Sierra was so absolutely right. There was a timeline for getting to know the father of her baby. She'd already put it off for four days.

And timeline or not, the man drew her in.

Unsure whether she was being smart or stupid, she climbed back out of the SUV, went to the stairs, and began her ascent.

CHAPTER THIRTEEN

At the top of the stairs, Hayden paused for a mental check as to whether she wanted to reverse her decision and hightail it out of there.

Maybe she should, but she didn't.

She knocked on the door and waited, her heart pounding as it always did when she was close to Zane.

The only sounds came from the street on the opposite side of the building, where people were coming and going to the businesses that were still open. Zane's apartment was silent, so she glanced at his sports car below again, making sure it was his, even though she knew very well it was.

It was hard to tell from this side whether any lights were on in the apartment because the only window was the tiny one in the back bathroom. It was dark, but that didn't mean the living room was.

Again, she knocked. And waited. And admitted to herself he wasn't going to answer.

Instead of going down the stairs again and driving off, she pulled out her phone, deciding to take advantage of the blanket offer he'd made to crash in her bed here when she was too tired to drive. Technically, she was pretty damn wiped out. She typed in a message.

I'm at your place. Too tired to drive home. See you soon?

She stared at her screen for a few seconds, willing the three dots that would signify he was replying to appear, but they didn't, and she frowned.

Okay then. Less sure of herself, she dug in her purse for her spare key, then let herself in.

"Zane?" she called out just in case he was asleep or out on the balcony or had headphones on.

His bedroom door was open, the room dark. The only light was from a lamp in the living room, on the dimmest setting. Once there, she looked into the master bedroom—hers, sort of—also dark, and then went into it, glancing around to make sure he wasn't there. Of course he wasn't there. And he still wasn't replying to her message.

"Guess I'm on my own for a while," she said out loud, tamping down the internal voice that said she should drive home.

When she flopped on the sofa, moaning at the relief, her stomach rumbled with hunger. She hadn't eaten since lunch, and she decided to order something for delivery.

"Something healthy," she said, grinning as she thought about her discussion with Zane about healthy food. She could get extra for him, for whenever he showed up.

With a Google search for organic restaurants, she found one, ordered two teriyaki bowls from her phone, mourned the lack of fries, and forced herself off the couch so she wouldn't fall asleep without dinner.

After checking again for a reply from Zane, she wandered through the apartment to see what changes he'd made. The biggest one was the food in the fridge. There were veggies in the vegetable drawer, a bunch of bananas on the counter, and meat in the freezer instead of processed meals in boxes. The man was missing out.

Hayden couldn't resist peeking into his bedroom and wasn't shocked to find the bed was made and the entire room was spotless. The only sign of it being lived in was a book on the nightstand with a bookmark sticking out—and when she realized it was a second copy of one of the pregnancy books he'd bought her, she melted a little bit.

He might've gone silent toward her, but he wasn't blowing off their situation.

Conscious of invading his privacy, she backed away from his doorway and made her way to the master bedroom, still half-full of her clothes and belongings. The main difference was that she'd given it a quick cleaning before giving Zane a key.

After closing the door, she shed her professional clothes and pulled on leggings and a tunic-style sweatshirt. When she went back out to the living room, she felt a little strange about getting so comfortable in what was technically Zane's house, but he'd told her she was welcome—before.

What if something had changed?

What if he'd met someone?

What if he was out with another woman right now and that's why he wasn't replying to her?

She checked the time—after eight p.m. Prime date time.

Feeling panicked, she lowered herself to the edge of the sectional. What if he brought someone home with him? Not only would that be mortifying but...she couldn't deny the sinking in her chest at the thought.

A knock came from the back door, sending her heartbeat into a frenzy for a moment before she remembered that Zane, with or without a woman, wouldn't knock, and the food delivery person would.

Absently, she set the food on the kitchen counter, still trying to decide whether she should get the heck out of there or hide away in the master bedroom and do what she'd told Zane she was there to do—sleep.

With an exhale, Hayden remembered she was no longer completely alone in her Zane dilemma, and she picked up her phone to get Sierra's opinion.

Having already explained Zane's open-ended offer when he moved in, she typed, *I went up to Zane's but he didn't answer, so I let myself in. Freaking out that he might be out with someone else. WWYD?*

Almost immediately, the three dots appeared.

I just left my husband at Clayborne's, Sierra replied, *carrying on with all four of his brothers. Zane told them your news and they're doing shots. I've never seen those boys quite like this. Trust me, he won't be finding anyone else tonight.*

She ended it with three laughing emojis.

The beginnings of a grin tickled Hayden's lips at the thought of the five oversized, loud, drunk North brothers.

Hope they don't get kicked out, she texted, leaning against the kitchen counter in relief.

Considering Hunter is with them, highly unlikely.

Does Hunter know I'm pregnant? Hayden asked, a little alarmed.

I'm guessing so, but now that he and Cole are brothers-in-law, he's been indoctrinated as family. Hunter won't let it slip except to Kennedy, and you know Kennedy will keep it quiet.

The more people who found out, the more real it became, and yes, that freaked Hayden out a little, but she trusted Kennedy, who was due to give birth in another month. That made her ask, *Is Hunter drunk too?*

No. Smart man. He's on call. My sister would kill him if he was incapacitated and she went into labor! Do you want me to come over? I'm still parked in front of the bar. I can be there in two minutes.

The offer brought tears to Hayden's eyes, which was ridiculous but proof that she was an emotional mess. An extra-tired one. *No, but thank you. I got food and I'm going to do what I told Zane I was here to do—crash in my own bed. Love you. Drive safely.*

Sierra signed off with Xs and Os, and Hayden belatedly noticed the food aroma wafting through the room. Her stomach growled.

She put one of the dinners in the refrigerator and took hers to the table, feeling calmer but still a little embarrassed by her decision to crash here. However, not embarrassed enough to trek down to her SUV and drive all the way home. When she finished eating, she cleaned up after herself, then crawled into her own bed and fell asleep within minutes.

———

HAYDEN AWOKE to a loud crash and bolted up on her elbows, trying to get her bearings. It took her several seconds to remember she was in her apartment—Zane's apartment—and to realize it was most likely him getting home.

She heard masculine voices at the other end of the place, then laughter, then another bump and a curse. Fully awake now and curious, she went out into the living room and stopped in her tracks at the sight of Zane being supported by Drake and Gabe as they stumbled into the kitchen.

"Are you okay?" she asked, torn between amusement and concern.

"Smells like food," Zane slurred without looking at her, and Hayden's brows shot up. "Needta eat. Drink some water. Be fine."

"Hello there," Drake said, sounding much more coherent than his twin. "We're good. Well, Gabe and I are. This one"—he rubbed Zane's head vigorously—"was overserved." He laughed, just sloppily enough that Hayden knew he wasn't sober either.

Zane seemed to realize for the first time that someone besides his brothers was in the room, and he stood up straighter, untangled himself from Drake and Gabe, and approached her.

"Hi," she said when he was a foot away, squinting at her as if he was seeing double or triple.

Several seconds passed as he studied her with his dreamy blue eyes. Hayden's brows rose again as she waited for him to say something, a grin tugging at her lips.

Zane finally lifted a hand and pressed it to the side of her face and clumsily ran it down her cheek. "You," he said slowly but intently and definitely drunkly, "are the mos' beautiful girl in the world." *Beautiful* came out as only two syllables.

His brothers laughed and shook their heads, and Zane, holding on to the counter to support himself, whipped around to them and insisted, "She is," but it came out sounding like *shiz*.

"Hayden is beautiful and you're shit-faced," Gabe affirmed.

"Jus' need some food. Water," Zane said again.

No one asked why she was there. Hayden was glad for the reprieve.

"I ordered you some healthy food," she said, brushing past him and going to the fridge. "Organic."

"'Mazing," he said as he watched her remove the carryout container, set it on the counter, and take off the lid. Then he looked at her and said, "You're 'mazing."

"I get that a lot," she said lightly. "Sorry, I didn't get you two anything," she said to Gabe and Drake. "Zane has some bananas though."

"I'm good," Gabe said, and Drake helped himself to a banana. "He ate dinner," he continued, pointing to Zane.

"Can't feel it," Zane informed him, taking a fork out of the silverware drawer and digging into the cold teriyaki bowl.

"I can heat it up," Hayden said, but Zane shook his head, leaned over the counter, supporting himself with an elbow, and shoved food in his mouth, still wearing his winter coat.

"Your manners are atrocious," Drake said to him.

"Fuck you," Zane slurred, then took another bite.

"Do you guys need to sleep here?" Hayden asked Zane's brothers, figuring she could sleep on the couch if necessary.

Gabe shook his head. "Already called an Uber."

"Where are the others? Sierra said you were all at Clayborne's."

"Hunter drove Mason and Cole home."

"Are they as bad as he is?" She pointed at Zane.

"Nowhere near," Drake said. "And Hunter's fine."

"How'd you get so messed up?" Hayden asked Zane, who was still eating as if he hadn't for a week.

"These assholes." He gestured at his brothers, then stood and helped himself to a glass of water.

"All four of us assholes. Plus Hunter," Drake said with a grin. Addressing Hayden, he explained, "He told us about the baby. Come here." He hugged her carefully. "I know it might not've been your first choice, but welcome to the family."

"I'm not fam—"

"You're brewing our niece or nephew," Gabe said. "You're

family, no matter what this schmuck does." He flicked Zane in the head.

"Uber's here," Drake said when his phone buzzed a couple of seconds later. He frowned at Hayden. "Are you going to be okay with this lug? He might need help getting to bed."

"Or a kick in the ass," Gabe added.

"Fuck you," Zane said nonchalantly again.

"Your tolerance for liquor is in the cellar, bro," Drake said.

"I'll be fine. Hayden'll be fine. Quit hugging her."

Drake, who hadn't touched her for a minute or two, just the one quick hug, held his hands up in surrender. "All yours, Z. Chill the fuck out."

"We have to go," Gabe said. "I've got a hot wife at home."

"Same," Drake said. "Let us know if you need anything," he said to Hayden.

She laughed and nodded, thinking they wouldn't be much help to her if she did. But she didn't. She suspected, as soon as Zane finished stuffing food in his face, she could guide him to his bed, and he'd pass out cold.

She saw Gabe and Drake out the door, spotting a waiting car in the alley, then locked up and went back to the kitchen, where Zane had finished his cold after-dinner "snack."

"Take your coat off. Let's get you to bed," Hayden said. "Tomorrow's going to be rough."

"Nothing to do but sleep it off," he mumbled. He removed his coat, tossed it on the opposite kitchen counter in a very non-Zane move, squinted again and took in his surroundings, then pointed toward his room. "That way." He said it as if reminding himself, and Hayden hid a laugh.

As she followed him to his doorway and flipped on the bedroom light, he asked, "What're you doing here?"

"Did you get my text? I was too tired to drive home. I was sleeping in the other room. I hope that's still okay."

He stopped just inside the room and felt in his back pocket, fishing out his phone. From beside him, she saw the black screen and realized he'd turned it all the way off, not just muted it.

"Doesn't work," he said, handing it to her as if he couldn't care less that his brand-new iPhone was faulty.

"It's not turned on, Zane."

He shrugged and moved farther into the room, and she held the power button down until it came to life. Clearly he hadn't relied on a cell phone for some time.

When the facial recognition screen came up, Hayden held it up to his face.

"Magic," he said with a boyish smile when the phone unlocked. She handed it to him, and he set it on the nightstand next to the pregnancy book without glancing at it.

"You're a cute drunk," she said, reaching up to touch his cheek.

"Nope. Magical." He laughed at himself, and then, before Hayden could register what he was doing, he whipped his shirt off.

Sweet mother of all things holy, that chest. Yes, she'd seen it before, but that was irrelevant. It was so…just right. Just wide enough, just muscular enough, just sprinkled with masculine hair enough.

She was still trying not to swallow her tongue when it registered that he'd undone his jeans and was pushing them down his legs. When her glance lowered, she realized he was shedding jeans and underwear as one.

"Nope," she said in a panic. "You have to keep your boxer briefs on."

"Sleep naked," he told her and stepped out of both. He held on to the bed as he bent over and removed his socks, and Hayden was torn between arguing and taking in the view.

Her eyes were locked on him as he crawled into the bed, giving her a primo view of his butt, with its round firmness, topping off those perfect thighs…

Hayden swallowed hard and switched the light off. "Night, Zane," she managed, her blood pounding through her. "I'll be in the other bedroom."

"Sleep in here."

She froze at the doorway. "You'd regret that in the morning."

"Why?"

"Because we're supposed to be figuring us out slowly. Not sleeping together."

He was quiet for several seconds and she wondered if he'd passed out. Then he said, "Jus' sleeping. Nothing else. Please?"

She wanted to. So much. He was tough to resist on a good day, but tonight, with his adorable boyish grins and his walls lowered?

"You have to put your underwear back on."

"Then you will?"

Biting her lower lip, she tried to talk herself out of it, but going back to her room at the other end of the apartment seemed so lonely. "Then I will."

He didn't reply, didn't stir, and she realized his breathing was deep and even.

"Zane?"

Still nothing.

Hayden let out a silent laugh and shook her head. She walked out to the kitchen, threw away the empty carryout container, and turned out the light. She hesitated, facing the living room and her bedroom in the darkened apartment.

Zane was out. There wasn't any danger of him getting frisky, not in his condition, and she sure wasn't going to initiate anything. But the thought of being so close to him all night, sleeping next to him…

She took a quick detour to her bathroom and brushed her teeth in record time—because frisky or not, she didn't want to be gross. Then she went back to his room, walked around to the far side of the bed, and slid on top of the sheet but under the comforter, her back to him, keeping that single thin barrier between them, just in case.

Within a minute, Zane rolled closer and put his arm around her, loosely spooning her and then returning to deep, even breathing.

Hayden closed her eyes and, in spite of the fact that the man holding her smelled like a distillery, fell asleep, more content than she could remember being in ages.

CHAPTER FOURTEEN

There was a science experiment going on in Zane's mouth, and his head was pounding in time with his heartbeat. He cracked one eyelid open and saw nothing but darkness.

The next thing that registered was the body beneath his arm, a soft, warm one.

What the fuck?

Rolling away from the woman, he racked his brain to remember where he was and how he got here and who...

It was Hayden, he realized.

He was in his apartment, and Hayden was in his bed.

His asshole brothers had been all too eager to keep buying him shot after shot. And he'd been all too willing to down every last one of them.

Zane had well and truly "cut loose," as Gabe had recommended, and it had accomplished exactly nothing, unless you counted humiliating himself in front of Hayden.

He didn't remember much of anything about getting home last night, didn't know exactly what he'd said to her, but he must've said something, because here she was next to him, and he was buck-ass naked—and hard.

Striving not to wake her, he swung his feet to the floor and eased his way up to sit on the edge. A wave of nausea came and went, and the throbbing in his head intensified.

Feeling around for his phone, he found it on his nightstand, held it up so the screen came to life. The time was 4:27 a.m. He had not one clue how long he'd been sleeping.

Once he'd unlocked the phone, he angled the dim light toward Hayden, who hadn't stirred. She was sleeping on top of the sheet, her arm on the comforter, allowing him to see she wore a sweatshirt.

She was still dressed.

That was a good sign, right?

If he was going to sleep with Hayden again, he wanted to be fully aware of every second.

But he wasn't going to sleep with her, not anytime soon, anyway. They'd agreed.

Disgusted by himself—the smell of liquor, the taste in his mouth, the furry feeling on his tongue—he crept to the bathroom. There, the light from the back porch, which he'd apparently never turned off, shone in enough that he could see the sink, his toothbrush.

He brushed his teeth, thinking he should buy a new toothbrush after this, took a couple of acetaminophen, then turned on the water in the shower, the lights still off. Turning the setting to cold, he stepped in and sucked in his breath against the shock.

He did a full but quick shower, including shampoo and plenty of soap to wash off the eau de drunk, leaning against the wall halfway through when another wave of nausea overcame him. One thing he wasn't doing tonight was throwing up, dammit.

After drying off fully, he downed a glass of water, then went back to his bedroom. Maybe it'd be smarter to do just about anything else, but with this headache, he didn't give a fuck about smart. He crawled back into the bed, making a point to keep to his side and not touch Hayden.

———

THE SUN WAS up when Hayden opened her eyes. It took a few seconds for her to remember what day it was—Thursday—and that she was at Zane's. In his bed.

She sat up, trying to gauge what time it might be based on the daylight filtering into the hall outside of the windowless bedroom. It wasn't too long after sunrise, she didn't think, unless it was particularly overcast. Since she had to work this morning, she eyed Zane's phone. She'd left hers in her room when he'd come home.

Carefully, she reached over his body, everything but one of his arms covered by the blankets, making a point of not touching him, and grabbed it. It was just after six thirty.

As she set the phone down, Zane grasped her waist, startling her and sending a thrill through her at once. When she met his eyes, he had the slightest smile on his lips.

"Hey," he said in a sexy, just-woke-up growl.

"Hi. I was trying not to wake you."

"I'm sorry as hell about last night."

His lids were half-open, the look in them earnest and embarrassed. There was a little scruff on his jaw, and hell's bells, did she like that scruff.

"What are you sorry about?" She herself was feeling pretty damn victorious that nothing had happened between them.

Shaking his head, Zane said, "I don't even know. Anything. Everything. I don't remember much."

His fingers were still at her waist, beneath her sweatshirt, and he brushed one over her bare skin. It was a subtle touch, but it shot heat through her as if he'd stripped her naked and run his tongue over that spot.

"There's nothing to be embarrassed about," she said, her voice coming out huskier than before as she lost herself in those mesmerizing blue eyes that were fully open now, the black centers larger. "How are you feeling?"

He blinked, as if gauging his condition. "Better than I did at four thirty. I showered and took something for my head."

Because she was having trouble focusing on anything besides the feel of his fingers on her skin—and the question of whether he was still naked—she reclined to her side of the bed and pulled the comforter over her against the chilly air. What she really longed to do was crawl under the sheet too and snuggle up to his side…

No. That was a lie. What she really longed to do was crawl under the sheet and roll on top of him and sate the throbbing ache deep within her.

"So you told your brothers about the baby last night," she said, rolling on her side to face him, which put her closer but still not touching. "How'd that go over?"

"About like you'd guess. I took a little shit, then they were all about accepting it—and you—and being supportive. Unfortunately, a lot of their support was in the form of Mezcal."

"Evidently." She grinned, not too surprised based on what she knew of his brothers. "And Hunter?"

"He's in on it but he'll keep it quiet. How'd it go with Sierra?"

"She was shocked, of course, but exactly what I needed." Propping herself up on an elbow, she continued, "We had an interesting experience. We stopped by my dad's to get his address book, and we interrupted a date. With your mom."

He whipped his head to her. "So it worked. Your setup."

"Um…" She pressed her lips together, choosing her words carefully. "I'd say so, considering your mom's overnight bag was sitting on his sofa."

"Whooo," he said on an exhale. "You think they're sleeping together already?"

"I don't think she was planning to sleep in the guest room." She told him about the intimate wine and dessert scene.

"Hurricane Hayden strikes again," he said, and she thought she heard affection in his tone. "I hope they find happiness together."

"Me too."

He rolled to face her, giving her a closeup of his handsome, scruffy face in the dim light.

"I can man up and say it: You were right. They apparently hit it off. Good call, Hay."

Hay. It was a nickname hardly anyone called her. Sierra,

sometimes Kennedy, a few others, but no man had called her that before, and…she liked it. When Zane said it, it felt intimate and personal. Lying in his bed helped that illusion along too.

She couldn't resist running a finger down his jawline, over the rough overnight growth of stubble. "I love a man who can admit when I'm right," she said, the tips of her lips curving into a smile.

"I love anything that makes my mama happy."

He caught her hand on his face, stared into her eyes with his panty-scalding blue ones—if only she were wearing underwear—then pressed kisses to the pads of her fingers, one at a time. As she registered the needful dampness between her thighs, he tugged her head closer and did exactly what she ached for—he kissed her.

Well, *some* of what she ached for.

She was dying for more contact, more than just lips and tongues and teeth. She'd never felt this kind of burn-her-up physical need before, and as he made love to her mouth, she wondered if it was Zane or some kind of pregnancy hormones. Whatever it was, it begged to be quenched.

"Zane," she said when they took a millisecond to breathe.

"I know. Asking for trouble. We'll keep the blankets in place and not get carried away."

With her oversensitive breasts heavy and in need of his touch and her pulse pounding a rhythm of desire deep inside of her, she shook her head. "I think we messed up."

With a sexy rumble of a laugh that vibrated through her, he said, "Sleeping in the same bed wasn't smart—"

"No," she said curtly. "I mean deciding no sex. That was… short-sighted. Stupid. We're trying to get to know each other, and I, for one, am dying to climb on top of you and put out this inferno that's raging inside. I mean…" She paused to breathe and consider that maybe she was alone in this urgent need. God help her. "Maybe it's just me and these pregnancy hormones."

Zane growled as he pressed his forehead intently to hers. "There's never been a woman who shatters my self-control the way you do, Hayden Eloise Henry. I'd like nothing more than for you to climb on top of me and fuck me till the cows come home."

Her exhale came out as a shaky laugh, heavy with relief and a need that ratcheted even higher with his crude words. "I don't know a thing about cows, but your wish is my command."

Still fully clothed, she slipped under the sheet and moved over him as he went flat on his back and welcomed her with both hands on her skin, beneath her shirt. She centered herself on his erection that was, indeed, still naked and quite impressive, and she couldn't resist grinding her lower body into his as she kissed his lips and pressed her breasts against his chest, relishing the feel of his hard chest even with her shirt between them.

Zane's hands were all over her beneath the sweatshirt, then he worked it off and tossed it aside. She moaned as she reveled in the heat of his skin against hers.

When he gently grasped both of her swollen breasts, his rough thumbs rubbing over her nipples, she caught her lip in her teeth and held her breath. There was a direct line between his thumbs and the spot deep between her legs that pulsed sharply with need.

As she rotated her hips, trying to assuage that need, Zane trailed those large, talented hands to the waistband of her leggings and pushed them down over her cheeks. He paused the task to palm and caress and massage her butt. One of his fingers strayed between her legs, and shot fire through her, making her gasp.

He rose slightly beneath her to push her leggings farther down her thighs, to her knees, and Hayden crawled to the side to pull them off the rest of the way.

They practically lunged for each other, their bodies aligning and pressing together as if there was a powerful force compelling them to each other.

Their mouths connected in an urgent kiss, and Zane's hands were back on her butt, clasping her. Hayden took a couple of seconds to appreciate every inch of his toned, strong body against hers, then she attempted to rise slightly on her hands so she could get him inside of her.

Zane had other ideas, though, and he rolled them over until Hayden was under him, the sheets pushed aside. He trailed a path with the tip of his tongue up her jawline, sending a shudder through her, and then he said, in a rough voice just above a whisper that curled her toes, "Just figured out the upside of pregnancy. No need for birth control, right?"

"Mm-hmm," she purred, unable to take another second without him entering her bareback, with nothing between them.

As ready as she was, he still stretched her in a delicious way, making her eyes roll back in her head.

He paused once he was fully inside of her, and she felt him studying her face. "You okay?"

With an exhale that was part laugh, because hell's freaking bells, she'd never been this flipping okay in her life, she repeated, "Mm-hmm. I feel like I'm getting to know you *much* better already."

A lust-heavy laugh rumbled out of him—Zane North, laughing during sex—and she pulled his mouth down to hers and devoured it, their tongues swirling as his hips began pumping, slowly, thoroughly, maddeningly. Hayden added her attempts to drive him higher still by meeting his thrusts, rotating her hips, arching her body upward. She was torn between wanting this to last *until the cows came home* and needing to explode right this instant.

As Zane's tempo increased—*thank you, sweet mother of all things holy*—she locked her legs around his waist, closed her eyes, lost all ability to think, and surrendered herself to the magic this man was working with his gorgeous, god-like body.

Her body went hot with a magical, telling tingle as she climbed higher, closer to that edge of bliss, and then Zane said into her ear, "Let go, beautiful." Three words plus another thrust that rattled the headboard were all it took, and she plunged over and called out as a kaleidoscope of a thousand colors burst behind her lids and seemed to hum through her blood.

When she opened her eyes, she found his gaze locked on her face, and then his lids squeezed shut, his body went stiff, and he plunged into her one final time and held himself there. He let out a strained "Fuck yes," and then he let his upper body collapse over hers.

She felt his body still pulsing inside of her, his breath on the side of her face. She released her legs from around him and palmed his sweet, perfect ass with both of her hands as she'd been longing to. That butt was quite the tactile treat, she decided with a satisfied grin.

As she continued to come back into herself, she waited to see if a pang of anything less than pleasurable popped up inside of her, like regret or worry. *Nope,* she thought. *Everything's afterglow, and holy shit, this man just rocked my existence.*

A few seconds later, Zane rolled to the side, pulling her with him, pressing kisses to her forehead as he wrapped his arms around her. "So," he said, still catching his breath. "First time wasn't a fluke."

"First time was not a fluke," she repeated with emphasis, basking in the likelihood that she'd blown his mind just as much as he'd blown hers.

"Sorry I wasn't here when you showed up last night," Zane said.

"Nothing to apologize for. We had no plans."

"I didn't expect to see you for a while. You went silent after Saturday."

"As did you."

He nodded once. "Guess I was trying to process everything. Lots to consider."

She let out a laugh at the understatement of that. "Same."

He started caressing her side in a slow, soothing motion from hip bone to rib cage and back. "Did you figure anything out?"

"About…?"

With a slight grin, he said, "Anything. The baby? Us? Global warming?"

"Well, I made my doctor's appointment for next week."

"Good. That's the one I can't go to, right?"

"Right. Because I probably have to get naked."

"I do like you naked." He trailed his hand down over her butt and squeezed as he said it.

"I like you naked too. But not in a doctor's office."

"You have a point. So what else did you figure?"

It was really early in the morning for such a conversation, and she did need to get going soon. She was due downstairs first thing, with a long list of tasks to finish before the store opened. So avoiding all her jumbled thoughts on babies and dual parenting and their future, she simply said, "I figured out, last night when Sierra dropped me off at my car, that I wanted to see you."

"Ahh. So you came to see me and not to sleep?"

"Yessss," she said indulgently. It made her uneasy to let herself be even that little bit vulnerable, but one conclusion she'd come to was that honesty was key, particularly in their situation. Games would get them nowhere.

He took a break from touching her body to run his fingers through her hair, pushing it out of her face as he peered into her eyes. "I'm glad you did."

She felt those four simple words in her chest.

"Me too."

"We, uh, changed the rules. That changed everything."

That statement made her uneasy. Hayden sat up and pulled the comforter over her. "Sex? Not everything. We're still just getting to know each other. Sleeping together doesn't mean we'll end up with a future romantically."

He came up on his elbow beside her. "Do you want one? A future with me?"

"Romantically? I don't know. I barely know you. I do want you in our child's life. But that's separate."

"Do they have to be?"

"Absolutely." She frowned. She'd thought they were on the same page about that. "You don't think so?"

"I think Mezcal did something to my ability to think straight."

"Even with a Mezcal disadvantage, you still seem like an intelligent guy. One thing I'm sure about: getting married for the sake of a baby usually doesn't work out. How well do you know Eliza?"

"Not well yet. She seems like a really good mom to Calvin and the perfect person for my uptight oldest brother."

"He doesn't seem quite so uptight lately."

"Which proves my point."

Hayden nodded. "Her parents got married because her mom ended up pregnant. They managed to stay married, but they were never happy. Her dad worked all the time in order to escape his marriage, like, to the extent he missed most of Eliza's childhood, and then he died of a heart attack really young."

"Let's not do that," Zane said.

"Let's not."

Look at them agreeing on things.

"So back to getting to know each other," he said. "Plus sex."

"You don't think sex counts toward getting to know each other?" Hayden asked, grinning as she reclined next to him.

"I do." He rolled toward her, partway on top of her, until his lips hovered just above hers. "Want to get to know each other some more right now?"

With a laugh, feeling his erection press into her leg, she mimicked him. "I do."

Half an hour later, she did know Zane better. She knew he was unselfish and thorough and was already learning what she liked.

She also knew she would have to take the fastest shower in history and wear her hair up today if she was going to be on time.

With one last kiss on his talented mouth, she rushed through the apartment to her room, thankful she'd picked out what she would wear last night as she always did, and climbed into the shower before it was hot.

On her way out, she stopped by Zane's room, where he was still in bed, drowsy and probably paying for last night more than he'd admit. She pressed a kiss to his lips, intending it to be a quick goodbye peck, not wanting to deprive him of more sleep, but he grasped her arm and held her there for more.

When they paused to breathe, he said, "Hurricane Hayden, you turn my world upside down."

Her insides went warm and mushy at his words, and she smiled down at him. "Likewise. But as tempted as I am to crawl back in bed with you, I have to get to work."

She took one last look at his sleepy, so handsome face, then stood to leave. At the door to his room, she paused, turned back around, and said, "You, Zane North, almost make me believe in Valentine's Day," then she left to get her overpacked workday started.

———

WHEN ZANE WOKE up again a couple of hours later, the first thing he noticed was the faintest hint of Hayden's lingering scent on the pillow next to him. He pulled it into his face without opening his eyes, letting the rest of reality seep into his brain.

He'd lost all semblance of control last night at the bar. The bone-deep regret that washed over him now was like one of those weighted blankets, except instead of easing anxiety, it was suffocating him. He wouldn't be doing another shot of anything anytime soon.

The problem was that *nothing* in his life was in his control. He thrived on control, needed it as much as oxygen, and knew, without it, bad things could happen. Ever since he'd set foot in his hometown, he'd been like a ship with no anchor. Not a damn aircraft carrier but a small fishing vessel, out on the open water, engine stalled, no idea when the wind would get around to blowing him to shore...or even which shore it would be.

It was time for him to take charge of whatever he could.

Mason was a prick for holding him off on the job front, but Zane could out-stubborn him and outwait him. In the meantime, he needed to fill his days so he wouldn't be desperate for a diversion the way he'd been last night.

He would get back to running, every day, starting today. He'd talk to Drake about a gym to join as well. And after a run, he'd head over to the Harrison North Baseball and Softball Foundation, the organization Cole had created to offer coaching and lessons to kids whose families couldn't afford them otherwise, to see what kind of volunteer opps they had.

No more sitting around this apartment during the days with too much time on his hands.

The nights, though…

As he rolled over, he took Hayden's pillow to the other side with him, hugging it to him, breathing in her scent again. Did he hate that he'd succumbed to his need for her this morning?

He sat up and took stock of himself. With the exception of being thirsty as hell, he was okay. His headache was gone. Even though Hayden had left more than two hours ago, he could swear there were still endorphins swimming through him.

No, he didn't hate it. It was impossible to regret something so good.

While sex had been unplanned this morning, they'd decided together the rules had changed, and he could find no reason to fight that change. If he gave himself permission to be with her, it was one more aspect of his life he was taking control of.

Zane set aside Hayden's pillow and popped out of bed with renewed energy, thankful to have a plan once again.

One of the first items on that plan? To rock the hell out of Valentine's Day for Hayden this weekend.

CHAPTER FIFTEEN

Saturday morning, Valentine's Day, Zane had his V-Day plan for Hayden mostly in place. Since he'd tuned in to the holiday so last minute, he'd decided to cook dinner for her at his place instead of fighting to get a reservation someplace where they'd be stuck in a noisy crowd.

Instead of flowers, he'd arranged to have a half-dozen cupcake "bouquet" from Sugar Babies delivered to her with a note that included an invitation to join him after work. He had the rest of the day to shop for ingredients and prep for dinner.

First, though, in the name of taking control of his life, he had business with his twin. Business that he'd avoided for a dozen or so years. He'd texted Drake earlier, and when he'd found out Mackenzie was at a spa with Sierra for several hours, he'd invited himself over.

As Zane approached Drake's front door, he took in the place with a new eye, one that had dipped a toe into house hunting for himself for the first time yesterday. The neighborhood was clearly a family one, with a couple of those motorized kiddie vehicles outside, a soccer ball in one yard, and more than a few minivans parked in driveways. The house itself was only a few years old, a cute, quaint, two-story style with stone accents.

Zane had never considered living in a neighborhood like this so soon, but he could see the allure now that he had a kid on the way. The one thing he knew was that a second-floor apartment on a busy commercial street was not an ideal place to raise a kid, even if only half time.

After he rang the bell, Drake let him in, his expression friendly but curious. Drake waited only until they were in the kitchen, where he got them each a vitamin water, to say, "What's going on, Zane? You're not usually one for social calls."

Zane eyed the connected dining room. "Can we sit?"

Drake made a *come on* motion with his head and led him into the living room, where a hockey game was on the TV with the sound muted.

"Capitals and Penguins?" Zane asked.

"Penguins are schooling 'em." He gestured to Zane to sit as he lowered himself to the sofa.

Zane sat on an armchair and checked the score, then reverted to small talk. "You taking Mackenzie out for Valentine's tonight?"

"Of course. She and I are going with Cole and Sierra to Sin's at the Wentworth. They're having a big, formal to-do the girls talked us into. They're at the spa getting pampered and, as they said, prettied up for it."

"Nice move, man," Zane said, grinning and more than a little glad his plans were more private and less of an ordeal.

"Are you taking Hayden out?"

"We're staying in. She'll be tired after working all day. She's pretty much perpetually tired because she works eighty-hour weeks."

"On top of being pregnant," Drake said, shaking his head. "She needs to slow down."

"Preaching to the choir. She's working on it, she says." Zane bit down on saying anything else, because it was a topic that perpetually concerned him. He told him about the cupcake bouquet he'd sent to invite her.

"Sounds like you've turned a corner and you're going all out to woo your woman."

Zane narrowed his eyes and said, "I wouldn't call it wooing. Just cooking her dinner."

"On Valentine's Day. The day of *love* and *romance*," Drake said animatedly.

"It's not love. I've only known her for a few weeks."

Drake's brows shot up. "She might get the wrong idea if you're going all out."

With a frown and a knot forming in his gut, Zane said, "I'm just trying to take care of her, treat her to a relaxing evening after a long day of work. Doesn't have to mean more than that."

"You doing the whole candles and placemats and roses thing?"

"I thought I was doing well to plan out the meal." Zane made a mental note not to pick up any candles or flowers at the grocery store. "I don't know where Hayden and I will end up as a couple, but I don't want to mislead her."

"Fair enough. Just beware that V Day can come with expectations."

Zane wouldn't deny that he was hoping the evening ended in a sleepover, but that—and what it meant—was between him and Hayden. So far, she'd been pretty okay with not defining things.

"I signed up at Jim's Gym yesterday. Thanks for the referral."

"Did you talk to Jim himself?" Drake asked.

Zane shook his head. "Some guy named Kyle. Built like a brick shithouse."

"Good guy. I'm trying to get him to sign on as a personal trainer for NBS."

"I thought maybe I'd run into you there this morning," Zane said. It would've been easier to talk at the gym. This felt like making it a big deal, and it didn't have to be. There was an underlying strain between them, and when they were with the rest of the family, they could cover it up, ignore it, but one-on-one, there was tension in the air, in spite of the friendly discussion.

"I don't get over there too often these days. I've got most of the equipment I need downstairs." Drake stood. "Come on, I'll show you my gym."

Zane clung to that stall and got up and followed his twin down the stairs to a finished walkout basement. They went through a decent-sized room with a pool table and a bar and ended up in an even larger room full of workout equipment.

"Damn," Zane said. "Nice setup."

Drake laughed. "I get a few perks. You're welcome to use it anytime."

Zane sized him up. "Am I?"

"Of course. I wouldn't say it if I didn't mean it." Drake lowered his brows. "Why are you here, Zane? You didn't come over to see my gym or talk about valentines."

Zane paced over to the sliding glass door and peered out at the patio, which had a giant deck for a roof. "You're right." He turned to face his brother. "I've blown this off for long enough. I owe you an apology."

Drake had bent down to adjust something on one of the weights, and now he stood, looking puzzled. "For what?"

Zane let out a snort. "I'm sorry for keeping my intent to go into the military all those years ago secret. I know I let you and Ezra down on our plans to room together, play ball together."

Drake sat on the seat of the multipurpose weight machine and frowned. "It was your life, Z. Your decision to make."

"But by not warning you, I screwed up your plans and hurt you. Don't deny it. There's been a distance between us ever since."

"I didn't understand why you couldn't trust me enough to tell me you were even considering the military."

Zane walked over to a different machine, one where you stood and pulled weighted handles toward you or down, depending on what muscles you wanted to work. Absently, without checking what weight setting it was on, he pulled the handles down, feeling it in his pecs. "I don't know why I kept it private. Mom knew. She helped me work out my visit to the Naval Academy. It ended up I could tack it on to the Model UN trip to DC." Letting the weight go after a handful of reps, he faced Drake. "You and Ez were all about partying and women and the social scene. I always felt different."

"You had your share of partying and girls in high school."

With a half grin, Zane said, "I can't deny that. But I always felt like I was just passing time until I could get serious about life and start flying."

"You've always been about the flying. I understood that, so if you'd just said, hey, I think I'm going to join the military so I can fly sooner, I would've been cool."

Zane nodded, realizing now that was probably true. "I was a stupid eighteen-year-old, I guess. Even though I hung with you and Ez, I always felt like a third wheel. Maybe I convinced myself you wouldn't care. I don't know. We don't make the best decisions at eighteen."

"Got that right. I never knew you felt like a third wheel. You're my twin."

"But we're opposites. Always have been."

Drake laughed. "Truth. It's ancient history now."

"It is, but I needed to air it out and give you a long-overdue apology now that I'm back. I never should've kept you in the dark. I'm sorry for that. I'm sorry if I broke your trust. I wish I had a better excuse than I was a stupid kid. I mean, now it looks like my decision to go to the military at all was a bad one."

"You have regrets?" Drake asked, and it was a more personal question than his brother had asked for years and years.

"I don't know what I have. I thought I'd be in until retirement. More eighteen-year-old cluelessness." He shrugged. "Anyway, I needed to clear the air. Now that I'm back, we don't need any decades-old tension between us. Life can throw new shit at us every day, so I just thought it was best to put it to rest."

Drake came over to the stand-up machine where Zane still stood and rubbed Zane's head vigorously, messing up his hair. Zane reacted with an elbow to his twin's chest.

Laughing, Drake said, "Thanks, brother. For apologizing."

"We're good?" Zane asked him.

"We're good." Drake went over to the bench press. "You ever figure out how to bench more than a hundred pounds?"

"Asshole," Zane said, laughing, feeling like a weight had been lifted off his chest. "I can still out-bench you."

"Doubtful." Drake stood back and gestured to the bench.

"Let's see what you've got. Winner foots the bill for the other one's Valentine's date."

"You're on, motherfucker."

Zane had never guessed it could feel so good to take shit from his twin, but it did.

CHAPTER SIXTEEN

hen Hayden had said the bit about Zane almost making her believe in Valentine's Day, she hadn't meant it as a challenge. She sort of loved that he'd taken it as one though.

It turned out Zane could rise to a challenge like a boss.

As she put her dirty plate into the dishwasher in his kitchen, she said, "If North Brothers doesn't work out, you could probably hire out as a chef. I can't get over how perfect the steak was. The whole meal, in fact."

He'd made the most tender steak with garlic-butter sauce, rice pilaf, and broccoli.

"You're still high on sugar," Zane said with a laugh.

"Maybe." She laughed too because he knew her weakness and had completely indulged her—all day. "Just because I ate four of the six cupcakes before I even got here…"

"And half a pint of Moose Tracks ice cream," he said as he turned off the spigot and leaned over and pressed a kiss to her lips.

"After you went to the trouble of remembering my favorite and tracking it down, I was sort of obligated." She couldn't keep a straight face, because there was no way she would've said no to dessert even after her afternoon cupcake fest.

"At least I got some broccoli down you to balance out the sugar a little."

"The cheese sauce was a good play." She went back to the dining room to retrieve what was remaining, then took it to the kitchen. "This was honestly the best Valentine's Day I've ever had. Thank you, Zane."

He was scooping the leftover rice into a container. "I didn't think it was right for a pretty girl like you to not believe in Valentine's Day."

"You're sweet. That was just my baggage rearing its head."

"And what exactly is your baggage, Hayden Henry?" He kept busy as he asked, making it seem like a nonchalant request, which she appreciated.

Though she didn't love talking about her past mistakes, she figured the sooner she explained them to him, the sooner they could forget about them. With a courage-building inhale, she answered as she continued clean-up duty.

"My baggage is two different suitcases, each a rotten decision on my part."

"Exes, I take it?"

Hayden nodded as she rinsed a serving spoon.

"How recently?" he asked.

Her stomach turned. "Suitcase number two, if we're talking chronologically, was just over two years ago. Brian Jergen. We were together for almost a year and a half and pretty serious. Or so I thought until I walked in on him with someone else. How's that for a cliché?"

Zane's eyes narrowed as he leaned against the counter, giving her his full attention. "I'm sorry. What a jackass. Were you living together?"

"Not officially, but I stayed at his place most of the time. I had a key."

She refused to think too hard about Brian and how angry she'd been—for quite a while after her discovery. Anger at him, of course, but also at herself, for being naive enough to trust someone who didn't deserve her trust.

"I suspect he was cheating on me all along," she said.

There was a tic in Zane's cheek as he clenched his jaw. "I wouldn't mind running into that son of a bitch and teaching him a little something about monogamy."

Hayden was far from a fan of violence, but coming from Zane on her behalf? Her chest went all warm and bubbly. She closed the dishwasher door that separated them, then pressed herself into his body and kissed him.

She broke the kiss off and said, "That story is mild compared to suitcase number one."

"I'm guaranteed to not like asshole number one then."

"Patrick was my college boyfriend. And I mean almost all of college. We met sophomore year, dated until a few months after graduation, at which point he went to grad school, and I got a job in the design industry. We'd moved in together senior year, and even though we were both really busy, we spent all our free time together."

"Sounds like you were close," he said with a frown.

"So I thought. It was right after Christmas that first year post-graduation that he planned a dinner for the two of us at a fancy restaurant. I couldn't help wondering if he was going to propose. It turned out my instincts were both spot on and completely off. He'd bought a ring and had *planned* to propose." She closed her eyes and longed for another bite of Moose Tracks, because this part of the story needed something sweet to counteract it. "Instead, he broke up."

"What the hell?"

"Right? He said he just couldn't do it. He wasn't ready." She scoffed. "Wasn't ready, my ass."

"Did he come back begging?" he asked as he caressed her back soothingly.

Hayden let out a caustic laugh. "Oh, no. Not begging. He and my roommate from sophomore and junior year were in the same graduate program, and they both studied abroad that spring semester after we broke up. That summer, when they got back to the States, they were engaged."

"Jesus. That sucks, Hay."

His endearment once again flipped something inside of her,

made the memory of her asshole ex almost not register on the painful memories scale anymore.

She ran her fingers over Zane's sandpapery jaw and shrugged. "I know *now* how right he was. We were never going to work out. But it took me a long time to get there."

"What about the girl? Are you still friends?"

Hayden shook her head. "We had a big scene where she apologized and insisted there was nothing between them before their trip."

"Did you believe her?"

"I did, actually. At least on her part. Whether he had feelings for her before that, I don't know. Whatever. I'm over it."

She was *mostly* over it. Except for the fact that trust still didn't come easily to her outside of her family and her close-knit stable of friends. She needed to trust her baby's father, though. Was starting to think she might be able to trust Zane.

"Thus ends the tale of why I have a hard time with trust." She laughed to lighten things up. "What about you?" she asked. "Do you have a long line of exes who broke your heart?"

Zane traced a finger over her upper lip, distracting her even though she was really curious about his romance history. "I'm afraid not."

"You must have been the heartbreaker in your relationships then."

He let out a low rumble of a laugh that she felt throughout her body, the full length of which was touching his. "No. I haven't had what I'd call a serious relationship. On deployment, relationships were against the rules. When we weren't at sea, I didn't have a lot of spare time. I had a few casual things but nothing that lasted too long. No one who tempted me, I guess."

Did she experience a little jolt of a thrill that he'd never been in love? Yes, she did. Did she think he was in love with her? No, she didn't. But there was a part of her that wanted him to be...

Slippery slope. Premature thoughts. Danger zone.

What was much easier than her thoughts was tending to this man's body.

With a growl, she leaned closer still and noticed his body

responded as she rose toward his lips. "Speaking of tempting..." She ran her hands under his shirt, thrilling at the feel of his chest yet again. "Would you like your Valentine's treat in the kitchen"—she teased the corner of his lips with the tip of her tongue—"or the bedroom?"

———

A COUPLE OF HOURS LATER, they'd in fact been naked in both the kitchen and the bedroom, and Zane didn't have to think very hard to conclude that this was *his* best V Day too.

Now they were in his bed, bodies still recovering from round two, the apartment dark and mostly quiet, though every once in a while, they heard sounds from the street. The outside noises couldn't intrude on his contentment as he pulled Hayden into him, both of them on their sides, face-to-face.

"Double happy V Day," Hayden said in a drowsy, well-sated voice.

He growled his agreement as he buried his face in her hair and inhaled deeply, loving the feminine scent that would forever get his blood revving.

"We should start the dishwasher," Hayden said. "Later."

"Definitely later."

There wasn't much that could get him to move from her side right now, his body still buzzing from her magic and their nest under the blankets warm and cozy.

A car door sounded right out back, and Zane barely registered it until Hayden said, "Sydney's date must be over. It was just supposed to be dinner but it's going on midnight. Must've gone well." Her voice was filled with speculative happiness for her employee.

"Maybe she got a happy ending too," he said, grinning.

"She deserves it. She doesn't go out a lot. Works too hard. Which obviously is to my benefit, but still."

"Do you have to get up for work in the morning?"

"Of course," Hayden said. "I know," she added in a rush,

before he could say anything about taking a day off. "I'm working on how to work less. It's a process."

"I wish there was something I could do to help you."

"You help me in other ways. Like cupcakes." She kissed him. "Have you heard anything new from Mason about working?"

He growled again but this one was irritated instead of content. "Of course not. As far as he's concerned, he said two months, so it's settled."

She ran a finger back and forth over his chest affectionately. "Can I ask you something?"

Her tone told him it was something she knew he wouldn't like. "You can ask."

"Why did you leave the military? I could understand if you only intended on doing it for a few years in the first place, but I get the impression you never intended to resign when you did."

Zane went still, probably even stopped breathing for a moment. He didn't remember ever admitting that to her, so her instincts were spot on. The question was, how much did he want to tell her? He'd never told a soul what had really made him leave.

His instinct was to button up about it and continue to keep it to himself. But then he thought of Hayden explaining her past boyfriends to him. There was no doubt it had made her uncomfortable, but she'd done it. She'd let him in. She'd trusted him when trusting a man went against everything inside of her. He needed to trust her with his deepest secret.

"It's…not a happy tale," he warned, thinking maybe she'd let him off the hook, but of course, she just lay there quietly, expectantly, her breath fanning out over his chest. "I told my brothers I started thinking about it when our mom had a heart attack."

"That wasn't the truth?"

"It wasn't a lie." He rolled to his back, tense but determined to get the story out. "Getting that email that said we'd almost lost her… I'd never felt so helpless. Seven thousand miles might as well have been seven thousand light-years."

She squeezed his upper arm. "That must have been awful. And you were stuck there by yourself."

"By the time I got the message, she was through heart surgery and on her way to recovery, so that helped. I still had almost a year on my commitment, so once I knew Mom was home and getting stronger every day, I let the idea take a backseat." The pressure of being a pilot on a carrier every day had been more than enough to worry about.

"So your mom wasn't the reason?"

"More like the thing that planted the idea." He pressed his lips together, thankful for the darkness because this was where it got hard. "Andre Weber came into my squadron a couple of years ago. Quiet guy, lots of promise. We bonded because, like me, he wasn't all about how hard he could party in his off hours, the way a lot of pilots are."

"Plus the whole quiet thing. Two peas in a pod," Hayden said softly.

Zane nodded. "Guys can be dicks to the nuggets—the newbies. I took him under my wing, I guess you could say."

"You're a good guy."

He winced a little. "About seven months ago, his wife told him she was pregnant."

"Ohh," Hayden said, excitement in her voice.

"He was so fucking happy about it. Like, bouncing on his heels happy." His voice cracked and he snapped his mouth shut. Spent several seconds collecting himself.

Fuck.

After a steadying breath, he managed, "That evening, we were up for night landings." He swallowed and didn't bother to explain how god-awful night landings could be. He'd be doing well to get the rest of the story out.

"Oh, no," Hayden said, as if she had some knowledge about them or some warning that what was coming wasn't good.

"On his third attempt to bring it in, Andre flew his plane into the back of the carrier."

Hayden gasped and clutched on to him. After several seconds, she said in a quiet voice, "Did he die?"

Zane managed to nod, and he squeezed his eyes shut, fighting, fighting, fighting that wave of blackness that threatened. He drew in a slow, measured breath, then exhaled it just as slowly. "Conditions weren't bad as night landings go, and Andre was good, one of the best at them."

"You think he was distracted by his wife's news?"

"I'll never know for sure, but yes, I suspect so. You can't have anything but the job up there with you." It was one of multiple reasons he'd never done relationships. When your emotions were jacked around by someone else, whether good or bad, it could affect performance.

Finally, he said, "I was still in the air and had to land after that."

"Oh, God."

Blocking out the memories, he recited, rotely, "I was the last one to land. It took me four passes. They had to send up the tanker to refuel me, which means there's yet another plane that has to land and I put one more pilot at risk."

"I can't imagine trying to land after...what happened," she said.

"It wasn't pretty, but the LSO didn't say a word." With another shaky inhale, Zane turned his focus to the woman next to him, shutting down on anything related to that night on the carrier. After years and years of practice, he was an expert at shutting down.

"I'm so sorry you lost a friend, Zane," Hayden said. He felt her shake her head and burrow into him. "Did you take some time off?"

He shook his head. "I had a flight the next day and the day after that. I was glad to have something to keep my thoughts under control."

She was quiet for several seconds. "You have to grieve when you suffer such a loss."

He stiffened and shook his head. "I'm not so good at that," he admitted. "I'm much better at locking it out."

Hayden lifted her head and peered at him in the darkness, and he was glad for such little light. "So you never grieved Andre?"

He shook his head.

"The only way around grief is to get through it," she said quietly, and he suspected she spoke from the experience of losing her mom. "What about your dad…?"

At the mention, he slammed down on what felt like an inferno of bad shit threatening to engulf him, same as always whenever his dad's death came up in conversation. Taking a moment to make sure his voice was even, he said, "I put all my energy into taking care of my mom, the family, the house."

"You were just a teenager…" She let out a quiet moan he suspected was supposed to be sympathetic.

"Everybody's different. Burying hard stuff is how I handle it. Only way I know to handle it," he said unapologetically.

She ducked her head into his chest, her hand on his cheek, and said, "Oh, Zane," and he longed for a subject change. "Emotions—even the hard ones—are what make us human."

"I've been in a job for the past twelve years where, if you don't keep a lock on emotions, bad stuff can happen. People can die." He'd been hyperaware of that long before Andre's tragedy.

He felt her take in a long, slow breath and wondered if she was going to keep arguing her point.

"So Andre's death made you decide to resign?"

"Not directly. But something changed after that. I made more mistakes than I ever had before, got worse landing grades, got chewed out by the LSO more times than I could count. No matter how much I shut out what happened to Andre, it messed with me. I lost my edge, and I lost any desire to do the job."

"Did you like your job before?"

He didn't reply right away because the answer wasn't simple. "At first I loved flying. But in the Navy, the pressure is high every single day, the days are long, and the longer I was in, the more I questioned what I was doing there, what we were doing, everything. I wouldn't say I was happy doing what I was doing even when I was only a couple years in. Then my mom, then Andre's accident, and no matter what I tried, I couldn't seem to get my edge back. So I got out."

"I can understand that," Hayden whispered. "You have nothing to be ashamed of, Zane."

"I'm not ashamed," he rushed to say. "It's just…*my* business."

Hayden was silent for a while, and then she said, "Thank you for telling me."

He felt itchy from doing so, so he merely nodded again, shutting out any remnants of the topic, then turned his full attention on her beautiful, tempting body.

Rolling over her, he took her nipple into his mouth, swirling his tongue around the tip, nipping at her, eliciting a moan from her, and slid into much more comfortable territory, literally and figuratively.

CHAPTER SEVENTEEN

February turned into March. The weather became nicer in general, with the spring winds not so brittle. Tulips and daffodils were starting to pop up everywhere, and it wouldn't be long until the landscaping service on Hale Street put out colorful pots of flowers along the brick sidewalks.

Thanks to Elena's invaluable help, the Wilsons' design project was finished, and the customers were thrilled with the results—and spreading the word. The Johansens' project was coming along nicely, and Hayden had booked three new jobs over the coming months that would keep them hopping. She wasn't sure how she would handle it all, just that she would.

Since Valentine's Day, Hayden had stayed at Zane's more often than not, and she could lie to herself and say it was just easier to go upstairs at night than to drive to her house. Or she could be honest and admit that she looked forward to going "home" to him every single night.

The things that man could do to her...and yet sex was only part of the allure. She was learning he was so much more than an unselfish, toe-curling lover. He was, deep inside, a nurturer.

Though she'd long been a stubborn woman determined to take care of herself, there were times she couldn't deny him, couldn't help herself from giving in to his care. She found him so damn irresistible on a good day. Then there were the bad days, when she got a *no, thanks* from a potential design client after spending hours on a proposal or dealt with an irate store customer who insisted on the owner making things "right" or didn't finish the day's work until after ten o'clock. Who could resist a home-cooked meal and a foot rub after a day like that? Not this overtired pregnant girl.

Several times, Zane had carefully brought up the topic that made her want to kick and scream and go fetal—even though she knew he was one-hundred-percent right. She needed to offload her responsibilities before she worked herself into a coma, for her health now and so she would have time with their baby later.

Since she knew she couldn't physically continue this pace at work, she had finally worked up the courage to take action. Step one was promoting Sydney to store manager, which she'd done yesterday. Step two was the focus of this evening, the reason she'd left work by six o'clock and driven to her own house.

She'd broken down and called in the big guns—her middle brother, Seth, who had a business degree and ran Henry's Restaurant. He'd built the modest eatery from a beloved local burger joint in a small town that barely paid its bills in the off-season into a thriving year-round contender, thanks in part to their oldest brother Cash's reputation as a talented chef. She had full confidence that he could find ways to help her free up her time while not letting either of her businesses falter.

"Just so you know, I see through the bribery here," Seth said as they sat at the farmhouse table in her dining room.

"Not trying to hide it in the least." Hayden set out the takeout containers of cashew chicken, governor's beef, beef lo mein, and pork fried rice and put serving spoons next to each. "If Dragonfly ever gets a Chinese restaurant, my power will be greatly diminished."

"I've been offering to help you since the day you first mentioned opening a business. You know I'd do it free of charge."

"Shut up and let me pay my way with crab rangoons."

"Whatever helps you sleep at night, Hay Bear." His voice was full of affection as he dug into the food. "Seriously, though, why are you suddenly taking me up on the offer? What's changed? As far as I can tell, you're still the fiercely, stubbornly independent little hellion we know and love."

Hell's bells. She'd planned to tell him her pregnancy news tonight. He was the brother she was closest to by far, always had been. She needed to come clean with her family, particularly because Zane had told his mom last Sunday, and Faye and Hayden's dad seemed to be seeing a lot of each other. Still, they'd barely sat down. She could've used a little more time to work up to it.

Like, a decade maybe.

As soon as she had food on her plate, she shoved a bite in her mouth to give herself a few more seconds for mental prep—even though she knew Seth would be caring and accepting and not condescending.

"Since you're already sitting down," she said, then paused for a drink of tea.

Seth narrowed his eyes and sat back as he chewed, eyeing her expectantly. "Hayden…"

"Okay, okay. I'm pregnant."

There. Let him chew on that while she chewed on some deliciously fresh cashew chicken.

"Oh, shit." He continued to stare at her, his meal momentarily ignored.

"Yep," she said with feeling. "So working sixteen-hour days is no longer an option. Nor is closing down either business."

"Hold on," he said, annoyed. "We're going back to you're pregnant. I have questions."

"The father is Zane North, Cole's brother. He knows about the baby, we're working on things, and he has plenty of money to support the baby," she said in a rush. "Does that cover it?"

"Not even close. He was the one you were paired up with at the wedding, right?"

Hayden nodded. "Pretty sure you met him briefly." She told her brother the story of Zane driving her home when her car wouldn't start, skipped over the few hours directly after he'd taken her home, and finished with, "He says he wants to be in the baby's life."

"You should've called me when your car wouldn't start."

"You'd been gone for two hours by that time. Sound asleep, I'm sure. I didn't want to wake you. Besides, Zane was right there at the right time."

"Of course he was," he muttered to himself.

"Seth, stop. I'm thirty-two years old. I make my own decisions. Zane was my decision." She sure as heck didn't need any of her blockhead brothers acting as if her virtue had been compromised.

"How about getting knocked up?"

She slapped his arm lightly. "Don't be a jerk."

"Sorry. Give me some time to process that my baby sister's going to be a mom. I'm going to be an uncle."

Hayden smiled at that thought, because Seth would be a wonderful uncle. He was the quiet one of the bunch, the brainy, introverted one who'd always held the most promise to succeed in life. While Cash was the hell-raising rebel and Holden was the incurable socializer, Seth was grounded. Stable.

So much more stable than Hayden had ever felt.

"So maybe you could problem-solve while you process?" she suggested, knowing she wouldn't be alert for longer than a couple more hours tonight, no matter how much she wanted to be.

"Is he going to marry you?" Seth asked, ignoring her question.

"No, he's not going to marry me. We agreed we don't want to marry for the baby's sake. It's never good for anyone." As she said that, she tamped down the little voice in her head that squeaked about marrying for other reasons. Better reasons. Legit reasons.

"I suppose that makes sense. As long as he—"

"Seth." Hayden let out an emotional moan. "Please. Like I told you, Zane and I are working on things. We've got time. There is *no* need to big-brother this situation."

"So that's a verb now, huh?"

"It's been a verb since I was born." Instead of pleading with him to get to business, literally, she savored the next few bites of her dinner and let her well-intentioned brother take time to absorb her situation.

He apparently eventually did, because a few minutes later, he said, "So what are you needing from me exactly?"

"I need to work less somehow." She filled him in on making Sydney a manager and her plans to promote Elena as well and hire assistants for both her and Elena.

"How are your businesses doing right now?" he asked as he —*finally*—ate.

Setting down her fork, Hayden popped up and stretched to grab a folder. "I suspected you'd want these." She took out some pages from within. "I printed you a financial summary for each one."

"Good move." Seth took the sheets from her and studied them as he continued to devour his food.

The fried rice was empty, the chicken was nearly gone, and her brother had made quite the dent on the other two containers when he said, a little later, "You're doing really well, Hay Bear. Look at you."

She couldn't help feeling pride at his praise. None of her brothers gave it out unless she earned it.

"You shouldn't let this much money just sit there," he continued.

"I know," she said halfheartedly.

She was by no means an expert on business, not like Seth. She'd taken classes specifically on running a design business as part of her studies, but they'd given her just enough knowledge to get by. She did sort of know she shouldn't let her money sit there doing nothing for her, but she wasn't sure what, exactly, to do with it. As far as she was concerned, it was a good problem to have. "I haven't had time to figure it out."

When more than two-thirds of the food was gone, Seth sat back in his chair, and she could practically see his mind churning, coming up with an actionable plan for her.

An hour and a half later, they had a plan, lots of plans, and

Hayden could weep with relief. She'd be hiring an accounting firm to take care of all things financial, including advising her on investing and capital improvements and tax write-offs and all the things that made her mind swim. She'd also hire out all of her marketing, which would mean extra time for a few weeks as she got someone up to speed on her needs but would save time in the long run.

Seth helped her come up with an official list of job duties for Sydney and convinced her to promote or hire two others to assistant manager positions. They wrote up job descriptions for more hourly employees and posted them to job sites.

"You have to get yourself out of the day-to-day at the store," he'd insisted, and though she'd argued for a good fifteen minutes about it, she knew he was right. It was just…difficult. In the end, she'd agreed to it after a month-long transition where she would still oversee, help train, and make sure for herself that her employees could handle their new responsibilities. And then she would step away to focus on Henry Designs.

"You need to quit at the restaurant ASAP," he told her.

"I'm not taking any shifts right now. I'll cross that bridge when the season starts," she said, clinging hard to the thought of contributing to her family's business.

"Be realistic, Hayden. Even with all we're taking off your plate, you're still going to be working full-time hours and more. How are you going to add in even one eight-hour shift on your feet?"

"But—"

"No buts. You're not being fair to yourself or to Holden. You need to tell him what's going on and that you won't be working. He deserves to know that going into the season so he can hire the right number of people."

If she was honest with herself, the idea of standing for eight hours behind the bar made her want to throw up. She inhaled deeply, staring at her brother, and then said, "Fine. I'll quit."

"And you need to tell the family about your pregnancy."

Yeah. That.

"I will."

"You need to do it soon."

"You need to not be so bossy," she flung back. What was with all these men in her life bossing like a boss?

"You invited me over and buttered me up with Chinese food so I would tell you what to do. You can't have it both ways."

"Mean," she said, crossing her arms over her chest and trying not to grin.

"You love me that way."

"I might stop," she threatened pointlessly.

"Hayden." He used his don't-fuck-with-me big-brother voice, which made her roll her eyes.

"I'm going to tell them. Soon. I just need to be sure none of you will go off half-cocked like in the past."

"That was never me," Seth said.

"No. So you can help me rein in Cash and Holden."

"Has Zane hurt you?"

"Of course not."

"Then he should be fine. They've only gotten physical when some asshole breaks your heart."

It was the truth. Holden had run into Patrick at a bar that summer after he'd returned from studying abroad, and he'd gotten in Patrick's face, had him pressed up against a wall, daring him to say the wrong thing. Thankfully that's as far as it had gone. Cash, on the other hand, had tracked Brian down a couple of weeks after Hayden had caught him cheating and had lured him into a fight. It'd only taken her oldest brother a single punch to have Brian on the ground, crying for his mom. At least that was the way Cash told the story.

She loved her brothers to the moon and back but hated when they went all ass-kicky big brother. Mostly. If pressed, she'd admit to some satisfaction that Cash had broken her ex's previously perfect nose.

"You look like you might collapse from fatigue," Seth said. "Promise me you're not going to work any more tonight, Hay Bear."

"I'm not going to work." The thought of her bed was too tempting.

"Not even a little? Promise?"

"Seth! I love you and I'm grateful for all your help. Now go home so I can go to bed."

He pulled her into a hug at her door. "Let me know when you're going to break the news to the others. I'll help you keep them in line."

"Thanks."

"Welcome. All I ask in return is that you name the kid after me."

Hayden laughed. "I won't rule it out."

"And bring Zane. I'd like to get to know him better. The look on your face when you talk about him makes me think he must be pretty damn special."

"I don't get a look on my face."

He merely raised his brows, kissed the top of her head, and said, "Take care of yourself, Hay Bear."

She saw her brother out the door, then flopped onto the cream-colored love seat, shutting down any thoughts about the impending talk with her family and instead wondering how, exactly, she looked when she talked about Zane.

CHAPTER EIGHTEEN

Zane reached across the front seat of his Jag and grasped Hayden's tightly clenched hand. That and her uncharacteristic silence for the hour-long drive to Dragonfly Lake were the only outward signs of how nervous she was to tell her family she was pregnant.

There'd been other signs of even higher than usual stress in the week since she'd broken the news to Seth and he'd insisted she tell the others soon—a shorter fuse, even less organization than normal, and he knew firsthand she hadn't been sleeping well.

Zane would be lying if he said he wasn't uptight too.

All he knew about her brothers was what she'd told him. Seth, the middle, he'd met, though he couldn't say he remembered anything of import about the guy. Seth already knew their news, and Hayden said he would be the most amenable of the three. Her oldest brother, Cash, was overprotective, unpredictable, and could be volatile. Holden, the youngest of the brothers but still older than Hayden, was also overprotective, plus outspoken and opinionated.

And here he was, the guy who'd gotten their baby sister pregnant.

Zane had also been introduced to Mr. Henry at Sierra's

wedding, but telling Mr. Henry their news would be an entirely different, more uncomfortable situation.

Hayden had asked Zane to go with her, so he was, in spite of his own worries. He'd willingly share the burden and take whatever blows he could for her. Hopefully the Henry men would limit it to verbal blows, but if any of them swung a punch, he'd be ready. Hayden's tales of what her brothers had done to her two worthless exes had him on alert—and at the same time, ready to shake their hands for roughing up the assholes who'd hurt her.

"It's going to be okay," he said into the crushing quiet. "No matter what they say or do, we'll get through it, and then we'll drive back, and I'll take you to the bakery."

That got a half smile out of her. "You definitely know how to sweeten the deal. Take a right up here."

They arrived in the town of Dragonfly Lake, where Hayden had done half of her growing up. It was small enough that it wouldn't take more than a handful of minutes to get to Henry's Restaurant, where they'd arranged to meet with her dad. They were banking on all three brothers being there because they usually were on Monday afternoons.

"There it is," Hayden said not long after, pointing to the left side up ahead.

As they drew nearer, Zane spotted the Henry's sign. Through trees and evergreens, he caught glimpses of the lake on the other side of the building.

"There must be quite a view," he said as he pulled in.

"The best on the lake," she said, and there was pride and love in her voice. "There's a lakefront deck that stretches the full length. It fills up every good-weather day of the summer. And if it's raining or off-season, the entire back wall is windows, so there's a view from every table inside."

"Impressive. Sounds like they do quite a business."

"Between Cash's food and the view, it's turned into a destination spot. When my brothers took over from my nana, they did an extensive remodel and added on that whole wing," she said, pointing to the left side of the building. "Cash insisted on a bigger kitchen."

She was more animated talking about her family's restaurant than she'd been for days.

"Looks like they're all here," she said, her tone back to worry and nervousness. "That's Holden's Mustang, Seth's Subaru, Cash's ancient Ford—"

"And your dad's truck?"

"Right. I know you're worried, but my dad is the most reasonable out of all of them." She squeezed her eyes shut as Zane pulled the keys out of the ignition. "Okay." Her eyes popped open and she glanced over at him and nodded.

Zane got out of the car and hurried around to her side. He offered her a hand even though she was still flat-bellied and slender. She was around eight weeks pregnant now, and he couldn't help but wonder when he'd be able to see that she was expecting. Her breasts were larger, fuller, more tempting than ever, and according to her, more sensitive "in a good way," so Zane made a point of giving them plenty of attention.

Aaaand…he needed to stop thinking about her tits as he was walking into the firing squad known as her brothers.

He focused instead on the restaurant itself, taking in every detail of the place that meant so much to Hayden.

The restaurant was an A-frame with wings on both sides. On this side, away from the lake, there was a wide stone chimney that stretched from the ground level up beyond the two-story-high roof point. In front of it was a patio with inviting wooden benches. The double entrance doors were to the right of the chimney, and Hayden led him up to them.

"Here goes nothing," she muttered before pulling one open.

Zane fought the urge to take her hand, as she was barreling forward and he wasn't sure how she wanted to handle the "them" part of the equation yet. They probably should've discussed that.

Through the door, there was a hostess stand with no one behind it, not surprising since it was just after two p.m. Hayden had worked hard to get away from work this afternoon because it was their slowest time at the restaurant. She claimed getting the family together for dinner was nearly impossible since three of them were usually consumed with running the place.

Another open doorway took them into the bar. There was a long counter on the outside wall with low-backed stools along it, plus a handful of high-top round tables scattered through the intimate room. The decor was simple and homey, with rough-hewn wood and metal and glass accents. As her dad and Seth entered the room from a doorway next to the bar, Zane's inspection halted and his stomach balled up into a knot.

"Dad," Hayden said and went forward to hug Mr. Henry.

Seth walked up to Zane. "Zane," he said, holding out his hand. He had about an inch on Zane's six feet. Hayden's brother was studying him with his eyes slightly narrowed, definitely sizing him up with more interest than when they'd previously met.

Worked both ways.

"Hey, Seth. Good to see you."

Seth gave a nod but didn't smile. "Hay Bear," he said then and hugged his sister while Simon Henry shook Zane's hand and greeted him warmly.

We'll see how long that lasts.

"Hey, Hayden." A third man came in from the dining room, which Zane noticed had a wall of windows that did, in fact, give an excellent view of the lake. Zane didn't take the time to notice more details as his attention went to the third Henry.

"Holden," Hayden said, then hugged him too.

"You brought a friend." Holden looked Zane over curiously.

"This is Zane North. Zane, Holden, my youngest brother."

They shook hands and Zane said, "Pleasure."

"Likewise. You guys going to eat?" Holden directed the question to Hayden.

Hayden looked to Zane, and as much as he wanted to try everything on the menu, he said, "Up to you."

"Just drinks. At the bar. Where we can talk," Hayden said.

Her refusal of food was telling. He'd never seen her turn down food. She must be even more nervous than she'd let on.

"That sounds serious," Holden said as he went behind the bar.

"What sounds serious?" Henry number four came through the same doorway Holden had. He was taller than the others by a couple of inches, his voice lower, face less friendly.

"Hi, Cash," Hayden greeted as she sat on a stool and motioned to Zane to sit to her left.

"Hayden doesn't want to eat. Just wants to talk," Holden announced gravely.

Cash wore a white chef's coat over black pants. He had dark brown hair and brown unsmiling eyes that took in Zane as if he were studying a complex dish to figure out what had gone into it. As he walked by his sister, he pressed a kiss to the top of her head. "Everything okay, Hayden?" he asked, his eyes still on Zane as he went around the end of the bar and joined Holden on the other side.

Hayden introduced Zane, and Cash's response was an unfriendly nod from several feet away, no handshake. If Zane were any kind of coward, these guys could be called intimidating. Their scary big-brother act didn't work on him though. Or he liked to think it wouldn't if he hadn't gotten Hayden pregnant practically before he knew her last name.

Zane offered a "What's up?" to Cash's nod.

Seth sat on the other side of Hayden, and Mr. Henry remained standing behind them.

Hayden turned to him. "Why don't you sit, Dad? We want to talk to all of you."

At that pronouncement, the tension in the room climbed noticeably. Mr. Henry took the stool on the other side of Seth. It was clear their father was the quietest of the family.

"What's going on, Hayden?" Holden said as he lorded over the bar, arms spread wide, hands perched on the edge of the long wood counter.

"I'd like an Arnold Palmer, please," she said primly, giving nothing away.

Holden's eyes ticked slightly narrower, then he looked to Zane. "What can I get you?"

Zane asked for an iced tea, unsweet, and Holden poured tea for both of them and added lemonade to Hayden's as the silence stretched on. Zane felt Hayden's hand land on his knee beneath the counter, and that cue was all he needed. He took her hand in his and kept it there, out of sight but not hidden.

"What's on your mind?" Holden asked Hayden as he set both their glasses in front of them.

Hayden made a point of taking a long drink, then bit her lip and looked at Zane. He could feel himself sweating down to his balls. He squeezed her hand, as if to say, *I got you.*

Her chest rose as she inhaled, and then Zane got his gaze the hell off her chest and looked at Cash. The gruff guy leaned against the back counter, arms crossed, watching his sister, waiting.

Hayden sat up straighter and said, "I'm pregnant. Zane and I are having a baby."

"Jesus." Holden leaned into the back counter next to Cash, who was glaring at Zane. "How in the hell are you going to handle a baby?"

"I'll handle a baby just like everyone else handles a baby," Hayden snapped. "It's not like I'm seventeen years old. I'm thirty-two and used to taking care of my responsibilities—"

"I think what he means," Seth interjected, eyeing Holden as if to send him the message to turn it down, "is how are you going to find time and energy for a baby? Nobody's saying you won't be a good mom."

"You work a hundred hours a week," Holden said. "A baby's a full-time job itself. You need to cut something out."

"She's got me," Zane said. "She won't be alone in this."

"And what do you do?" Cash finally spoke, and his tone was low, not giving away any emotion. His face though…

"Starting next month, I'll be working for my family's company," Zane said.

"His family owns North Brothers Sports," Hayden said as if daring them to question more.

"No shit?" Holden stepped forward in interest.

Zane nodded once. "My dad and uncle were the original

North brothers. My oldest brother's the CEO now, and all my brothers and cousins work for the company."

"But you don't," Cash said in a low rumble. "Why not?"

"I just got out of the Navy."

Everything on Cash's face changed. "Yeah? I was Navy too. What did you do?"

"Pilot. How about you?"

"Culinary specialist. Something caught." He nodded at his chef's jacket.

Zane felt his tension lighten slightly as he shook the guy's proffered hand, and they compared notes to find they'd served on the same carrier, just at different times. As Cash was older, he'd been there before Zane had finished flight school.

While Zane and Cash talked, he was ever aware that Holden was hammering Hayden with questions, so he kept hold of her hand. Seth interjected every so often, clearly used to forging peace between the two youngest Henrys, and Mr. Henry sat there quietly, his brow furrowed.

As much of a relief as it was to strike a chord with Cash, Mr. Henry's silence kept Zane on edge.

As Hayden was insisting to her other two brothers that she was finding ways to work less, Zane reentered the conversation.

"I'm holding her to that," he assured the rest of the family. He made a point of making eye contact with Hayden's dad, as if that could reassure the man everything would be okay. "Work in progress." He squeezed her hand to let her know he was on her side.

The tension in the room had lessened significantly, and Hayden left Zane with her brothers as she pulled their dad aside. As the guys peppered him with questions about fighter jets and flying, Zane was half-conscious of her and her dad's too-low-to-decipher conversation on the other side of the room. When he saw Mr. Henry pull her in for a long hug, he relaxed further and agreed to let Cash give him a tour of the place.

Twenty minutes later, Zane had seen the state-of-the-art kitchen, where two employees were busy prepping for dinner. He'd been blown away by the views and the rest of the property.

They stepped out on the sprawling deck, which had two large heaters for early-spring and late-fall dining.

There were two tables of people in the main dining room, closer to the homey flames of the giant stone fireplace than the windows, but otherwise, there was a calm-before-the-storm feeling.

Cash verified that when he said, "Duty calls. Expecting a full house tonight."

He extended his hand and they shook again as Zane thanked him for the tour.

"Quite a place you've got here. I'll be back for the food when Hayden has more time."

"No need to wait for her," Cash said. "I'm here pretty close to seven days a week."

With a grin, Zane said, "Must run in the family."

Cash didn't return the lightness, his expression going even more serious. "That she's let you in speaks volumes, man. Hayden doesn't let anyone run her life, but you seem like you have some influence."

"Influence is a strong word," Zane said.

With a nod, Cash said, "Don't fuck it up," and then he excused himself to the kitchen.

That's the goal, he thought.

When Zane wandered back into the bar, Hayden grasped onto his arm, her face tight with emotion.

"You okay?" he asked. Holden had his back to them, a phone pressed to his ear, and Seth and Mr. Henry were gone.

Hayden nodded tightly and said, "Just ready to go."

As much as Zane was itching to try the food, that flew out of his mind with one look at her.

"Need to say goodbye?" he asked.

"I already told Seth and Dad. Holden's busy. Let's just go."

Confused and concerned, he took her hand and got her out of there with a quick glance over his shoulder at Holden. He was still on the phone, so they walked out without a word.

He still held her hand as she lowered herself into the Jag's passenger seat, and it hit him in that instant that not only would it eventually be tough for a very pregnant woman, stubbornly independent or not, to get in and out but the Jag would also be useless for a family with its lack of a backseat. He'd need to buy something more family friendly.

His mind was still on vehicle shopping when he walked around the car, got into the driver's seat, and realized Hayden's shoulders were shaking and she was silently sobbing, her hands covering her face.

"Hey," he said gently, confused. "What's going on, Hayden?" He pulled her into him and put his arms around her as best he could in the small space.

"Drive us...away please," she said between gasps. "Don't want them"—*hiccup*—"to see me crying."

Zane started the car and drove off with one hand on the wheel, one holding on to her as he struggled to figure out what had set her off. Last he'd known, it was going okay, all things considered.

As soon as he was out of Dragonfly Lake, he took a right turn on a random country road and pulled onto the shoulder.

"Come here." He pulled her awkwardly into his arms over the console and let her cry it out.

When the sobs slowed to a random hiccup and sniffle, he kissed her temple and said, "What happened while I was with Cash?"

Hayden squeezed her bloodshot eyes closed and let out something between a laugh and a wail. "Nothing. I'm a stupid mess and I'm sorry. It's just..." She shook her head and looked about to break down again. But she took in a slow, deep, shaky breath. "It all just...got to me. I was so freaking scared to tell them, and my dad was so incredible and supportive, and Cash ended up being your BFF, and even Holden chilled out and stopped being an ass, and I guess I just...had all of this pent up..."

"And you don't like your brothers to see you crying," he guessed.

She nodded. "They don't handle it well."

He pulled her in again, understanding that she'd been on the edge for a week, probably for longer than that. Maybe even since the positive pregnancy test. He suspected she hadn't taken time —hell, probably hadn't *had* the time—to let all the emotions out, and this was the result.

The need to help her somehow pulsed through him and he racked his brain for how. Ideally, he'd fly her somewhere for a weekend away, but he knew without asking she wouldn't be able to leave for that long. Not yet. But maybe an afternoon…

An idea blossomed as he rubbed her back, periodically kissed her head, her temple, her cheek. He could get her away without actually getting her away, in a sense. He just needed to get her to go for the idea.

"What are you doing Sunday afternoon?" he asked, hoping, if he could convince her to do this, that he could get all the other details to align. There were a handful of them.

With a sort-of laugh, she said, "Working."

"I thought you were making a point of not working on design clients on Sundays?"

"I am. I'm planning to go into the store. It'll be Gayle's first day."

"Your parents' friend?"

"Mm-hmm, so I want to be there."

"But Sydney will be there to start training, right?"

"Yes, but—"

"But you promoted her to handle things like this, right?"

With another inhale, Hayden nodded.

"I was wondering… This guy I know has a plane and offered to let me take it up anytime. Would you go with me?" All of that was true. What he didn't need to admit to was that when Brandon Fleming, a former classmate of Mason's and retired baseball pro Zane had connected with at Cole's foundation, had made the offer, he hadn't been tempted to take him up on it. Now…he might be ready. In large part, for Hayden.

"You're ready? To get up in the air again?" Her brows rose and her entire face lit up. He sensed her excitement was for him and not herself, and that would work just as well. Whatever it took to give her the gift of a couple of carefree hours away from reality.

He allowed himself to really consider the question. "I believe I am." In fact, he felt that familiar rush in his blood at the thought of it. It was time. He needed a flying fix—and if he could get Hayden to go with him, so much the better. "But I'd rather not go alone. What do you say? Are you up for it?"

She looked pensive, obviously thinking about whether Sydney and her employees would be okay without her, and then she said, "I'd love to."

Zane kissed her, then held on to her hand as he drove them back to Nashville, hoping like hell he could get all the pieces in place by the weekend.

CHAPTER NINETEEN

atching Zane pilot an airplane might just become Hayden's new favorite hobby.

His strong, capable hands played over the controls, and his brilliant mind seemed focused and more than competent as the nose of the plane lifted and they took to the air. If she'd had any fears of going up in such a small craft, Zane's obvious mastery and confidence would put them to rest.

The airplane, which could hold four passengers and two crew, looked shiny and new. It belonged to Zane's former-baseball-player friend, who apparently had retired to Nashville and kept the aircraft at a small airport on the north side. Zane had spent the morning at the airport with his friend, checking it over, familiarizing himself with the ins and outs, then he'd picked up Hayden. His mood even in the car had been light, excited, like a little boy who'd gotten a new bike. And she'd thought the serious, almost broody version of Zane was hard to resist...

The sights out the window were incredible as the green-and-brown-patched earth receded from them, but her eyes were glued to the fantasy-worthy man next to her. They both wore headphones, and Zane was communicating periodically with air traffic control, so completely engrossed in his task that she wasn't sure he remembered she was sitting to the right of him in the cockpit. Which was perfectly fine, as she preferred a safe flight to his attention at the moment.

They climbed higher, and Hayden turned her focus to the scenery outside, the river lazily twisting below, the buildings of downtown looking miniature, the roads winding like ribbons, the cars like ants.

Eventually, Zane adjusted several controls then hit a button on the dash marked AP, and he leaned back into his seat, blew out a breath, and smiled widely—none of that half grin stuff today. As he took in the vista, he reached over and linked his fingers with hers.

"No hands?" she asked, more curious than alarmed.

"Autopilot."

With another glance around them, she saw that they were still pitched upward but their wings were level and the plane felt very...in control. She checked Zane's face again and saw complete relaxation. Relief?

"You look...happy," she said, unable to keep from smiling. "Like I've never seen you before."

He let out a laugh, looking carefree as he gestured to the open sky out the windows. He opened his mouth and shook his head, as if he couldn't immediately find words. "Just...look at this."

"It's beautiful up here."

"It's unlike anything else anywhere. Not the sea, not land. It's...freedom. Relief. It's truly getting away from your problems for a couple of hours, which is why I wanted you to experience it. You need it. You deserve a break from everything. I hope you can find some kind of relief from stress, even if only for the afternoon."

She pulled his hand to her lips and kissed his knuckles, her insides going warm and melty at the sentiment. With another look out at the clear, endless sky, she took in a slow, belly-deep breath like she'd learned at yoga class the few times she'd managed to go, felt her tension fade away, and nodded. "Thank you. Can I kiss you without us crashing?"

He laughed again and said, "Autopilot's got us. When we get to ten thousand feet, she'll level us out."

Hayden unbuckled her seat belt, leaned across the console, and planted a slow, heartfelt kiss on his lips. He caught the back of her head and held her there for a few extra seconds, then released her.

When she was back in her place with her belt refastened, holding his hand again, she said, "I did a lot in the past three days to help lower my stress, actually." She hadn't had a chance to update him since she'd stayed at her own house the past two nights—Friday because she, Sierra, and Mackenzie had done girls' movie night and Saturday because she'd spent the day on a custom refinishing project that she'd promised one of her regulars. It was the last refinishing she'd do until after the baby was born, as she not only didn't have enough time but also didn't want the exposure to the fumes. "I signed the contract with the accountant on Friday, finalized things with the marketing person Kennedy recommended, and yesterday, Sydney and I finalized her first two hires."

"How'd it go?" he asked, knowing this wasn't only the first time Sydney had been in charge of hiring but also the first time Hayden had given over the reins for the process, settling for final approval powers but nothing more.

"Really well," Hayden said with enthusiasm. "Andrew's the kind of guy you can't help but like immediately, and Irina has a great design eye, especially for not having any training. With Gayle, that doubles the staff to six, not counting me."

"Because you're not part of the staff now," he said. "You handling that okay?"

She was still heavily involved in her retail business, but she was working on untangling herself from it, gradually giving up the day-to-day, no longer putting herself on the shift schedule. Sydney was proving to be amazing, both patient with Hayden's struggle to give over control and competent with the running of the store.

"Mostly. I spent so many hours at the Johansens' this week I didn't have time to think about not being at the store. I only worked past seven one time, and that's because the crew ran into problems with the wet bar."

Zane squeezed her hand supportively. "I know it hasn't been easy. The extra sleep's paying off though. Your eyes look more alive than they have in all the weeks since I met you."

With a laugh, she said, "Good to know I was walking around with dead eyes."

He gazed into said eyes. "Your baby blues are beautiful either way."

"Flirting at ten thousand feet?" she asked with her own flirtatious grin.

"Just being honest."

"You're spoiling me. Please don't stop."

After a quick kiss to her lips, he turned his attention to the dash, and she realized the plane had leveled out. She watched as he made some adjustments and moved back into concentration mode, and hell's bells, his mind was as sexy as those hands.

This man truly was spoiling her. Each night she'd been able to stay with him, he'd had dinner waiting for her. Dinner, sometimes a bath, and always his bed.

At first she'd tried to reciprocate by ordering dinner for them, bringing him a cupcake during a work break, delivering hot breakfast from Frank's Diner. After ongoing insistence from him that she needed to take extra care of herself to nourish the pregnancy, she was getting better at accepting his caring gestures without keeping score. She was starting to grasp that cooking for her truly made him happy. He left no doubt their nights together were as amazing for him as they were for her.

When he pressed the autopilot button again, she asked, "Are you sure you don't want to fly for your job? Instead of North Brothers Sports?"

"I heard from Mason this morning, actually."

"You did? Did he finally give in?"

"I start two weeks of training April first. Going to work in the IT department, doing something under Logan. I'll have a steep learning curve, but they'll teach me whatever I need to know."

"That's fantastic," she said, gauging his expression closely, watching for a spark.

She didn't see one. A smile, yes, but it seemed shallow.

"Yeah." His tone was upbeat, relieved. "About time." He rolled his eyes over Mason's stubbornness now instead of swearing about it.

"You're sure about it though?" she tried one last time. "Have you truly thought about jobs that would let you fly? An airline or a private pilot or even giving flying lessons?"

"I've always planned to end up with my family's business. Flying… I love this. But having it as a job took the fun out of it. I wasn't sure I could get this enthusiasm back, and I don't want to ruin it."

She studied him for several seconds and saw he believed that. And she believed he truly wanted to make his family's company work, somehow felt he owed it some time. Maybe it would end up okay. At least now he'd have a chance to find out.

"Fair enough," she finally said. She took a drink from the bottled water they'd brought up with them. "So I'm dying to know your call sign. Please? Will you tell me?"

Zane eyed her stoically. "That's classified."

"I'm having your baby. Squeezing your child out of my nether region. It seems like that should grant me access to your secret."

Zane laughed. "When you put it that way…" His eyebrows shot up and he hesitated.

"Just say it. I already know you think it's embarrassing."

He closed his eyes and said, "It's Pucker."

"Pucker?"

Zane nodded once, not looking at her, and now she had to laugh.

"Like, as in, this is sour, pucker up?"

"Like, as in, pucker factor. Something that comes into play when you're landing on the boat in a black-ass night, and you can't see shit, and the deck is pitching like a son of a bitch. Pucker factor doesn't refer to the lips."

She grinned, fighting not to let out a laugh. "Like, butt cheeks?"

"Like that."

"And why exactly is that your call sign?"

"Goes back to a particularly hairy landing in crappy conditions." He shook his head, a hint of a grin curving his lips upward. "My CO claimed he had to change his pants afterward."

"But you made it," she said.

"No choice but to make it." He took out his phone and spent a couple of minutes searching, then held it up, displaying a photo.

Hayden took it from him. It was of a pilot sitting in the cockpit of a fighter jet, and his name and *Pucker* were painted on the side of the plane. "Is that you?"

"In the flesh."

"And that's your plane?"

"In a manner of speaking."

She studied it more closely, in awe of him in his flight suit, so handsome and capable and hot, even if he was wearing aviator glasses and a flight hat that made it tough to identify him.

"Sexy," she said, drawing another laugh out of him. She loved that sound, and she treasured that he'd shared his call sign with her.

They flew for more than an hour, trying to pick out familiar landmarks in the countryside below and then veering too far from home to recognize much, but that was okay. It was all pretty and peaceful.

Somewhere over Kentucky, he turned the plane back toward Nashville. They discussed how far this little plane could go without refueling, how often his friend used it for leisure trips, and Hayden found her imagination getting carried away. An image popped up in her mind of them, the three of them, Hayden, Zane, and their child, taking frequent trips in a plane piloted by Zane. Weekend getaways, summer vacations, family trips centered around business conferences—

Whoa. That was a really clear picture—well, all except for the baby details. What was she doing imagining that far ahead with Zane? She'd promised herself she'd be wary, careful.

She had been careful, actually. Was being careful. Maybe too careful? Yes, her history said that trusting a man got her hurt in the end, but…not every man was a bad ending, right? Look at Sierra. And Mackenzie and Eliza and Lexie too. They were proving the North boys had some staying power, and what she knew of Zane suggested he was a good, responsible man who maybe…cared for her too?

Slow down, crazy girl. No reason to get ahead of yourself. We still have seven months before the baby's born. Seven months to see how it goes.

All that mattered right now was today. It was a good day, and she intended to appreciate it for what it was, without borrowing trouble about the future.

"We should be on the ground in a few minutes," Zane said lightly, oblivious to the way her thoughts had momentarily derailed.

He wove their fingers together again and pulled her toward him for a lingering kiss, which was a compelling argument to savor the present moment…and maybe the very near future.

"Yeah? And then what?" she asked with a flirty look as they kissed again.

"Well, I've been ordered to bring you to dinner tonight—"

"At your mom's?"

"The one and only."

She couldn't deny that a shot of joy pumped through her at being included in a North family dinner. So what if it was his mom asking—or ordering. It was a start, an in, and she was finding it harder and harder to fight her doubts, which were getting quieter and quieter.

"Okay. This guy I know convinced me to take the entire rest of today off, so I could probably make that."

"Seems like a pretty good guy."

She laughed as she said, "Pretty good for sure."

He glanced at his watch. "We'll have a couple of hours to kill before we have to go to dinner. Little-known fact…flying a plane? Makes me hot and bothered." His eyes sparked with desire as he said it.

"That is such a coincidence," she said, holding his gaze,

"because, little-known fact, watching you fly a plane? Makes me hot and bothered."

A low, growly rumble came from his chest. "Guess we better get this plane back on the ground so we can head for my place."

Grinning, she said, "Guess we better."

CHAPTER TWENTY

Since Zane had started working last week—or rather, training—at North Brothers Sports, time was moving a lot faster.

Today was *the day*. He and Hayden were en route to her ob-gyn appointment, her second, his first. She was almost through the first trimester, and there was a good chance they might hear the baby's heartbeat. He couldn't quite wrap his head around it.

He was starting—finally *starting*—to feel like he was getting his life settled and on track. Having a job to go to every day did wonders to help him feel less in transition, less like a drifter. Even more, getting back up above the clouds made all the parts of his existence "click" better.

Since his first flight with Hayden in Brandon's plane three-plus weeks ago, Zane had been able to go up every Sunday, and he no longer knew how he'd gone without flying for two months after leaving the Navy. Time in the air without the relentless pressure of the military was an altogether different world and one he vowed not to do without ever again. He was playing with the idea of buying his own plane. It wouldn't be cheap, but it would be priceless.

Better yet, Hayden had been in his bed nearly every night, some nights just sleeping, some nights so much more. While he loved showering her body with attention, he was also fully on board when she fell asleep as soon as her head hit the pillow. At least when it was his pillow, he knew she was getting rest and taking good care of herself. She'd worked nearly double time to enact the strategies Seth had helped her with, and she was finally starting to see some relief. Finally starting to be able to work closer to a forty-hour week.

"Are you nervous?" he asked Hayden after she'd hung up with one of her suppliers about an order change.

She exhaled and closed her eyes. "Truth? I haven't had time to be. Mrs. Johansen's changes have put a crimp in everything. Let's see, where are we going?" She grinned at him to show she was kidding about the last part.

He reached across the Jag's console, took her hand, and squeezed it wordlessly.

"Don't worry," she said. "I'm staying calm about work. Mrs. Johansen will be paying extra, and I made it clear it will extend the timeline. Besides, your mom is taking excellent care of me."

For the past three Sundays, Hayden had gone with him to his family dinner, and predictably, his mom hadn't hesitated to welcome her into the fold. Though he'd reassured his mom he was doing his best to take care of Hayden, she'd gifted the mother-to-be of her next grandbaby with a weekly prenatal massage package that would last the entire pregnancy. He was pretty sure the old Hayden would've smiled and thanked her and then not been able to take the time for pampering, but it seemed like she was fully on board, grateful, and had already scheduled the first month of appointments.

"Massage on Friday?" he asked.

"Massage on Friday. Bliss."

It wasn't until they were in the exam room forty-five minutes later, had finished with the nurse, and were waiting for the doctor that Hayden said, "Okay, now I'm nervous," as she lay on the table.

Zane stood next to her and took her hand. "About hearing the heartbeat?"

As she nodded, there was a light knock on the door and then it opened.

"Hello." The fifty-ish female doctor entered, wearing a white coat and a smile. "How are you doing, Hayden?"

"I've gained three pounds," Hayden told her, sounding worried.

"That sounds about right, my dear. Pants tight?"

"I can't button them," Hayden said. "Thank God for yoga work pants."

"Best invention ever. Good work, Mama." She turned to Zane and said warmly, "And you must be Hayden's support system."

"This is Zane," Hayden said. "The father."

With a nod, the doctor said, "I've learned not to make assumptions. It's nice to meet you, Dad. I'm Dr. Stone."

Zane replied in kind, reeling internally at being called Dad but shoving that aside to focus on Hayden and the doctor.

She asked Hayden several questions about how she'd been, whether she was sleeping, what her stress level was like. When she asked about diet, Hayden looked sheepishly at Zane.

"This guy is making sure I eat lots of vegetables."

"Excellent," Dr. Stone said. "Sounds like he's a keeper."

"I still require cupcakes," Hayden confessed.

"A cupcake here and there is good for the soul. As long as you're getting good nutrition the rest of the time."

"I'm doing my best," Zane said lightly. "We compromise a lot."

"It sounds like you two will work well together as parents too. You're at"—the doctor tapped a few keys on her device—"almost twelve weeks. Congratulations on finishing your first trimester."

"Thanks," Hayden said. "I know a lot of people are sick the whole trimester, but I've felt pretty much normal. Except tired."

"And hungry," Zane said.

"For sure hungry," Hayden agreed with a laugh. "Sometimes I even forget I'm pregnant."

"That's just as normal as the people who throw up for three months," Dr. Stone said. "And a blessing. Have you told anyone else your news yet?"

Zane met Hayden's gaze and they both grinned. "Our families know," he said.

"We both have big, loud families, but as far as I know, they've kept it on the inside," Hayden added.

"Now that you're entering the second trimester, it's safer to tell people outside of the family. Soon you won't be able to hide it even if you wanted to. That'll help it start to feel more real for you," Dr. Stone said.

Zane's eyes went to Hayden's sexy middle, and he tried to imagine her with an obvious bump there. He took her hand, intrigued by the thought of watching her body change.

"Today we're going to see if we can hear the heartbeat," the doctor said as she pulled out a handheld device that Zane assumed was the fetal Doppler. "Now"—Dr. Stone looked both of them in the eye as she spoke—"it's early and we might not hear it today. That does not signify a problem at this stage. It just means we try again next time. Understood?"

They both nodded, and even after all Zane had read that said the same thing, the doctor's warning was reassuring.

Dr. Stone lifted Hayden's shirt, revealing her abdomen, which was possibly just barely starting to show the slightest curve to it, in spite of Hayden's inability to fasten normal pants. Her stomach was normally so flat that the slightest change might be noticeable to her.

After gelling up the end of the wand, the doctor pressed it to Hayden's skin, moving it around, and there were sounds of swooshing, like white noise, but Zane heard nothing that sounded like a heartbeat.

Hayden frowned as they listened, the doctor searching, her own expression giving away nothing—not concern and not optimism. When Hayden met Zane's gaze, he could see the worry in her eyes, so he squeezed her hand and raised his brows as if to say, *Just wait*, even as his own disappointment seeped in around the edges, surprising him. He'd familiarized himself with the odds of hearing the heartbeat today, but he hadn't realized how much he was hoping they would.

"If we can't hear it today, how long do we have to wait to come back?" Hayden asked.

Dr. Stone held up a finger as if to signal she wasn't giving up yet and continued to move the wand around. When she probed around Hayden's far left side, she paused the motion, her brows shooting up.

Then Zane heard it too, the rhythmic *whoosh, whoosh, whoosh* that was undeniably a tiny little heart pumping away.

Hayden gasped. "Is that it? That's the heart?"

Dr. Stone nodded, grinning widely. "That's your baby's heart."

Hayden's eyes went huge, her face lighting up. "That's... Oh, my God. There's really a baby in there."

Zane laughed, blindsided by the awe that overcame him. In that moment, it hit him like it hadn't previously that he and Hayden were going to have a *child*. A little human being who would grow into a bigger human being, with a beating heart, his or her own thoughts, feelings...

"Incredible," he said quietly, overcome, unable to find any other words as he stared at Hayden's belly and tried to grasp the miracle that was happening inside of her.

"This never gets old," Dr. Stone assured him. "Baby's heartbeat is one thirty. Right in the middle of healthy."

"Wives' tales would say it's a boy," Hayden said, her eyes sparkling.

"Other wives' tales say fighter pilots only have girls," Zane challenged, grinning.

"Ooh, who will be right?" the doctor asked, watching them.

"We need to start thinking of names soon," Hayden said. "Alexander. Maxwell. Samuel..."

"Alexandra, Maxine, Samantha," he teased, just to make a point about the gender, suspecting they would take weeks to come up with their favorites.

"Not Maxine." Hayden wrinkled her nose. "And nothing that starts with H."

Because the baby's last name would be Henry, he surmised,

and for the first time, it bothered him that it wouldn't be a North. His grin faltered for a moment.

They'd agreed not to get married for the sake of the baby. There wasn't a single doubt in his mind that was the right decision. But also for the first time, he started to wonder if they could marry for other reasons. Traditional reasons.

It was early to think that way. He and Hayden had plenty of time to figure that out before the birth, so he filed it away to ponder later.

The doctor finished up and made notes in her computer, telling them some of the most unique names of babies she'd delivered lately, some of the choices making them laugh and cringe in sympathy.

On their way out, they set an appointment for a month later, then headed to his car. Hayden chattered nonstop, her happiness and relief bubbling out of her. When he opened the passenger door for her, she threw her arms around him, and he was all too happy to pull her close, breathe in her scent, soak in her unfiltered joy, a joy that was so all-encompassing that it was nearly a foreign concept to him.

With Hayden, he wanted to experience it more. He couldn't deny it was seeping into him, just being with her, experiencing their baby's heartbeat with her, holding her.

"That was…" She shook her head, still pressed into his chest, as if she couldn't find a word to do it justice.

"Yeah. Incredible. And a relief."

Hayden nodded. "I've known on some level I was pregnant. Well, mostly. I was serious when I said sometimes I wondered if I really was. Now I know. Like, *know*. You know?"

"I do, actually."

"What do you say we go shopping this weekend to buy something for the baby. Anything. A little outfit or a crib or a diaper pail."

"A diaper pail?" He laughed that that was one of the first things to come to her mind. "As long as you don't buy anything blue just yet."

"No pink either."

"Agreed."

When she loosened the hug, Zane pulled her back to him and kissed her, pouring his reaction to the appointment into her the way he knew how, and then he held her hand as she lowered into the car.

CHAPTER TWENTY-ONE

For the three days since they'd heard the baby's heartbeat and everything had become *real* real, like on a new level, Hayden had gone into full-on baby-lust mode.

It was as if her desire for a baby had been simmering under the surface for some time now but she'd been afraid to let it out. She hadn't been in the right place in her life before Zane—it wasn't practical for a single girl with zero time to herself to wish for a baby. And then along came Zane and the big whoops, and she'd still been scared to think too hard about a living, breathing baby. Like she'd told the doctor, without any major symptoms, save for bigger, better boobs, there were days she could almost convince herself she wasn't pregnant.

Then…they'd heard proof.

They'd heard their little bean's heart, and everything got real. While nothing was ever guaranteed, if she was lucky, she was going to be holding a precious little baby in six months.

Nursery design ideas had started spinning through her mind at all hours. She'd finished reading one pregnancy book and started another. And today, she and Zane had made their first baby purchase—or six. She'd left work early to go to a heavenly late-afternoon prenatal massage, then Zane had taken her to dinner, and finally they'd ended the evening at a baby store so they could pick out an outfit. As if she could settle on just one adorable little outfit! Even staying gender neutral, she'd had a hard time narrowing it down to six.

The cutest thing? Zane was getting into it. Though she would never call him an emotional man, he was loosening up a little, getting into the search for baby clothes, being more affectionate than he'd ever been, indulging her even more. He seemed less antsy now that he had a job to go to every day, even if he'd only been in training sessions for the past two weeks.

He pulled into her driveway in his brand-new Toyota 4Runner, which he'd bought in addition to the Jag so that he'd have a place for a car seat.

"I think I love this thing," she said, tapping the dash of the SUV. "But I have to ask, are you and Drake officially in some kind of competition to see who can own the most vehicles?"

He scoffed. "There's no competition. Jag beats a Porsche any day. His Jeep is a little squeak toy compared to this big boy."

"What about his motorcycle?"

Zane let out a condescending but good-natured laugh. "What's the top speed of a crotch rocket? Close to two hundred miles per hour?"

Hayden shuddered. "I don't know, but our kid is never getting one."

"When you fly something that can go faster than the speed of sound every day for nearly ten years, what's the point of a motorcycle?"

He meant it as a joke, but still, as he peered at her across the front seat, wearing sunglasses and a cocky half grin, her lady parts stood at attention and begged her to treat herself to a full serving of Zane.

Later for sure, she silently promised herself with her own smile.

"You win," she said out loud as she opened her door.

Once inside, she flipped on the lights and briefly took in the state she'd left the place in. "Messy again."

"Is it again or still?" he said with a laugh.

"I keep thinking maybe it will clean itself up." She kicked the two pairs of shoes next to the door closer to the wall. "Come on back to the spare room. I can't wait to show you what Seth brought over."

Zane closed the door and followed her down the short hallway to the room that she'd always planned to turn into an office but hadn't taken the time to buy furniture yet.

"Cleanest room in the house," she said lightly as she flipped the overhead light on. Her eyes went to the only furniture in the room, and she shivered with excitement and love. "This is the rocking chair my nana used to rock my brothers and me to sleep whenever she took care of us." She went to it and ran her fingers over the floral and leaf design carved along the top of the back.

Zane was taking it in and nodding. "That's perfect, Hay. Both practical and sentimental."

"Sierra will give me a hard time for not keeping it the original wood color, but I'm planning to give it kind of an antiquated white paint wash. I'll add a cushion on the seat and a big throw pillow for the back— Oh!"

She went to the closet and slid the double door to one side to reveal a stack of throw pillows—as a matter of fact, she did kind of collect them—and scanned them for something suitable for a nursery. She pulled out a chambray blue one. "No blue or pink," she said to herself and stuffed it back in. "How about something like this?" She took out the extra-soft, extra-shaggy heart-shaped pillow similar to the ones she'd put out in her store for Valentine's Day except this one was the lightest shade of gray. "Or I could find a star-shaped one. I know I've seen them somewhere. We can have a star theme for the nursery, and Lexie can paint us an amazing mural in grays and yellows and— No, that won't work. Kennedy's is stars and moon. Did you hear she had a baby girl on Wednesday?"

When she glanced up at Zane, he dropped heavily into the rocker, looking like he'd seen a ghost.

"Zane?"

He didn't appear to hear her as he stared at his phone, his face pale, eyes haunted.

Hayden rushed over to him. "Zane, what happened?" She looked down at his phone and saw a photo of an adorable newborn baby boy with fuzzy black hair and light brown skin. Her pregnant heart started beating faster with affection, and she let out an *oooh*.

Zane didn't appear to be thinking *oooh* or anything good, and she promptly forgot the good feels that the photo gave her.

"Zane, you're scaring me. What's wrong?"

———

ZANE STARED at his phone but barely saw the photo now. A black wave of pain like he'd never felt before engulfed him, stole his breath.

When Hayden grabbed his arm and shook it, he registered that she'd asked him what was wrong. He tried to slam down on the bone-deep sorrow, tried to blink himself back to the present. Attempted to speak. Failed.

Hayden bent down in front of him, her hands on his legs, asking again what had happened. He didn't know how to answer that.

He took in a slow, unsteady breath, then blew it out, shook his head, wishing he could shake this off, bury it deep. Aware that he needed to try to explain before Hayden lost her shit, he opened his mouth. "I… This text came…"

"Who's the baby?" she asked when he didn't say more.

"It's Andre's." He barely got the words out before his throat closed up with grief.

"Andre— Oh, the pilot who…?"

He nodded, or at least he thought he did.

"Oh, God, Zane." She grasped both his hands, staring at him.

All he wanted to do was escape. He couldn't put a coherent thought together, couldn't breathe here. He removed his hands from hers and stood, trying to be gentle about it, when what he really wanted to do was yank himself away so he could fight the demons that were circling around him like a cyclone of hurt.

"So Andre's wife sent it to you?"

He nodded, pacing away from her, fighting between escaping and answering her questions. Speaking was a test. He swallowed hard and managed, "She wanted me to see my namesake, Zane Oliver Weber."

Fuck.

He squeezed his eyes shut and tried again. "Apparently Andre told her at some point he wanted to name their first son Zane. Because he—" Son of a bitch, he was gutted. "Because he looked up to me."

"Ohh, Zane." She came up behind him, cradled one of his arms, and leaned her head against him.

He knew she was trying to help or be there for him, but he didn't want help. Didn't want anyone there for him. He needed to be alone before he lost his mind.

"I need to go," he bit out as if his life depended on it, and it felt like it fucking did as his lungs struggled to fill. "I'm…sorry." He shook his head. "I can't… I have to go."

He disentangled himself from her, barely seeing her, so overcome with pain, with darkness, a cold, smothering darkness that was on the verge of suffocating him.

"You shouldn't be alone right now," she said, but he couldn't fathom staying.

"I'm…sorry. I need to go." He bolted out of the spare room as if it was on fire and strode through the house, to the front door.

The cool night air barely registered and sure as shit didn't offer an ounce of relief. Zane heard Hayden calling after him, pleading with him to stay with her, let her help him, but there was no helping him.

The pain he'd evaded for seven months had finally caught up and was leveling him.

He climbed in his SUV and backed out of the driveway. Instead of heading to his apartment, he drove toward the highway, destination unknown.

———

ZANE DIDN'T KNOW how much later it was when he drove through a Podunk little town somewhere in western Tennessee. It was dark, it was late, and he was a fucking wreck.

He'd managed to block out the bad shit enough to focus on the road at least on some level, but all he could think about was the fact that Andre wasn't alive to hold his son.

Zane's namesake.

He'd had no idea that was coming—how could he know? Andre hadn't lived long enough to tell him anything of the sort.

That man had loved his wife so fucking much, had been so elated that he was going to be a father. Now his wife, Sharice, was left to raise that baby all by herself. From the things Andre had said about her, Zane believed she would handle it okay, like a queen, but she shouldn't have to. And little Zane Oliver Weber…

He shouldn't have to grow up fatherless.

Anguish took his breath again as he pulled into a parking lot along the highway. He didn't know what town he was in or where he was other than he was a half tank of gas away from Nashville. Not far enough, but it occurred to him that continuing farther wouldn't do him a damn bit of good. The pain would follow him wherever he went.

The pain…fuck, the pain. It was a physical pain that made it hard to breathe.

He turned off the engine and sat there, on the outer row of a parking lot—the Motor Inn Motel, the sign said. There was no streetlight anywhere close, casting the 4Runner in darkness. Blessed fucking darkness.

For seven months, he'd managed to lock all this in a box, tell himself he was okay, that Andre wouldn't want him to break down or grieve him. It didn't matter what Andre would or wouldn't want. This shit was barreling in, heedless of what Zane himself wanted.

He longed to see his friend's wide-smiled face, in good spirits almost all the time. He'd give just about anything to hear the man's low, quiet laugh. Could imagine how he would beam with pride over his baby son.

Zane sagged over the steering wheel as his eyes filled with tears and he could no longer hold in the grief. Grief for his friend and, oh, hell, he couldn't deny it, grief for his father. His losses combined into one swirling, choking morass of sorrow like he'd never experienced before. By design, of course.

This was what he'd been fighting off all these years.

This grief felt like it had the power to suck the life out of him. All these years, he'd been right to avoid it. People said you needed to grieve someone in order to process a loss, but he didn't see how anything positive could come out of this.

It was the middle of the night when he sat up straight, empty. Fucking depleted. Still lost.

He walked to the office of the dumpy roadside motel, every muscle in his body aching but none more than his chest. Reserving a room was a quick matter once the owner stumbled out of the back room, obviously having been asleep.

Zane made his way to room number two and, still in his clothes, collapsed onto a bed that was harder than the bed in his cabin on the carrier. Didn't really matter. He didn't figure he'd be sleeping a wink tonight.

CHAPTER TWENTY-TWO

$\mathcal{B}$y Sunday morning, Hayden was a wreck.

She woke up in her bed, painfully alone, wrung out like she'd never imagined possible because she had yet to hear from Zane.

Nobody knew where he'd gone. Nobody had heard from him. His brothers were threatening to kick his ass when he turned up. His mother was ready to wring his neck, and that had nothing on what Hayden wanted to do to him. But even more, she just wanted him to walk through her door so she could throw her arms around him.

Except she wouldn't.

Because she wasn't sure she could let this go. She wasn't sure she could live with Zane shutting her out like this.

She heard Sierra in the kitchen, probably brewing coffee, looking for something to eat. Hayden thanked the stars above for her friend, her beautiful, steadfast friend, who'd spent the night in Hayden's guest room in case Hayden needed her.

Hayden understood that Zane was suffering. She was guessing he was grieving his friend for the first time, and she had enough experience with grief that her heart ached for him. Though she'd been heartbroken when he'd walked out on Friday night, in some ways, she'd understood. She knew everyone had to grieve in their own way, and while she couldn't fathom being alone herself, she could acknowledge some people preferred that.

So, fine.

She could forgive him for Friday night.

Now, though, she was worried out of her ever-loving mind about him to the point where she couldn't eat, and getting out of bed felt like an insurmountable task. If he'd just checked in, answered any one of her two dozen texts, at least she would know he was alive and breathing.

And today... How was she going to get through today?

Tonight was her dad's birthday party, and she'd never felt less like putting on a party dress and a smile.

She would. Of course she would, for her dad. But this day was going to be sheer agony. She was due at the restaurant at noon to start decorating and prepping.

A light tap came on her bedroom door, and Hayden croaked out a hoarse, "Yeah," pulling the blankets farther up around her, wishing to hide from the world.

"Hey, you," Sierra said quietly as she came into the room. "Did you sleep at all?"

"Eventually. A couple of hours maybe."

"Brought you some vanilla almond coffee." She set it on the nightstand.

Hayden got a whiff of the sweet aroma, closed her burning, weary eyes for a second, and garnered the energy to sit up, all in the name of a hit of caffeine. Leaning against the headboard as Sierra climbed into the other side of the bed and scooted up beside her, she picked up the mug and blew on the liquid, then took a sip. It tasted flat and half as sweet as it smelled, but she knew it was her that was off, not the coffee.

"What am I going to do, Sierra?" she asked in a dull monotone that belied the despair she felt. She didn't have the energy for anything, especially not for crying more.

She'd cried more in the past two nights than she'd ever thought physically possible.

"You're going to get through the day one hour at a time," Sierra said. "One minute at a time, if necessary. I'll be with you at the restaurant all day, and we'll make it pretty and get ourselves pretty, and we'll put on the best fake smiles ever so your dad has a good night."

"That's important." She nodded, staring off in front of herself. "And then what? I can't do this. What Zane's doing is not okay."

Contrary to what she'd believed thirty seconds ago, her eyes were indeed able to refill with tears, and they overflowed.

Sierra put an arm around her and pulled her into her side, then draped her other arm across Hayden's front in a hug. "I know, sweetie. He's obviously not in his right mind."

The sobs came again, but they were weaker now, because good God, she was so very empty.

"I can't believe I did it again," Hayden said. "I fell in love with someone who can't love me. And this time…" Her crying picked up, making it too hard to speak. The truth was too ugly.

This time the stakes were so much higher.

"I swear I'm going to borrow your Louisville Slugger and use it on him when he shows his face again," Sierra said with conviction.

"I swear I'm not going to stop you," Hayden forced out.

"And then, once he's confirmed that he's okay and has begged and pleaded for forgiveness—"

"I'm out," Hayden said with conviction. "I'm so fucking out, Sierra."

"I know you're devastated right now, but let's wait and see what he says."

"He can say all he wants to, but if he can't lean on me when he's going through hell, there's no future for us."

"That may be," Sierra conceded. "But maybe not. You have to hear him out."

"You're assuming he's going to show up. What if he doesn't?"

"Then we take your bat and hunt him down. But he's going to show up eventually. If nothing else, he has to be at work tomorrow."

Hayden wasn't sure that would matter to him. And even if it did, she wasn't sure *she* would matter to him.

"I feel so stupid," she said quietly, the crying a little more in control. "When I found out I was pregnant, I decided then and there I could do it alone. Somewhere along the line, I let him reel me in. Let him convince me I could trust him. Let him make me love him. I think I hate him." Even as she uttered the words, she knew they were a lie.

"You're hurt and mad and scared," Sierra said. "You have every right to be. And if you and Zane can't work this out, you *will* make it through. I'll be with you the whole way. I'll do anything you need—birth coach, middle-of-the-night mama relief, shoulder to cry on, you name it. You're a strong woman, Hay."

She felt about as strong as a piece of cheap plastic wrap with a tear in it. Sierra would do exactly as she said, she knew. Between the two of them and her family and her army of support, she would make it through without Zane.

But in the name of all that was holy, she didn't want to have to.

First things first…coffee, shower, superpowers, and a day full of faking happiness when all she wanted to do was dive under the covers and stay in bed.

———

ZANE WOKE UP FROM A SHALLOW, stress-filled sleep. He wasn't sure how long he'd been out, wasn't exactly sure what day it was, but the daylight coming in through the cheap drapes told him it was probably Sunday.

Shit. Another day had passed. Disoriented, debilitated with exhaustion, he blinked several times as his stomach raised holy hell with a loud rumble. After rolling stiffly to the edge of the bed and sitting up, he dug his phone out of his back pocket. He'd turned it off when he'd arrived at this hole-in-the-wall dump— his best effort to close out everything he could in order to try to handle what he couldn't.

He powered it up to verify what day it was—Sunday, late morning, nearly noon. More than thirty-six hours had passed in an utter, hellacious fucking blur of gutting sadness for both his dad and Andre. For himself and his losses. It was as if, once the grief had gotten a foothold on him, it all flooded him.

As soon as the bars registered a signal, his phone went berserk with notifications, possibly from everyone he knew. The name he zeroed in on, though, the face he focused on was Hayden.

Oh, hell. Hayden.

She'd sent nineteen text messages and left eight voicemails. With a lump in his throat the size of a grenade, he listened to the first one. At the first note of her voice, his raw, irritated eyes filled once again, and the headache that had been with him for two days became like ice picks to the backs of his eyeballs.

"Hayden," he said to himself in a voice that was rusty and barely more than a whisper. He ended the message and didn't move on to the next one. Didn't need to, because everything became clear within the first five seconds of listening to her.

There was worry and hurt in her thick, nearly unrecognizable voice that made him ache for her. He needed her. Needed to feel her in his arms, as much to ease her concern as to soothe himself. He longed to have her whisper to him that he would be okay, that he wouldn't always feel this god-awful, that tomorrow he might feel a little bit less horrific than he did today.

It hit him with the impact of an F/A-18 crashing into the back of a carrier—he'd fucked up epically.

Instead of opening himself to her comfort, instead of letting her be there for him, he'd shut her out, just as he'd tried to slam down on the emotions that had flooded in as soon as he'd read Sharice Weber's text message and seen that perfect baby boy's picture.

He braced himself and pulled up the photo now. There was still a sharp pang but it was less eviscerating. More bearable. He recovered in seconds instead of days and studied the baby's features. Little Zane's eyes looked like his daddy's.

Andre would never have the opportunity to sit and stare at those eyes, that face, the baby he'd loved wholly even when it was no bigger than a blueberry.

The pulsing pain gathered in his throat again, but Zane didn't try to escape it. He let it burrow in.

Harrison North had missed out on so much too. So many baseball games, so many anniversaries and birthdays, which he'd always made extra special. He would've loved meeting the women his sons fell in love with, and his grandchildren…

Zane's father would never have the chance to meet Zane's children, to watch them grow, to love them.

Nothing was guaranteed in this lifetime, and it'd never been more crystal clear to Zane that he didn't have time to waste. He'd been tiptoeing through life, fighting off anything that made him *feel*, but he'd bet Andre would give anything to have another year, another week, another day to *feel*, both the good and bad stuff.

At the sound of a housekeeping cart outside the door, Zane stood abruptly, his body feeling like he was ninety years old, but he had purpose like he'd never had before.

He needed to be with Hayden. He needed to apologize and grovel and beg her to forgive him. And he needed to spend the rest of his life loving her unfalteringly, through the easy, happy times and the roughest of seas.

Clueless as to how far from home he was, he did a search on his map app. Two and a half hours' drive. He'd be home by… Oh, hell. Today was her dad's birthday party. He had to get to her before that.

He had two and a half hours in the car to figure out how to get exactly what he wanted from life. The cornerstone was Hayden. He only hoped he could come up with a way to get her to forgive him, because he loved her and wanted to spend however many years or weeks or days he had left in this life making her happy.

CHAPTER TWENTY-THREE

It was forty-five minutes until Simon Henry's seventieth birthday party, and everything was nearly ready. Everything except Hayden.

She'd spent the past hour at Seth's with Sierra, Mackenzie, and Lexie, getting into her little black party dress—a halter-style top with a short, flouncy skirt that she'd been much more excited about when she'd bought it than she was now. Her makeup was flawless, thanks to Mackenzie, who, with a YouTube assist, had also worked a miracle with Hayden's hair, which was her usual straight but with an intricate braid ringing her head.

The girls were coming in a few minutes, but she'd returned to the restaurant ahead of them to do a final inspection of everything and check in with Cash in the kitchen, who was in the process of knocking it out of the park with the food.

The restaurant had closed to the public for the evening, and they were expecting nearly a hundred people to show. Knowing her dad's friends, a few would be early. She stood by herself near the unlit fireplace, surveying the rooms and working on her game face.

Hayden and her brothers had transformed the restaurant, removing half of the tables, adding some extra high-top standing tables like the ones in the bar, and placing six different serving stations throughout the three indoor dining areas—four for heavy appetizers, one as a second bar, and one for dessert, which was an incredible assortment of mini-cupcake towers from Sugar Babies.

The decorations were a mix of black, gold, and silver, and she and Sierra had collected photos of the birthday boy from all of his friends over the past few weeks and posted them in collages throughout. Some of his friends had yet to see him in person since he'd moved back, so she was certain there would be multiple joyful reunions tonight.

She hoped those would carry her through somehow so she could avoid breaking down—again—until later, when she was home alone.

Zane's entire family would be here, including two of his three cousins, who'd gotten to know Hayden's dad because he, too, had become a regular at the North family dinners most Sundays. The Steele Hearts tour bus had been scheduled to return to town this afternoon, so even Eliza would be able to join them, along with Mason and Calvin. They all knew as much about what was going on with Zane as Hayden did, and they'd agreed to forge ahead and give her dad a fantastic party. Though her brothers knew the situation, she hadn't filled her dad in, and she wondered how long it would take him to notice Zane wasn't there.

She'd deal with that when it happened.

Right now, she needed some space and some quiet to patch up the facade that she was okay. Holden was in the bar, making sure everything was stocked and ready, so she headed there.

"I'm going down to the dock for a few. Get myself ready for the show," she told him. "Text me if you need anything."

"Will do." He stopped what he was doing and met her gaze. "Hang in there, Hay. You're doing great."

The supportive words were not Holden's norm, and tears threatened. She blinked them away and shot him a blustery smile. "Only four hours till I can curl up alone. I'll be fine."

"Go. Breathe. This place looks amazing."

With a nod, she turned and headed for the door out to the deck before anyone else could stop her.

She went down the stairs from the deck to the paved path toward the lake. The sky was clear and blue, though the sun was casting long shadows and would set in the next couple of hours. The air was a little cool but fresh and exactly what she needed. With a deep, cleansing breath, she walked out onto the long dock that, in high season, could fit up to ten boats and often did, with people from all over the lake gathering for the best food around, by both car and watercraft.

She walked to the far end and stood, looking out over the calm water, endeavoring to soak in that calmness. It didn't quite work. She still felt twitchy.

A fishing boat went by, sending lazy waves toward the shore, and when they finally reached it, the water made several nearby docks creak and clunk with the motion. Hayden took comfort in the familiar sound.

Though she knew it wouldn't do any good, she unlocked her phone to send Zane one more text. She hadn't since last night, knowing it was futile.

Please check in soon. I'm worried about you. Hope you're okay.

She held her breath and hit send, then turned her face to the sky in a silent plea that he would surface soon.

"I'm okay."

The familiar voice several feet behind her startled her, and it took her brain a couple of seconds to process what her ears told it. She whipped around.

"Zane? You're here? What…?"

So many questions ran through her head that she didn't know what to ask first. Instead, she drank in the sight of him, gauging how okay he really was.

On the surface, he looked handsome, in gray dress pants and a navy-blue polo that stretched across his chest. But a closer look revealed that he'd had a hard two days. He'd shaved recently, but his eyes were slightly red and weary, and the area beneath them looked puffy, as if he, too, hadn't gotten much sleep.

The whole while, she resisted the urge to close the space between them and throw her arms around him. Because she also wanted to shove him off the dock, into the cold water, and swear at him for shutting her out and messing them up. Because they *were* messed up, and now that she knew he was safe, she would willingly join his mom in wringing his neck.

"I'm here." He took a few steps toward her. "I'm so damn sorry, Hayden." His voice gave out at the end of that, and he cleared his throat. "I screwed up, and I know I hurt you, and that fact is killing me. I'm sorry I shut you out." His voice was gravelly, thick with emotion and undeniable regret, and she had a hard time maintaining her anger.

She stood up a little taller and doubled down on her determination to stay strong. A few pretty words and an apology didn't mean they could suddenly handle a long-term relationship.

"I understand you got blindsided with that photo," she said. "I can only imagine what that did to you. I mean, I sort of saw what it was doing to you, and I just wanted to help you somehow. At least hold on to you. And you cut me off like I was the enemy."

"I didn't handle it right. I reverted to my go-to, or I tried. Tried to shut down on the storm of feelings Sharice's text evoked." He shook his head, averting his eyes to the dock. "The grief—" His voice cracked and she saw him swallow hard. "I've never felt anything like it. It leveled me. I thought I could shove it down like I usually do, but that photo… It was a gut punch."

"I can understand all that, Zane. I know firsthand what grief can do to a person. But I've been worried to death about you. Your family's been worried. Your mom—"

He closed his eyes in a shamed look. "I regret that more than I can say. Hurting you is the last thing I ever want to do."

She noticed the present tense and couldn't deny it made her heart perk up hopefully. She tamped down on it. "Where have you been?"

He shrugged. "Some awful little roadside motel a couple of hours west of Nashville. There was a convenience store across the street. I think I managed to eat two hot dogs and a donut since I left your place. The bed was a rock, but I barely noticed. I don't know how to explain my state to you, but I wasn't in my right mind. All I can do is apologize."

The thought of him doing that to himself, isolating himself, cut her to the bone. "Zane, if you'd just stayed—"

"I know." He paced a couple of steps, then back. "I shut down on the pain of losing Andre for so long, thinking I could avoid it."

"You can't," she said. "It has to come out."

He nodded. "I did the same with my dad." He clamped his jaw down, as if trying to keep himself under control, then he shook his head. "Fuck it. Locking down on emotion is how I've been for so long. I'm still trying to break the habit." He let out a slight laugh, and then Hayden noticed his eyes became glossy. "It felt like my dad's death was new. For sixteen years, I shut that out. It all caught up with me."

She would be inhumane to not ache for this man and what he'd been through the past two days. "I'm really sorry you went through that by yourself."

"My doing. My fault."

It was. She would've been there for him. *Had* been there for him, but he'd rejected her support. "The way you walked away from me…practically ran away… Not only did you make it harder for yourself but you *hurt me*. I was learning to trust you, Zane. That's not a small step for me—"

"I know, Hayden."

"Then you shut me out cold."

"I regret that like crazy. I'm sorry. I wish I could go back and do it over differently."

"Would you?" she asked, then held her breath. Because she wanted nothing more than to be able to believe in him. But she'd spent forty-eight hours—that seemed like forty-eight days—thinking they were over, that he'd added himself to the list of men who'd crushed her heart.

He straightened and gazed into her eyes with so much intensity she could feel it to her soul. "I would. I will. I promise you

I'll do my best to not shut you out ever again. I've promised myself I'll quit slamming down on my feelings. I'm a work in progress but I'm determined." He took her hands in his and she let him tug her closer. "I need you, Hayden. Need you to make my hardest times a little less awful and the good times even better. I want to be there for you too, for all of it."

The look in his eyes was imploring, shining with vulnerability like she hadn't seen from him before, and she could no longer let her history dictate her future. Zane was here, trying to make amends, trying to shore up a weakness of his, just like she eternally was.

She believed wholeheartedly he meant what he said.

"You *have* been there for me, Zane. You're good at taking care of others' needs, but you suck at taking care of your own."

He laughed quietly and leaned his back against the nearby lamppost, keeping their hands interlocked. "You hit the nail on the head." He sobered again and met her gaze. "Waking up today in that state and realizing what I did to you"—he blew out a breath—"I realized some life truths, Hayden. Andre will never get to meet his son, and that's a travesty."

She nodded sadly, her heart breaking over that and that the adorable little baby would never know his dad, who seemed like a really great guy.

"I'm still alive, even if I haven't been fully living. I owe it to Andre, and my dad, to start living the hell out of my life, to appreciate every day I have."

Again, she nodded, encouraged. Wanting to be the woman who was at his side every day, encouraging him when he needed it.

"I've been telling myself, as the father-to-be, it's my job to be there for you, take care of what I can for you, to ease the way for you because you're doing all the hard work. Convinced myself it was my *duty*. That made me more comfortable than bringing emotions into it. But screw all that. Hayden Eloise Henry, I love you. It's impossible for me *not* to love you, and I can't lie to myself anymore. Back at Cole and Sierra's wedding, when you jokingly said I was your hero, I didn't feel like anyone's hero.

Now, you make me want to be worthy of being called your hero."

Her heart took off faster than the six-seat plane Zane spent his Sundays in, and everything he said burrowed into her soul and told her she'd be stupid to deny herself this. Him.

"You're already worthy of it and I love you too," she said in an excited rush. "I tried to be careful too, but I can't help loving you, Zane."

He stared down into her eyes with his intense, sincere blue ones, and he slowly moved his lips toward hers, watching her the whole way. Her gaze was glued to his as each second brought his mouth closer to hers, had her anticipating contact, longing for it, for the warmth of his breath, the softness of his lips, the magic of all of his attention directly on her.

And then he kissed her, the gentlest, most love-filled kiss of her life, no tongues, just lips and breath, as if he was breathing his love directly into her, his hand at her nape, cradling her.

"I love you," he whispered and then pulled back slightly and continued, "As much as I want to press you up against this light pole and peel that dress off you and love you right here and now, I have more to say."

Her body went hot at his words, her mouth went dry with desire, and her voice didn't work, so she merely nodded.

Zane backed up a little more but kept his hands on her back, as if he wouldn't let her go if she wanted him to.

She didn't want him to.

"I had two and a half hours in the car today, thinking about everything, about what I want out of life. First and foremost, I want you."

"You have me."

He kissed her again, just a few seconds of contact of their mouths, like a silent thank you.

"Second, my job... I hate to give Mason any credit, but all that bullshit he was spouting about me figuring out what I 'burn to do'... It finally sank in." He paused for a second, brought her hand up to his mouth, kissed her knuckles, then laced their fingers together. "I've been so focused on fulfilling my duties, my responsibilities, because that's been my life for the past dozen years. Duty first. Even above my passion for flying, it was duty. Duty is more black-and-white than emotions. Duty was more comfortable."

"That makes a sort of sense," she said when he hesitated.

"As I was driving, I thought about my first day on the actual job tomorrow, no more training, the real thing. Sitting in the IT department. I thought I should be at least a little excited. I wasn't. It didn't feel right. And I've shut out that thought for two weeks now… Hell, probably more like two months."

"That doesn't shock me."

"I love being a part of North Brothers Sports, more than I ever thought I would. Being a part of something with my brothers and my cousins, something that's literally in our DNA, it got me here"—he touched his chest—"like I never expected it would. Learning the family's history, being a part of it on such an insider level… It was, in a way, similar to being in the military, the good parts of it, being part of something bigger than me, something I care about."

"That's important, Zane," she said, a little confused about where he was going, and more than a little curious.

"As I was driving along, I saw a plane coming into some tiny airport, and it hit me like a gale force coming out of nowhere that that's what I should be doing. Flying, like you said. Like my brothers said. But flying for NBS. The second night I was home, the night of Cole's wedding, Mason brought up me flying their jet, and I told him I didn't want to be his chauffeur, but that's not what it would be."

"I agree," Hayden said, smiling, loving that he wanted to fly, because she'd suspected he needed that in his life as much as possible.

"All of my brothers have come around to working for the company in their own ways. Mason was born to lead and has always planned on it. Gabe, he's such a people person, and HR is a good fit for him. With Cole, our black sheep, he did everything he could to stay out of it out of contrariness, but now he's doing NBS his way, leading all the construction projects. And Drake, hell, if my flighty, commitment-phobic brother could find a way to bring his skill set and interests to the company, it should be a no-brainer for me."

"It is," she said quietly.

"It is. Even if it took me a while to work back to it and accept it. I talked to Mason today, proposed making two pilot positions in-house full-time and hiring me to be one of them. He gave me shit for all the work they've done to make room for me in IT, then jumped on it wholeheartedly. Tomorrow's still my official first day on the job, and I'll be hammering out the position with my brothers and the board and overseeing the hiring of another pilot."

"That's perfect, Zane. I'm so happy for you." Hayden threw her arms around his neck and planted a kiss on him.

"Best part is still to come."

"Yeah?" she said, lowering back to the dock in her heels.

"Flying is what I burn to do, and you're who I burn to be with. I've never loved someone so much or needed anyone in my life the way I do you. It has nothing to do with the baby and everything to do with you. Only you."

When she thought he'd kiss her, he broke eye contact and lowered one of his hands, seeming to be momentarily distracted. He met her gaze again, then, before she could process what was going on, he stepped to the side slightly, watching where his feet landed, then lowered himself to one knee.

Hayden's eyes popped wide open, and some kind of high-pitched squeal came out of her as she looked down at Zane. She nearly melted on the spot when he pressed a kiss to her abdomen, as if acknowledging the baby, and then she saw the little box in his hands. He opened the lid to reveal a sparkling princess-cut diamond ring in white gold.

"Hayden, I want to be a family with you and the little bean and any other little beans we might be blessed with. Will you marry me?"

She bounced up and down on her toes and blurted out, "Yes!" without a single doubt in her mind or glance to her past. "Yes,

Zane. I'll marry you." Laughing, she bent forward to plant a kiss on his lips, then said, "And I'll bring the bean with me."

In a single motion, he stood and lifted her into his arms, and she wrapped her legs around his middle as their lips met in a promise for all of time. After a few seconds, he slid her down his body until her feet were on the ground, literally speaking, and he took the ring out and held it between them.

Hayden raised a shaking left hand and covered her mouth with her right one as he slid it on. "It's stunningly perfect. I love it, Zane. I love you."

"I love you too. Both of you. I'd love you even if we hadn't gotten pregnant. But you know what?"

She yanked her gaze from the gorgeous engagement ring on her finger to peer up at him. "What?"

"I'm glad we did."

"Me too," she whispered, and she meant it. Three months ago, it had seemed like a daunting situation, but it was interesting sometimes how things that seemed like a challenge often turned out to be the very best in the end. "He's going to be so very loved and adored."

"She is," he said, laughing as he leaned in to kiss her again.

When they came up for air, Hayden said, "We're getting married."

"Damn straight we are. Do you think our families are here yet?" He checked the time on his phone, and she saw it was seven minutes until six, which was when the party officially started. "I don't want to be the guy who steals the spotlight from your dad, but I'm dying to tell the entire universe you're mine."

"I think my dad'll be elated to hear the news. All of them will be."

"Let's go then," he said and took her hand in his.

They headed back up the dock. As they ascended the handful of steps to the deck, Hayden glanced through the floor-to-ceiling, end-to-end windows and realized there were quite a few people there already. Zane opened the door for her, and she stepped inside and noticed many of them were staring at her, at them, as Zane stepped next to her.

Applause sounded, and then a screech from someone—Mackenzie, she realized—and there were calls of "Congratulations!" from all sides.

Hayden laughed, looked up at Zane, who shrugged and pulled her close, his grin a mile wide.

Sierra came forward from the crowd. "When are we doing this wedding thing?"

"How did you all know?" She turned to Zane again and said, "Did you tell them?"

"I only told Mason—"

"I didn't tell a soul," Mason called out from somewhere.

"We'll discuss that later," Eliza said lightly, making everyone laugh.

"Mackenzie saw you two out there, and then we saw Zane go down on one knee, and then it was so obviously a yes," Sierra said, pulling both Hayden and Zane in for a group hug. "Congratulations, you two."

"Thank you," Hayden said, and as Sierra backed away so others could crowd around them, Zane pulled Hayden into his side.

Her dad came up to her and threw his arms around her. He pulled her close without a word—he didn't need words to show her how he felt about their news. Finally, he pressed a kiss to her forehead, then turned to Zane. He held out a hand to shake, then, when Zane took it, he pulled his future son-in-law in for a hug.

"Congratulations, you two," Simon said after the hug ended. "And good luck," he said to Zane with a laugh. "I know from personal experience, she can be a handful. But you seem like you're the best for the job."

"I intend to be," Zane said, his emotions all over his face like Hayden hadn't seen before.

As her dad went to Faye's side, Hayden stood on her toes again, leaned up to Zane's ear, and said, "Guess it's a good thing you didn't peel my dress off me quite yet."

Zane leaned down to her and replied, "Let's get through the party and go do that."

He kissed her, and then they were carried away by hugs and

family and congratulations and love from every side, and Hayden knew, without a doubt in her heart, that this was how their life would be. It might bring them ups and downs and good times and bad times, but through it all, they would love and be loved.

EPILOGUE

*O*ver the past few months, Zane had figured out a fundamental truth. The more he opened himself to emotion, the bigger the payoff could be. The lows were still hell, but the high points were more incredible than he ever could've imagined.

He couldn't fathom how he'd existed without the highs that Hayden brought into his life.

Tonight, his first Christmas Eve with his wife and child, was one of those that would stay with him for the rest of his days.

The entire North family, all twenty of them, including all the wives, all three cousins, Calvin and the three babies, Aunt Liz, and their honorary aunt Geraldine, plus Hayden's dad, Simon, had flown to Colorado to spend Christmas at Gabe's mountain lodge. Zane had piloted the corporate jet, and they damn near maxed out its capacity of twenty-five. When you included Drake and Mackenzie's two adopted mutts—and you had to include them because they weren't the kind of puppies that curled up in a corner and stayed unnoticed—they were a rambunctious, noisy crew, and that held true even now.

Zane stood in the warm, crowded, overflowing-with-good-cheer family room that was decked out to the hilt for the holidays. During daylight hours, the floor-to-ceiling windows offered a breathtaking view of white-peaked mountains. Tonight was all about twinkling lights, sprigs of holly, and a tree and Santa motif throughout that Hayden had helped Lexie with.

A fire crackled in the fireplace on the far wall. Faye and Simon sat on one of the couches with Logan, the middle cousin, who was strumming background holiday music on his guitar. Sierra and Cole sat on the floor against the hearth, seemingly in their own little bubble, feeding each other the gourmet chocolates Sierra had ended up with in the white elephant gift exchange after their traditional North family Christmas Eve dinner of spaghetti and meatballs and garlic and cheese bread. The real gifts would be opened tomorrow.

Mason was at the dining table with Calvin, helping him with his brand-new LEGO Christmas set.

Zane's other cousins, Miranda and Connor, were in the open kitchen with Liz, Geraldine, and Drake, some of them cleaning up dessert plates, some mixing drinks.

With Gabe at Zane's side, Mackenzie on the other, he was absorbed with watching Hayden, Eliza, and Lexie as they posed the three newest Norths for a group photo under the main twelve-foot-tall Christmas tree.

He'd never been so full of love and admiration for his wife as he'd been since she'd become a mom. She was incredible, and his love literally grew every damn day and blew his mind.

Their son, Harrison Andre North, had been born three days after his due date in a highly dramatic day-and-a-half labor that ended in an emergency C-section. The baby had gone into distress, necessitating the operation, and until they'd gotten him out and Zane had been reassured both Hayden and the baby were okay, it had been one of those hellacious lows. Followed quickly by the most incredible moment of his life, when he'd watched Hayden take their baby into her arms for the first time. They'd agreed months ago to name their boy after his father and his squadron mate and were planning a spring trip to take him to Seattle to visit little Zane Weber and his mom, Sharice.

Mason and Eliza's son, Jasper Andrew, had won the cousin race, defying his later due date and being born one day before Gabe and Lexie's son, Wyatt Wilson. The three cousins, plus Calvin, who was now five, would be raised close, almost like brothers. That's how the North family was, how it'd been with him, his brothers, and Connor, Logan, and Miranda. That's why they were all together now, just as they usually were for holidays and birthdays and Sundays.

"That is so adorable that *my* ovaries just did a little squeeze," Mackenzie said as she watched the photo shoot.

"Don't get any ideas," Drake said, laughing as he came up next to her. "We've got our hands full with Tank and Gunner."

The dogs, both less than a year old, had been banished to a bedroom for the past half hour so they wouldn't ruin the photo shoot. The Lab/St. Bernard mix and the Lab/shepherd mix were in training and making progress but full of energy and were works in progress on the obedient doggy front.

The new moms had planned the shoot to the smallest detail. All three of the chunky baby boys were shirtless, with Santa hats pulled up over their diapered lower halves, and they each somehow slept through the chaos and noise on a thick white fur blanket, one baby's head resting on the next baby's backside, like three fallen dominoes.

"Absolutely precious," Geraldine said as she handed Christmas martinis to Faye and Simon.

"Have to admit, I thought they were being over-the-top with the idea," Gabe said, "but that is a Kodak photo contest winner right there."

"You're not biased or anything," Connor called out.

"Biased but confident I'm right," Gabe said.

"Heavens, the cuteness! This grandma agrees, Gabe," Faye gushed.

"Everybody, look!" Calvin called out from the table. "We did it!"

"I question who enjoyed it more, Daddy or son," Drake muttered as he spun around to admire their brickwork. "That looks awesome, little dude!"

"Calvin, you're so fast at LEGOs," Mackenzie added.

"My dad helped a little bit," Calvin said, perched proudly on his knees on the dining chair, chest puffed out. "This is the people's house," he continued, pointing out parts, "and this is the snowman they made, and here's their outside Christmas tree, and they have an inside Christmas tree that you can see inside of the windows, and here's the Santa!" He held up the red-clad LEGO figure.

The adults oohed and aahed and admired and praised, and Eliza promised she'd be over soon to check it out, as Lexie snapped shot after shot of the babies.

"Two years from now, Christmas is going to be a new level of madhouse," Aunt Liz said as she watched the slumbering models. "Nothing will be safe."

"I can't wait to show Kennedy these pics," Sierra said, standing to see better.

"I bet you're missing little Stella," Miranda, who'd come into the living room, said to her.

"We Facetimed earlier," Sierra said of her niece, Kennedy and Hunter's nine-month-old daughter. "You should see her Christmas dress." She took out her phone and started scrolling through to find a picture.

The photo shoot came to an abrupt end when Jasper woke up and let out a squall that could shatter eardrums.

"He gets that from his mom," Mason said, garnering a group laugh.

"Country crooner to be," Eliza said as she scooped up her boy.

Lexie lifted Wyatt to her shoulder, and Hayden did the same with Harrison. Zane went over to assist.

Hayden handed Harrison off to him, arranging a blanket over the baby's shoulders. Her cheeks were flushed with happiness as she stood on her toes and kissed Zane. He wondered how long before it would be acceptable for them to close themselves into their bedroom for the night so he could peel off her festive Santa hat, ugly Christmas sweater, leggings, and whatever treats lay beneath them.

Zane caught her at the waist and, as he settled his son into his shoulder, went in for another kiss.

A few minutes later, Eliza had come back from feeding Jasper and putting him and Calvin to bed, and Gabe had taken Wyatt to the crib in their room and returned. Harrison still slept on Zane's shoulder, and he probably could've taken him to his own crib, but he loved the feel of his boy snuggled in, so trusting and warm and loved.

Lexie was making the rounds, showing off the photos she'd taken, when Simon, standing next to the overladen Christmas tree with Faye at his side, his arm around her, cleared his throat loudly.

"Can I have your attention?" Simon said in his quiet voice, which didn't quite do the job with this bunch.

Drake was nearby, and he took over. "Yo, everybody! Shut up and listen!"

Hayden's dad laughed and said, "I wouldn't have put it that way, but thank you." He cleared his throat again as the chatter quieted. The man's uncharacteristic nervousness caught Zane's attention, and within a millisecond, he knew.

Judging by his mom's raised brows as she watched the man she loved, she did *not* know.

Zane moved in closer, along with everyone else.

Simon again cleared his throat and smiled and looked at Faye. "Thank you, Faye, for inviting me to spend Christmas with your fantastic family." He nodded around him. "It's not even Christmas Day yet, and already it's one of the best holidays I've had in years. Because of you." He pushed his glasses higher on his nose as he jammed his hand in his pants pocket. "I hope we can spend many more together, with your family, with my family, with both families together." He nodded at Hayden and Zane and there were laughs all around. Without further fuss, he took one of Faye's hands in his and, with his other, held up a ring with a large diamond. "Faye, will you marry me?"

With grace and a beaming smile and love radiating from her, Faye pressed one hand to her chest and let out a quiet sound of joy. Her eyes shone with tears as she gazed at Simon. "I thought you'd never ask! Yes, Simon, I'll marry you. Yes!" She lunged toward his chest, placed her hands on both of his cheeks, and kissed him as the room went up in cheers.

"About time you make an honest woman out of our mom," Drake said as he gave Simon an affectionate slap on the back.

Their mom threw her arms around her intended and giggled like a happy teenager.

Simon's grin was as wide as his face, and though Zane couldn't hear him over the ruckus, he read the man's lips when he told their mom he loved her.

As hugs and congrats were exchanged all around, Sierra beelined for the kitchen, saying something about champagne, and soon everyone had a flute of bubbly.

"To another addition to the North family," Mason said when everyone looked to him expectantly. "Will you go by Simon North?"

Again, there was laughter, and Faye sipped her champagne, flicked her oldest son on the chest, then hugged him.

Hayden crowded up to her dad and said, "Congrats, Dad. Well done."

Zane narrowed his eyes at her. "Wait a second. You don't act surprised."

She laughed. "I might have gone with him to pick out the ring."

"And you didn't tell your husband?"

"I was sworn to secrecy."

"She told me," Sierra announced. "How else would we have champagne chilled and ready for the occasion?"

"These two," Cole said to Zane as he came up to his side, shaking his head.

"Can't leave them alone together for a second," Zane said.

It was finally his turn to carefully hug his mom, Harrison still on his shoulder, and officially welcome Simon to the family.

"Zaner, wanna trade white elephant gifts?" Miranda asked him several minutes later, when most of the champagne was gone.

"What'd you get?" he asked even though there wasn't a

chance in hell it was something he wanted more than the two front-row tickets to a Steele Hearts show.

"She got the dumb sexist book about porn for females," Logan said.

"Nothing dumb at all about fully dressed good-looking guys doing housework," Mackenzie said. "I'll trade you my drink cozy mittens for it. You can use them at football games. Keep your hands warm and your drinks cold."

"Deal," Miranda said. "If Zane's not giving up the tickets."

"I'm not giving up the tickets," Zane confirmed. "Can't wait to see my sister-in-law get her fiddle thing on now that I'm all country."

"Mmm, sorta country," Hayden said as she sidled up to the side Harrison was on and made googly eyes at him even though he was still sacked out. "I'll put him in bed. I have no idea how he's still sleeping."

"I'll come with you," Zane said, ready to close a door on all the noise and have his gorgeous wife to himself.

Zane told everyone good night and followed Hayden and Harrison down the stairs to their room in the finished basement.

Once the baby was in his crib, lying on his back, his little head turning slowly to the side as he slumbered on, Zane and Hayden stood at the side of it, still mesmerized by their son. Zane nestled up behind his wife, his nose burrowed in her silky hair, arms wound around her middle, eyes on the little miracle that had forced them to give each other a life-altering chance. He let out a quiet, contented groan, and Hayden tilted her head back into him, resting her arms on top of his.

"He's been such a good boy," she whispered.

"He's perfect," Zane responded. "You're perfect."

Though he'd made a conscious decision to stop fighting emotions so hard, to let them in, he still wasn't the kind who bubbled over or wore his heart on his sleeve. Except when it came to Hayden and their son.

"Come here," he whispered to her, giving Harrison one more love-filled glance before taking Hayden by the hand and pulling her closer to the bed, away from the baby. "God, I love you." He drew her to him, slid his arms around her, feeling for the thousandth time like two puzzle pieces clicking into place. It would never get old.

"Love you too," Hayden said. "This was the best Christmas Eve ever. I miss my thug brothers and wish they weren't all so alone in the world, but they've got each other. I feel like a part of your family—"

"You are a part of my family. The most important part of my family. You're everything to me, Hay. You and that little watermelon over there in the crib."

"You can't compare our baby to a fruit!" she gasped as if scandalized, making him laugh.

"I love watermelon."

"And I love cupcakes—"

"Way to get your own white-elephant contribution back, by the way."

She'd brought a half-dozen Sugar Babies cupcakes for the exchange and stolen them from Geraldine, who'd stolen them from Lexie, who'd stolen them from Mason, who Zane couldn't even remember who he'd stolen them from.

"Play of the evening," Hayden said proudly. "As was eating the best two so that no one could get the cherry almond or the s'mores."

"That's the holiday spirit," he joked. He ran his hands down her back, under her sweater, over her skin, his body going rock hard like it always did. He fought to focus. "You know I'm not a fan of mushy, but I want to say thank you, Hay."

"For? Did you steal one of my cupcakes?"

He laughed. "I'm trying to be serious."

She sobered exaggeratedly. "You shouldn't have let me drink the champagne on top of the two Christmas martinis then."

"I don't let you or not let you do anything. That's all you." As much as he was being serious, he couldn't keep the smile off his face, because this was what his wife, all these months later, still did to him. She made him so fucking happy he couldn't even be cool about it. "Hayden?"

"Zane." This time she did get serious as she looked up at him in the dim light.

It was his turn to reach into his pocket and pull out a tiny blue-foil-wrapped box with a silver bow on it. "Merry Christmas, my love."

"We're doing this tonight? Your present is upstairs under the tree."

"Yours is too. This is extra."

"Ooh, I love extra." She took the box, removed the bow, stuck it on the top of his head, then ripped the paper off like a pro.

When she lifted the lid off the box, she gasped. "Zane. It's beautiful."

"It's a mother's ring, an opal for our October baby, set in an infinity loop. That represents our family."

"I love it," she said in an awed whisper. She took it out of the velvet nest and slid it onto a finger on her right hand. "It fits perfectly. Thank you." She threw her arms around his neck and kissed him, and Zane held her to him, returned the kiss, then ended it so he could get what he wanted to say out. So he could move on to the stripping-her-naked part of the night.

"Thank you, Hayden. For being brave. For embracing him"—he nodded toward Harrison in the crib—"when it wasn't the easy way. For nourishing him with vegetables and cupcakes. For making me the luckiest man alive."

"Back at you. I'm the luckiest girl."

"One more thing."

"Yeah?"

"You gave my mom her happily ever after too, with your determined senior setup all those months ago."

"They are sort of adorable, aren't they?"

"I've never seen her so happy. I mean it. Thank you for that."

"You're welcome. My dad is crazy about her too."

"Something you should be aware of," he said.

"Yeahhh?"

"Any girl who makes my mama happy? Has my heart forever."

Her tone went flirty when she said, "Just your heart?" Her

hand trailed down to his buckle, fingers dipping into his waistband.

His voice turned hoarse. "Not just my heart," he gritted out as his blood pounded south.

Hayden growled as she went up on her toes and said into his ear, "Seems like you have yet another problem I could solve, mister." She grabbed the bulge in his pants. "But what are you going to do about that? There's a minor in the room."

Grinning, he hoisted her up into his arms, eliciting a squeal from her. After checking the crib to make sure their son was still asleep, he whispered in her ear, "I'm going to whisk you away to the en suite, take you to the shower, and have my way with you."

"Zane?" She curled her legs around his middle, bringing her soft core right where he needed it. He managed to get them to the bathroom and close the door, then he lowered her to the granite countertop, not letting an inch of space come between them.

"Mm-hmm?"

"Not to take away from your caveman act or anything, but in situations like this? Your way is the same as my way."

He let out a gravelly laugh. "Just one more reason you're perfect for me."

NOTE FROM THE AUTHOR

Thanks for reading *True Hero*! I hope you loved Zane and Hayden's story.

You can order the first book in the Dragonfly Lake series, Unraveled, now! Unraveled is the story of Holden Henry (Hayden's brother) and Chloe Abrams.

If you missed Cole and Sierra's story, you can order or download it right away! Find out what happens when Mr. Socially Awkward spontaneously volunteers to be his beautiful boss's fake date.

You can also read Kennedy and Hunter's story right away. Find out what happens when bartender Kennedy's new boss, Hunter, has her shaken *and* stirred.

"I loved this story—from beginning to end, it had me!" —5-star reader review

———

If you liked *True Hero*, I hope you'll consider leaving a review for it. Reviews help other readers find books and can be as short (or long) as you feel comfortable with. Just a couple sentences is all it takes. I appreciate all honest reviews.

———

True Hero is part of the North Brothers series, which includes these stand-alone stories:

- True North
- True Colors
- True Blue
- True Harmony
- True Hero

North Brothers is a spin-off of the Hale Street series, which includes these stand-alone stories by me:

- Sweet Spot
- Sweet Dreams
- Soft Spot
- One and Only
- Last First Kiss
- Heartstrings

ACKNOWLEDGMENTS

Thank you to author Geri Krotow, who graciously helped me with military and Navy information, and for her excellent workshop on military characters. Any errors regarding military details are entirely my own.

Thanks to Scott Gorden, my pilot friend who answered countless questions on flying a small plane. Again, errors concerning flying are mine alone.

Thank you to Shayla Black for generously helping me write an engaging book description for the back cover blurb—and by helping me, I mean taking it by the reins, cutting most of what I had, and making it a thousand times better!

Thank you to Kay Lyons, for being the first one to lay eyes on this story that gave me so many fits and for reassuring me that there IS a lovable story there after all.

Thanks to Rachel, Kathy, Meshanna, Lisa, Edie, and Heather for your continued dedication, feedback, and enthusiasm for my stories. Your suggestions help make my stories stronger, and I'm beyond grateful for your generosity with your time.

Thanks to my Booktrippers girls—Melissa Chambers, Amanda Torrey, and Christine DePetrillo—for daily writerly support, marketing conquests, encouragement, laughs, and love. I'm so thankful that we've connected and can't imagine this journey without you all.

Thank you and love to Natasha Lake and Emily Leigh, who started as my writing lifelines and morphed into some of the best friends I could ever ask for. We've stuck close through snake chases, plot adversity, dead smoke detectors, Really Bad workshops, killer baby bird drop-ins, blurb writing hell, blue cocktails, treacherous wooden stair challenges, four-seltzer nights, and some of life's biggest, hardest bumps, and my life is so much richer because we're in it together.

And as always, thank you to my family for supporting me always. To my mom for reading every one of my books and sharing them, to my sons for believing in me even though you wouldn't be caught dead reading my books, and to my husband, who gives so much behind the scenes to help me plot the books and advance my career that you've nearly earned a by-line. I literally couldn't do it without your love and unwavering support.

ALSO BY AMY KNUPP

North Brothers Series

True North

True Colors

True Blue

True Harmony

True Hero

Hale Street Series:

Sweet Spot

Sweet Dreams

Soft Spot

One and Only

Last First Kiss

Heartstrings

Hale Street Box Sets:

Meet Me at Clayborne's

Clayborne's After Hours

Island Fire Series:

Playing with Fire

Heat of the Night

Fully Involved

Firestorm

Afterburn

Up in Flames

Flash Point

Fire Within

Impulse

Slow Burn

Island Fire Box Sets:

Sparked (books 1-3)

Ignited (books 4-6)

Enflamed (books 7-10)

OR

Island Fire: The Complete Series

ABOUT THE AUTHOR

Amy Knupp is a *USA Today* Best-Selling Author of contemporary romance and a copy editor for Blue Otter Editing. She loves words and grammar and meaty, engrossing stories with complex characters.

Amy lives in Wisconsin with her husband and has two sons, four cats, and a box turtle. She graduated from the University of Kansas with degrees in French and journalism. In her spare time, she enjoys traveling, breaking up cat fights, watching college hoops, and annoying her family by correcting their grammar.

For more information:
www.amyknupp.com

If you'd like to know when her next book is available, you can join Books, Beaches, and Bellinis, her Facebook readers group, or sign up for her newsletter at amyknupp.com.